# WINGED ISIS

## JEAN STEWART

# Bella
## BOOKS

Ferndale, Michigan
2001

**Bella Books, Inc.**
P.O. Box 201007
Ferndale, MI 48220

Printed in the United States of America on acid-free paper
First Edition

Editor: Lila Empson
Cover designer: Bonnie Liss (Phoenix Graphics)

**ISBN** 1-931513-01-5

*As ever, this is for Susie,
the best thing that ever happened to me.*

*With great thanks to Barb Doran,
Karen Sanders, Julie Davis, and my mom, for the
love and encouragement.*

*Thanks to Beth Mitchum for the early
editing contributions,
and to Robin Houpt, for the proofreading.
Thanks to Lila Empson for the final edits.*

*Last and most important, thanks to
Kelly Smith for sharing the dream.*

## Other books by Jean Stewart

The Isis Series:
*Return to Isis*
*Isis Rising*
*Warriors of Isis*


Fiction/Romance:
*Emerald City Blues*

# Prologue

Once, there was land called America. Vast and varied, the land rolled from the Atlantic Ocean to the Pacific, and energetic, hopeful people populated it. For over two hundred years it was a haven for liberty, a land of free men and women.

Then came a virus called AIDS. For several decades after it was first discovered, the disease existed in certain groups of people, but most of America was unaffected, and so ignored it. Then, around the year 2000, the AIDS virus mutated and bonded with a virus called genital herpes. AIDS had, in America, for unknown reasons, nestled into gay male and then poor minority populations in preference to others; in contrast, AGH made its chosen home among heterosexuals.

The mutation went unnoticed for about seven years, until

1

large numbers of young, sexually active heterosexuals came down with odd forms of pneumonia and reproductive tract cancers. Throughout the medical world, research and drug development efforts were mobilized, but a cure was not found. By 2009, AGH was well on its way to becoming the worst plague since the Black Death of the Middle Ages. Young heterosexuals were dying in record numbers. In the midst of the resulting panic, America took extreme measures.

Societal behaviors that had developed during the AIDS crisis became driving forces. Instead of trying to cure AGH, people blamed the victims.

In June 2010, a select group of white men, the Aryan Procurators, joined forces with a group of religious zealots called the New Order Christians. They convinced the U.S. President that something radical had to be done. He issued the Laws of Public Safety. Originally conceived as a temporary measure, the Laws of Public Safety ended up superceding the U.S. Constitution. Liberty and personal freedoms gave way to a code of strict regulations, and fundamentalist interpretations of the Bible crushed democracy. Not surprisingly, the Aryans and the New Order Christians ended up with all the power. They called the new nation Elysium, the Greek word for paradise.

They began to kill. At first, they killed just AGH carriers, but they soon killed anyone else who wasn't wanted: anyone who wasn't white, heterosexual, and an avowed fundamentalist Christian. A tide of refugees raced west. The states in the middle of the continent, already swamped with their own health emergency, were simply overrun. By 2011, cars at a standstill, with nothing but corpses at the wheel, clogged the highways. Orphaned children ran in small herds, raiding supermarkets for canned goods or eating rodents when they couldn't find packaged food. Rumors of cannibalism abounded.

Once-affluent, pristine suburban towns became armed forts, cut off from the less fortunate. Yet, when the plague struck them, too, those same forts became ghost towns, littered with the debris of discarded loot and decomposing bodies.

The far western states, meanwhile, rebelled against the Laws of Public Safety. Their leaders met in Las Vegas to plan a resistance, and sent a cable to Washington, D.C., stating that they were a "free land." A civil war, later called the Great Rift, erupted. America split in two, into Elysium on the East Coast and Freeland on the West Coast.

In 2013, the Elysians dropped a hydrogen bomb on Las Vegas to eliminate western resistance. The fallout from radiation multiplied the devastation from AGH; anywhere the wind blew became a death zone. Anyone left alive fled Nevada. The entire center of the continent became an unpopulated Wilderness. In the east, AGH killed two in ten people, but in the west, AGH killed two in three.

AGH ravaged the world. Over one-third of the global population was gone by 2017. By 2030, the United Nations, or what was left of it, met in France and announced that over one-half of the world's population was dead and many more were dying. In the hardest hit areas — Russia, India, Brazil, China, and much of Africa — the plague meant annihilation. Contact between countries was reduced to a tribal affair, and out of fear of encountering some new mutant strain of the virus, contact was, for the most part, shunned.

In keeping with this sentiment, in 2013 Elysium's military-industrial complex created an invisible photoelectro-magnetic shield, an oval of light beams controlled by NASA satellites in space, to provide a Border that rose out of the Atlantic Ocean. Impenetrable by land or sea, it fell across the Gulf of Mexico and the center of the continent. Like a huge, unscalable wall, the Border sealed Elysium into its own world, so that no one came in and no one went out. After they'd hunted down and exterminated every AGH carrier they could find, the Elysians were sure they would be safe.

It was not to be. No matter how many AGH carriers were executed, the disease continued to move through the populace like a foul smell. Finally, the Elysian leaders began to understand they could not stop the plague with their extermination program; they also began to understand the importance of having a productive work force, even a sick one. There were jobs to be done and no one to do them. Because there were no longer enough healthy women to assure a future Elysian civilization, the leaders turned AGH-free women of childbearing age into Breeders and kept them in "breeding pens." Men and other women were allowed to become citizens in the walled, feudal towns that the new government erected outside of the polluted, corpse-filled city centers. New York City's elite class relocated to West Point. Washington's politicians moved to Bethesda, Maryland. All over the east, people abandoned the large cities and left them to ruin. Officials enacted laws that decreed AGH-infected people were serfs to be sequestered on farms in rural areas, far away from "normal" people. They were doomed to slave away their remaining years, providing food for their oppressors.

In Freeland, one group of people survived in vast numbers: the nonheterosexuals. When the plague first started, some women in the Pacific Northwest had had the foresight to organize. Via mass electronic mailings over the Internet, these women encouraged lesbians to prepare for the worst, to turn their savings into supply stockpiles, and then to relocate to communes hidden deep in the national forests. Among stands of century-old trees, the lesbians set up sperm banks, medical clinics, and water purification works. Carpenters among them built small but sturdy structures for housing. As the Great Rift began, lesbians all over the west seemed to disappear. Too much else was going on for the authorities to worry about a crazed network of survivalists camping in the national forests.

After the Border went up in 2013, lesbians began to resurface and assert their presence. Mounted troops of armed and well-trained warrior women came out of the Cascade, Olympic, and Sierra Nevada Mountains. During the next

4

decade they methodically subdued vandals and gathered survivors. They built new settlements and created new life.

Civilization survived.

Patriarchy was gone.

Fierce women, later called the Mothers, contributed without reservation to the welfare of their city-colonies. They developed inventive methods of food production, expanded medical resources, organized schools. Women took on backbreaking tasks, had large families, and passed on the concept of woman-strength to their daughters and sons.

Some of the sperm banks had no categorical descriptions attached to the sample. A woman bore a child and it was considered good fortune, the gift of a future. Racial hybrids were the norm. Other women chose to preserve their ethnicity. They searched the sperm banks until they were able to match the donor sample with their own heritage. Since the Elysians were promoting Aryan purity, it seemed essential to some that diversity be cultivated too. Japanese, Navajo, African, Vietnamese, Hebrew, Mexican — the differences were prized and preserved.

After witnessing the violence unleashed against the unwanteds and other acts of terror sanctioned by Elysium's fundamentalists, many in Freeland turned away from Christianity. New and old religions came into practice: Buddhism, Wicca, and belief in the Native American Great Spirit, among them. However, after the Elysian example of intolerance and its horrific consequences, religious tolerance became the overriding cultural maxim. Once-common Christian names were forsaken for the names of Amazons, ancient goddesses, and ethnic heroines. A culture once centered on Judeo-Christian beliefs and trappings, slowly redefined itself. Christians who remained steadfast were not fundamentalists; rather, they were followers of the loving and forgiving example set by Jesus.

At first, survivors congregated in tiny villages. Then, in an effort to marshal the meager populace that was left, seven city-colonies were formed. The city-colonies of Artemis, Boudica, Harvey, Morgan, Susan B. Anthony, Lang, and Tubman were arranged along the western coast and the southwestern edge of Old America. Artemis, Susan B. Anthony, and, years later, Isis, adopted women-only mandates, structuring separatist societies. A mix of lesbian and heterosexual peoples populated the other city-colonies. All were matriarchies, with the exception of Harvey, which drew a majority of gay males. No city-colony was larger than fifty thousand people, and a development program was created to publicly fund the founding of new city-colonies when growth demanded it.

The seven city-colonies adopted the U.S. Constitution as their governing document but amended the clause regarding the executive branch. Because the Freelanders had learned a bitter lesson when the American President caved in to special interests during the plague panic that preceded the Great Rift, they no longer would vest so much power and authority in one person. Instead, Freeland's executive branch was defined as a Council of seven Leaders, each one the elected Leader of a city-colony.

By 2040, Freeland, out of necessity, entered a technological revolution. The Mothers began collecting machines — all kinds of machines. At first, they were merely salvaging usable pieces from units that no longer functioned in order to build another unit from scratch. However, as the ranks of hungry children grew, they had to meet demands for increased productivity. With two-thirds of the former U.S. population gone and distribution systems in ruins, Freeland lacked sufficient people to do the necessary work. Manual laborers could not plant, harvest, and process all the food needed; they could not grow, pick, and weave all the cotton needed. The Mothers began designing new machines, machines run by computer programs instead of human beings. Computerized hydroponics sheds, cotton and clothing production, and manufacturing processes provided a wealth of necessities, from soap to construction materials. Within a few decades, Freeland was moving out of the shadow of the Great Rift.

In 2032, a Seattle doctor, Dr. Kea, had set up a team for intensive research. In one series of experiments, she had obtained from Native American healers an herbal mixture that had immunostimulator properties. While the active ingredients remained unknown, the extract had been used in the pre–Great Rift years for the treatment of various infections and was known to enhance T-cell activity. The research team found that a vaccine derived from dead AGH virus particles, when used in conjunction with the herbal immunostimulator, had a profound protective effect on bone marrow and resulted, ultimately, in the elimination of the virus from the infected patient. After Dr. Kea's death, ironically from plague, her research assistant, Dr. Satrina, perfected the treatment.

Once the three necessary medicine-plants involved in producing the immunostimulator were successfully introduced to a farming and harvesting regimen, only the actual production of the mixture became a problem. The laboratory preparation was time-consuming and needed a team of botanists and analytical chemists to attain desired results.

A young woman named Maat Tyler created the computer program that automated the preparation of the immuno-stimulator compound. The vaccine was manufactured and dispersed throughout the small but ecstatic populace of Freeland. By the end of 2058, within a decade of Maat's contribution, AGH ceased to exist in Freeland.

In Elysium, public funding for education had been one of the first expenditures dropped. Soon, the only knowledge in Elysium was what was passed down from father to son. Simple medical procedures were lost; computer skills disappeared. Illiteracy and ignorance abounded. By 2059, no one in Elysium knew how to control the Border. The wall erected to keep out the world now imprisoned them.

In Freeland, Maat Tyler returned her attention to solving

7

the mystery of how the Border worked. Maat had earlier discovered how to coordinate the satellite beams that kept the shield dome in place. She had then taken the design one step further and developed a means of breaking the light beams at certain points. These points, or weak spots, she called Bordergates. For a while, it had become stylish for the more daring Freeland warriors to go undercover in Elysium and gather information, coming and going via the Bordergates.

From this information, Freeland had gradually become convinced of the steady dissolution of Elysium's threat to them. Elysium was clearly destroying itself, strangled by its feudal caste system, sexist doctrine, scientific ignorance, and religious fanaticism. The Regulators, a gestapo police force, compelled obedience to the law, controlling the Elysian populace with storm-trooper tactics. And the AGH virus that had provoked it all was still spreading quietly among them, evading all attempts at quarantine.

By contrast, Freelanders had learned to cherish the differences in race, religion, and sexual orientation that enabled their mutual survival.

In the year 2095, eighty-two years after the Border was first erected, the satellites that control the photoelectro-magnetic shield were irreparably damaged. Freeland was about to lose the only thing that had stood between them and Elysium, their mortal enemy.

# Chapter 1

Whit gulped oxygen, the sound of her own breathing loud, even with a helmet covering her ears. The Elysian F-24 jet seemed tied to her tail, mimicking every evasive maneuver Whit's streamlined Peregrine was making.

Below her, the blur of dark, blue-green fir forest rippled away to the horizon of the granite-topped Cascade Mountains. To her left, Puget Sound was revealed in a bright glimmer of water. Beyond the Sound, the magnificent, snowcapped Olympics rose. It all looked wild, lovely, and untouched, and Whit knew that for the most part, it was. The crowded urban sprawl that had marked the corridor along Interstate 5 a century ago was hard to see from the air. Seattle was just another high-rise western ghost town, and the forest had reclaimed the suburbs with a voracious vengeance.

*If I could just get above him.* Whit anxiously scanned her datalink, evaluating the speed of the F-24 that pursued her.

Her Peregrine was a smart plane, its computer circuitry wired to sense the Elysian jet's coordinates and to configure multiple statistical outcomes, predicting where the enemy jet would go and what it would do next. Whit gave only cursory attention to the stream of color-coded information going by her right eye on the tiny helmet screen, however. Whit depended more on her own mystical combination of guts and intuition than on any scientifically correct computer prompts.

Ahead of Whit's Peregrine, another F-24 dropped out of a cloud bank, speeding toward Whit with deadly intent.

*Shit! Now there're two of them!*

Whit yanked her joystick right, sending her small fighter jet into a brief barrel roll. Relying on sheer instinct, Whit dramatically dropped speed.

Immediately, the datalink codes flickering on her helmet viewscreen went from yellow to fiery orange. The color change meant that she was only a few seconds shy of being targeted.

*Concentrate. Take them one at a time.*

She executed another barrel roll.

Cold sweat trickled down her neck and slid inside the high collar of her flight suit. Her heartbeat thundered in her ears above the quiet hum of the cold-fusion engines on her wings, her heartbeat was thundering in her ears.

Then the cockpit shuddered as the chasing jet plowed right by her. Shouting in triumph, Whit fought to stabilize her craft, riding his updraft and climbing above the F-24.

Before her targeting system could green-light her, she read the angle and squeezed off a rocket. Seconds later, the first jet burst into a huge fireball before her. Whit banked sharply left, scanning the orange data on the top right of her helmet's viewscreen. She knew the other F-24 was bearing down on her, but she was no longer certain where he was.

*Should I dive? Climb?*

Then, unbelievably, the data on the viewscreen turned blood red and the target alarm screamed. Whit peered through the canopy, as a slight, silver missile emerged from the blue sky to her left. Her stomach flipped.

*No! No!*

The noise of the explosion surprised her, as it always did, and the Peregrine dropped violently. The blue-green fir forest came rushing up at her. Whit gasped, using her elbows and knees to brace herself.

The computer announced, "YOU HAVE BEEN DESTROYED. END OF ARC SESSION NUMBER NINE."

A familiar voice came on the end of the computer message, startling Whit. "Hey, speed demon, come out of there. I have something to tell you."

"Kali," Whit responded, still trying to orient herself.

Smoothly, the Peregrine simulator settled and stilled. The enveloping blue sky and forest shimmering on the other side of the canopy disappeared, replaced by an oppressive black emptiness. Nausea, her body's usual response to a high-G workout, squirmed through her like a serpent. In stark white print, the viewscreen on Whit's helmet screen stated, "SHOT DOWN."

With a growl of frustration, she yanked off her helmet. Someone in the control booth must have keyed the canopy, for it slid back, and the dark cockpit was bathed in the dim, greenish light of the Artificial Reality Centrum. Whit snapped off the simulator controls, then released her seat belt. With the smooth coordination of an experienced pilot, she tucked her helmet under her right arm and hoisted herself free of the flight chair.

*That was pathetic.* Whit grimly raked a hand through her damp, dark hair. *I was indecisive. I was slow . . .*

Brooding, she stepped over the side of the Peregrine to the stub of its wing. With a practiced leap, she left the simulator and landed on the metal grill deck. She stood and glared at Danu's latest creation.

Mounted on powerful hydraulic posts and encased in what was essentially a huge wind tunnel, the Peregrine simulator was programmed to interact with a pilot in a challenging game of aerial chess. Thanks to the simulator, scores of novice and veteran pilots stationed in Isis had the opportunity to hone their fighting skills. Still, she hated losing to a machine.

Across the steel deck, a control-booth door opened, and then Kali was there, smiling at her.

Instantly distracted, Whit smiled back. *She's glowing. Wonder what that's about?*

Laughing, Kali rushed into her arms. Whit lost her grip on the ARC helmet, dropping it to the metal deck where it hit with a bang and rolled away.

Making a small, breathless moan, Kali hugged Whit closer, and arousal flared in Whit like fire in a drought-parched forest.

Laughing, Whit joked, "Hello to you, too."

In answer, Kali reached up and caught the back of Whit's neck, pulling her head down.

This was not their usual wifely greeting kiss. Kali passionately slipped her tongue across, then partially through Whit's lips, and Whit melted. Kali's hands brazenly ensnared Whit, unleashing all the seductive power that Whit often found in her lover's arms in the privacy of their bed.

Gasping, Whit caught Kali's hands and broke the kiss. She glanced significantly at the dark windows of the control booth, protesting, "Hey, we're giving everyone quite a show!"

Kali shook her head no, and her long, straight, blond hair shimmered in the strange half-light. "As soon as you blasted the first Elysian jet, I volunteered to shut down the works when you finished and then sent the simulator crew off for dinner." Smiling as if she had a secret, she offered, "I wanted some time alone with the great Leader of Isis."

Perplexed, Whit began, "I know my crazy schedule doesn't leave us much time anymore . . ."

"No," Kali inserted quickly. "I'm not complaining." She nestled against Whit again, possessively running her hands up Whit's arms to her broad shoulders. "Goddess knows, I've been just as busy. I've spent so many hours decoding my mother's satellite configurations that I'm doing math equations in my sleep."

Whit gave her a squeeze. "Thank Gaea we have you. Without your knowledge of Maat's original design, the satellite team would never have gotten away with manipulating Maat's Border program for as long as they have. As it is, we can keep the Border in place —"

Grimly, Kali finished, "For a short while longer."

Kali shivered, and Whit realized she was frightened. *For good reason.*

A saboteur had damaged the satellites that held the Border in place during a bizarre attempted coup six months earlier, in November 2094. It was now late April 2095. There were only so many reconfigurations available, which Kali had made clear when she proposed her stopgap solution and assembled her team of scientists. Internally, a deliberate power surge had overloaded the electrical circuits that ran each satellite, and steady deterioration had ensued. Soon the satellites would no longer function and the Border would fail.

*And when the Border fails, all-out war with Elysium is going to be inevitable.* Whit smoothed a gentle hand down Kali's back.

Kali stirred in her arms, and Whit kissed the top of her partner's forehead. "You said you wanted to tell me something." She smoothed a few stray strands of golden hair back from Kali's expressive face, waiting.

"Yes," Kali began, those deep brown eyes glancing up at her, and then away. "I ... um ... I ..."

*What is it?* Whit studied her. Kali was blushing and looking inexplicably shy. Whit heard her say under her breath, "I hardly know how to begin."

The door of the control booth slid open, revealing one of the younger members assigned to Whit's staff. Wide-eyed, the woman took in the intimate encounter before her. Kali moved out of Whit's arms and seemed to consciously collect herself. "Sorry to interrupt, ma'am."

"What's up?" Whit asked.

"General Medusa and her staff have just landed out at the airfield, ma'am. She's heading for the Leader's House as we speak. The General says she wants to see you ASAP."

"What?" Surprised, then annoyed, Whit replied, "I don't recall —"

Quickly, the clerk interjected, "This appears to be unscheduled, ma'am." She sent an apologetic look to Kali, then added, "She's very ... insistent."

"She is, is she?" Whit muttered, rubbing the back of her neck. *What kind of stunt is Medusa setting up now?* "Right," she said. "Call out to Cochran and ask my chief of staff to join us at the Leader's House."

Caught up in this new development, Whit headed for the door, then stopped and turned back to Kali. "Sweet Mother," she breathed, "I'm sorry, Kal." Whit extended her arm and with an affable shrug, Kali came over and slipped beneath it. "What did you want to tell me?" Whit asked, genuinely curious.

That same pleased, secretive smile stole over Kali's face. "It can wait till tonight."

"You're sure?"

"Yes," Kali said. "Come on. Let's go find out what old battle-ax Medusa wants with you."

Barely containing a laugh, the clerk led the way.

* * * * *

When Whit entered her office, Medusa's three military aides snapped to attention, hands over their hearts in salute. Whit, no longer an active-duty officer, knew it was a mere gesture of respect for her as elected Leader of Isis, but she still found herself snapping off an automatic salute in response. Old habits died hard.

General Medusa, who had been pacing by the tall windows, turned and scrutinized Whit. Approaching the woman, Whit took the opportunity to repay her in kind.

*After all*, Whit thought. *This is a Freeland legend in the flesh.*

In her dark gray warrior's uniform, the three stars on her collar gleaming, Candace Amanirenas Medusa appeared as rigid and formidable as an arthritic old grizzly bear. She was a tall, amply built woman. At five-foot-eight, she was only an inch shorter than Whit. Her white hair was close cropped, and the deeply ingrained lines in her dark skin betrayed the fact that she invariably wore the same disapproving frown that was on her face now. General Medusa seemed to be watching Whit with the keen, assessing eyes of a predator.

Whit launched into her standard welcoming speech, then introduced them to Kali, who stood calmly beside her.

Medusa's black eyes glittered as they flicked to Kali, and lingered there, moving over Kali's body with a subtle interest.

White was nettled. *Is she actually cruising Kal — right in front of me?*

"I knew your mother," the general told Kali with a slight bow. "I'd heard the resemblance was remarkable, but . . ." She cocked her head sideways and fell silent.

Then the general's regard shifted, and the dark eyes examined Whit's pale gray flight suit. "I've been informed that a small flight school is operating at your airfield." Dryly, she quipped, "Have you reenrolled, Leader?"

15

Whit met and held the sardonic eyes. "I like to work off job stress in the Peregrine simulator." She grinned slightly as she said, "Keeps my fighting reflexes sharp."

The coal-black eyes narrowed, and Whit knew Medusa heard the warning.

Expressionless, Whit waited. *You're the one who came busting in here making demands. Get on with it!*

General Medusa clasped her hands behind her back. "I've come to review your timetable, Whitaker."

"I assume you mean the timetable for the shuttle launch?" Whit returned.

Her voice soft yet impatient, Medusa hissed, "Yes."

Unexpectedly, Kali moved forward. "May I get you or your aides anything, General Medusa?" She laid a hand on Whit's arm as she passed, dispelling some of the indignation Whit felt. "Brew or a hot meal?"

Medusa politely refused, and again her eyes stayed on Kali.

Willing herself to courtesy, Whit explained, "I've sent for my chief of staff, Loy Yin Chen. She'll be here any minute with the latest dispatches from our launch site. Perhaps you've heard that we christened it the Jackie Cochran Space Center?"

One of Medusa's aides stirred, a small, pleased smile stealing across her face. "After the twentieth-century aviator . . ."

"Yes," Whit answered. "First woman to fly a bomber across the Atlantic. First woman to fly faster than the speed of sound."

The aide added, "To say nothing of directing the Women's Air Force Service Pilots during World War II. Damned fine naming."

Unsure just who this confident young major was, Whit inclined her head, accepting the commendation.

Medusa irritably cleared her throat. "We all know our herstory, Major Reno."

Motioning toward the comfortable armchairs nearby, Whit

turned back toward Medusa. "While we wait for Loy, I'll be happy to give you a complete update of our activities since the satellites were damaged last November."

Medusa ignored the chairs. "I'm listening." Her gaze once more drifted to Kali.

Kali made fleeting eye contact with Whit, and Whit recognized the glint of laughter there before Kali demurely dropped her glance and slid into a plush, dark leather chair.

*Yes, you're a fine-looking woman, but if she keeps eyeing you like that I'm going to . . .*

Kali shot Whit a censorious look. Kali was not only psychic, but she could also hear every wisp of a phrase that danced through Whit's head. *I'll never get used to living with a mage.* Whit smiled at Kali.

Whit ran a hand through her unruly hair, aware that everyone was waiting for her to begin. "As you know, General Medusa, Arinna Sojourner sabotaged the NASA satellites last autumn while trying to take control of both Isis and Kali. We managed to defeat Arinna, but the satellites appear to be permanently disabled."

Shifting her stance, Whit nodded at Kali. "With Kali's help, we were able to break down the Border program her mother wrote three decades ago, when Maat reworked Elysium's original system."

Kali spoke up. "One of the problems is that the solar-fed batteries are failing. Since the batteries fire the orbit-adjusting rockets, keeping the satellites aloft all these years, we've been trying to bypass the old ops programs with new ones."

Smiling proudly at her lover, Whit said, "Kali heads a staff of technicians who monitor the satellites and adjust data feeds to each one as needed. In doing this, we've managed to maintain the Border's integrity. It's nearly May, and city-colonies all over Freeland will be celebrating Beltane in safety tomorrow night. We've been able to stabilize the Border far longer than we dared hope."

Whit paused, letting this accomplishment speak for itself.

Major Reno remarked, "That *is* six months, General Medusa. Longer than anyone estimated."

The general rewarded this unsolicited observation with a withering glance.

Unfazed, the aide returned her attention to Whit.

For a moment Whit examined Reno, curious. The fact that she'd made major, while in no more than her mid-twenties, was intriguing enough. To compound it, she already had the lean, well-scrubbed look of a career soldier. With her mocha -colored skin and her gleaming, nut-brown hair arranged neatly in a long French braid, she was also a beauty. Increasing her attractiveness, the major's brown eyes were shining with some barely suppressed excitement.

*This one's ready for something. But what?*

Frowning, Whit went on, "Unfortunately, the satellites are still deteriorating. To be frank, we're still not clear what Arinna did to them."

Looking annoyed, Medusa chided, "Am I expected to believe these stories about Sojourner being a sorceress? That she sent — what? Magic? Hundreds of miles into space to wreak this havoc?"

"You can believe whatever you want, General," Whit replied quietly. By now she was used to the skepticism the report she had filed had provoked in the hierarchy of Freeland's military. "We here in Isis had the problem and we here in Isis dealt with it."

Catching the criticism in Whit's words, General Medusa asserted, "We sent you hundreds of warriors." An icy gaze swept over Whit. "As soon as the satellites began malfunctioning, the Eight Leaders Council issued a Code Red, and I've been readying our forces for worst-case scenarios ever since."

Whit took a step closer to the older woman. "While we were left to bring in Sojourner." She kept her voice even, but the hands at her sides clenched into fists. "We had to infiltrate an underground SAC installation in the North Cascades, a veritable fortress, where she sat like a spider with scanning devices and nuclear missiles . . ."

"I read your report," the general bristled.

"Two women died," Whit answered hotly. "Kali was nearly number three. Several friends of mine were seriously injured and may never fully recover." She took a deep breath and lowered her voice. "Sorceress or not, Arinna Sojourner was a killer, and we were lucky to stop her."

The general raised her eyebrows meaningfully. "You did not bring in a body."

Whit opened her mouth, then closed it, remembering.

She had been crouching behind a rectangle of insulated metal, clutching Kali desperately against her, as Arinna's blast of lightning ricocheted off the metal and rebounded on Arinna herself. Afterward, there had been nothing left where Arinna had stood. Nothing but scorched concrete. Everyone hoped that that meant Arinna was dead, but no one, not even Kali, was certain.

"I'm sure," Medusa drawled, "that I've never read a more outlandish report than the one you filed about Sojourner."

From her seat, Kali said softly, "General Medusa, let me clarify matters." She raised her large brown eyes and anxiously licked her lips. "Arinna and I were both Think Tank Babies."

Surprised, Medusa folded her arms over her chest and looked down with barely concealed aversion.

"I see you remember that enterprise," Kali went on. "My mother was convinced that her DNA experiments would enhance natural intelligence and build a more gifted gene pool." Kali leaned forward in the chair, resting her elbows on her knees and no longer looking at anyone directly.

Whit gazed at her, concerned. *She doesn't have to expose herself to their idiotic prejudice.*

"It's all right, Whit," Kali said. "I don't think there's any other way."

Sitting up straight, Kali half extended an arm, palm up. Seconds later, a tiny pale yellow light sparked up from her hand and gathered into a small, glowing ball. One of the general's three aides gasped, and Medusa herself stepped back as the fiery sphere hovering a few inches above Kali's palm steadily grew. The brightness writhed and flashed for about ten seconds, then, as Kali closed her hand into a fist, disappeared.

In the thick silence that followed, Kali clasped her hands together and gave a nervous laugh. "I don't think that's what my mother intended. However, it seems that Arinna developed an array of supernatural abilities. And to my surprise, I have . . . similar talents."

Her eyes suddenly alight, Medusa demanded, "What else can you do?"

"I'm still finding out," Kali returned. "Often I can't quite master a . . . trick . . . until I'm in a desperate situation."

Reading the vulnerability on her partner's face, Whit moved closer and rested a hand on Kali's shoulder.

Exhaling a small huff of breath, Medusa used a finger to tug at her uniform collar, muttering, "If I hadn't seen it with my own eyes, I would never have believed it was possible."

Blushing, Kali mumbled, "Neither would I."

At that moment, Loy Yin Chen strode though the door, followed by her attractive assistant, Hypatia Rousseau.

Loy greeted them with, "Came as soon as I could," then pulled a chip box out of her belt pouch. "Here's the latest," she announced, extending the chip box to Whit.

As Whit accepted the small box of data, she noticed the slight tremor in Loy's hand. Concerned, Whit lifted her eyes, examining Loy's face, then realized that the general was watching them. The hair rose on the back of Whit's neck, and she quickly pocketed the packet of information.

As Whit introduced her chief of staff, she caught the young major unabashedly staring at Loy. Once, Whit would have put it down to Loy's exotic good looks. Black-haired and almond-eyed, Loy had always turned heads. Now, however, Whit found even her own eyes fixed helplessly on the livid, sienna scar that ran along the right side of Loy's jaw.

*The plastic surgery repaired the worst, but Arinna still managed to leave her mark.* Aloud she said, "I know you've been on your feet all day, Loy. Have a seat."

Loy murmured to her assistant, "That's probably all for today, Hypatia. I won't keep you. See you out at Cochran in the morning."

If Loy had not observed Major Reno's continued scrutiny of her, Hypatia Rousseau certainly had. Raising her chin, Hypatia declared quietly, "No, that's all right. I'll see this meeting through with you, if that's okay."

Shrugging, Loy murmured, "Suit yourself."

Whit watched as her chief of staff moved to a chair across from Kali and settled in with casual ease. Looking determined, Hypatia went to the chair that flanked Loy's, removing her stylishly cut, knee-length coat as she went. She seemed to pause before Loy, all long legs and long, loose brunette hair, before she gracefully sat. Bemused, Whit caught the sharp, hard glance Hypatia flicked at Major Reno.

*Is Hypatia after Loy?*

Returning her attention to her chief of staff, Whit related, "Loy, General Medusa is coordinating Freeland's defense during the current satellite emergency. She needs an update on the shuttle launch."

"Ah," Loy remarked, tilting her head as she considered the general. "The FS *Independence*. Named, of course, after the seventy-four-gun ship of the line first commissioned in 1815." For a moment, Loy raised her eyes, contemplating the ceiling with an air of long-suffering. "Of course, we could have been outfitting a twenty-first-century ship of our own design — instead of this mothballed relic from Old America — but then the top brass at Warrior Central has been lobbying against space travel R&D for years now, so —"

Medusa growled, "There's only so much defense funding

designated in the national budget! It seemed a ludicrous waste of money . . ." All at once, the woman stiffened and shot a glance around the room, plainly annoyed to have been drawn into explaining herself.

"Loy," Whit commented with a meaningful look. *Please don't start pushing her buttons.*

With a small, forced smile, Loy met Whit's gaze.

Medusa merely narrowed her eyes, studying Loy as if she were a trespassing insect.

Crossing her legs, Loy leaned back and began reeling off information. Quickly, Major Reno stepped forward, keying a palm computer to Record mode and then placing it on the end table near Loy. As the major retreated, Whit saw her admiring eyes tracing over Loy. Clad in muddy construction boots, mud-spattered khakis, and a white T-shirt under a short-waisted leather jacket, Whit realized that even though filthy and very tired, Loy had the look of a woman who got things done.

". . . the shuttle is completely assembled," Loy was saying. "We also have the launch tower in place. By the way, Cochran is located in the Carbon River valley about ten kilometers from here. You really ought to come out and look it over while you're here." Running her fingers over the scar on her jaw, Loy paused.

"Right now, we're testing the cold-fusion fuel, trying to get the thrust factors worked out." She turned toward General Medusa. "As in most modern engines, we're using crystal drives, employing the power of prisms and endlessly refracted light to engender cold fusion. Once the light rays set the vibrational tone in the water-based fuel, small atomic nuclei in the water begin to fuse at room temperature, thus generating vast amounts of cheap, environmentally safe energy." Loy leaned forward and rubbed her eyes. "As a matter of fact, we probably couldn't pull this off without using cold fusion. Any rocket fuel we've been able to find in storage anywhere was completely unusable." Attempting a grin, Loy looked up at Whit and then Medusa. "Aside from charting completely new territory in trying to come up with the thrust factors of a cold-fusion space launch, we're running pretty much on schedule."

Hypatia inserted, "We expect to get the fuel factors worked out within the next day or so."

Brusquely, the general demanded, "You have selected a crew?"

"Yes," Loy said. "We hope to take a flight commander, pilot, mission specialist, and two payload specialists. But we might reduce crew if the amount of fuel we have to carry demands it."

The general asked, "And your launch date?"

"Approximate date, June 20," Loy returned.

Glaring first at Loy, then at Whit, Medusa repeated, "Approximate." She clasped her hands behind her back and pursed her lips as if she had just made a decision.

At last, Whit knew that her suspicions were correct. A serious power play was underway. *If only Lilith were here. But she's embroiled in that trade conference in Artemis.* Unhappily, Whit drew a deep breath, realizing that she was about to go one-on-one with a ruthless political veteran.

"I'm taking command of the shuttle project," General Medusa announced. She held out her hand to Whit. "I'll take that chip file, Whitaker."

Loy was on her feet. "It's a civilian project! The military has nothing to do with it!"

Hypatia sat forward in her chair, her eyes darting between the general and Loy.

"Loy," Whit said, her voice low but the tone of her command unmistakable.

Knowing well Loy's rebellious and headstrong nature, Whit did not really expect Loy to stop. After one glance at Whit, however, Loy bowed her head and stiffly sat down.

*She hasn't been the same since Arinna got hold of her,* Whit realized. *She's nowhere near as obstinate, but she's so*

23

*quiet now, and sometimes her hands shake. And according to Danu she's living like a nun.* Whit frowned, worried.

Encouraged by Whit's intervention, Medusa gave Loy a slight smirk. Whit decided to straighten out that misconception.

"General Medusa," she asserted, "my chief of staff has it right. I don't know what personal whim you rode up here on —"

Medusa bridled. "How dare you speak to me like that?!"

As if she hadn't heard her, Whit continued. "But I'd still need to see orders with the signatures of every member of the Eight Leaders Council before I could turn over control of the shuttle project. Since I am a member of said Council, and have signed no such document, I must assume you are operating entirely on your own."

Infuriated, Medusa demanded, "Are you accusing me of —"

"Circumventing the chain of command, yes," Whit answered, her voice firm.

Loy's face remained expressionless.

"Whit," Kali said quietly, "I'm sure General Medusa has our welfare at heart."

Collecting her temper, Medusa looked over at Kali and replied gallantly, "I do, my lady."

General Medusa's fist slowly met her palm several times in what appeared to Whit to be a nervous habit. "Freeland is in grave danger," Medusa suddenly confessed. "Despite the initial mandate for Isis to undertake the shuttle launch, the entire project is fast becoming linked to matters of national security. It is time the project came under my authority."

"Why?" Whit asked.

Medusa met Whit's expectant regard, then addressed her aides. "Major Reno, attend me. The rest of you, take positions outside the doors. Make sure nobody enters."

Major Reno, who had moved to reclaim her palm computer, went to General Medusa's side. The other two aides

24

marched briskly across the room, then closed Whit's office doors behind them.

Medusa looked from Whit to Kali, and then to Loy. "What I reveal cannot leave this room. Agreed?"

Loy sighed impatiently and leaned back in her chair. Hypatia checked Loy's reaction and then, in a milder version, mimicked it.

Her face puzzled, Kali nodded. Noting her lover's expression, Whit watched her for a moment. *She says she "hears" my thoughts like constant background music, but has learned to block the mind chatter of everyone else. But Kal isn't just waiting, like the rest of us, for Medusa to fill in the blanks.* Whit tilted her head sideways. *This whole situation has caught her by surprise, and that hasn't happened to my little psychic in months and months.*

Gesturing to her aide, Medusa said, "Major Mika Reno."

The young woman straightened.

"Tell them what you told me," Medusa ordered.

Reno stated, "At the current rate of deterioration, the satellites will fail before you launch."

Kali made a small, involuntary gasp.

"But," Whit argued, "expert scientists are reconfiguring the data, transferring functions from the damaged areas of the satellites to those circuits that are still operating."

Major Reno nodded gravely. "I checked with your satellite team and factored that into my findings. Regardless, the Border cannot remain intact beyond the second week in June."

A thick silence fell.

Disbelieving, Whit immediately looked over at Kali.

Kali's straight shoulders were hunched, as if expecting a blow. "I knew it would be close, but . . ." Her voice trailed off and then her gaze went inward. "Gaea! I should have known that."

General Medusa closed the distance between Whit and herself. "When the Border begins to disintegrate, it may manifest as a series of small holes in the overall screen. Or it may turn into large sections of open sky. Or the entire invisible wall may just suddenly be gone."

Loy spoke up. "Elysium is a primitive culture. Maybe they won't be able to detect the change."

"We can hope for that initially, but in the long run" — Major Reno gave a brief shake of her head — "it would be wise to prepare to defend ourselves. The Elysians will eventually attack."

Turning in her chair to look at the woman, Loy commented, "We *have* prepared. Why do you think Danu Sullivan designed and supervised the building of our Peregrine simulator? We've been training fighter pilots for months!"

Reno met her gaze. "May I remind you that you only have a small flight school and a few hundred warriors here."

Loy retorted, "You career warrior types think you're the only ones who know anything!" With an angry shove, she pushed out of her chair. "Whit and I are both pilots, both weapons experts, and we still hold our martial arts ratings! Kali, Goddess knows, could take on anyone in this room! Once you've served —"

"Enough, Loy," Whit interrupted.

At the same time, General Medusa rumbled, "Whitaker, call her off."

Fuming, Loy stalked toward the door. Hypatia hurriedly followed her. Mika Reno, who looked more than a little angry herself, briefly closed her eyes.

"Forgive me, but I'm starving," Loy complained. "Can we eat something before we get into this territorial slugfest?"

"Good idea," Whit agreed. "It's well past our usual dinner hour, and a good meal will probably put us all in a better mood." Attempting a cordial tone, Whit invited, "General, can I tempt you to sample the talents of our cook?"

After hesitating a moment, General Medusa accepted.

Loy stopped by the door, looking impatient. By her side,

Hypatia turned to glance back at them, tossing her dark brown hair.

"Then let's take this meeting in the dining room," Whit proposed. "I'm sure we can sort something out," she continued, as Kali stood up and moved to Whit's side. "Something that perhaps blends military and nonmilitary strategies of defense."

On the other side of Kali, General Medusa addressed Whit in a low growl. "Before or after the Regs arrive in half a dozen city-colonies, ready to rape and burn? Or have you forgotten what they did to Isis?"

Beside Whit, Kali, who already seemed paler than usual, went a sickly white. She reached out for Whit, and Whit caught her arm under the elbow. Soundless, Kali pitched forward in a faint.

# Chapter 2

Lunging, Whit barely managed to snag Kali's limp body around the waist and shoulders. Her breath coming fast, Whit knelt, gently lowering her partner to the floor.

For a moment, Whit's own head reeled. Then she shouted, "Loy, get a healer in here!"

Loy raised her wrist and rapidly sent a call through the tiny comline unit that was part of her chronometer.

Hypatia asked, "What's wrong with her?"

Loy motioned her silent.

Kneeling across from Whit, Mika Reno murmured, "With your permission, Leader." She leaned over Kali and began checking her vital signs.

Stunned, Whit glanced up at General Medusa, who stood just behind Reno. Consternation filled Medusa's eyes.

Looking down again, Whit was relieved to see Kali's eyelids flutter.

"She's coming around," Reno told Whit. She kept two fingers on Kali's throat, monitoring the pulse there as she stared at her chronometer.

Slowly, Kali's round, deep brown eyes opened and gazed up into the faces gathered around her. The dreamy, wondering expression in them quickly transformed to mild alarm.

"Wh-Whit?" she asked.

Tenderly, Whit stroked bright, yellow hair back from Kali's forehead. "You fainted," she answered breathlessly.

A rose-colored blush swept up from Kali's neck. "Oh no," she whispered.

Mika Reno moved back. "You seem all right now," she told Kali. "But you probably should see a healer —"

Brusquely, Loy interrupted, "Weetamoo caught the emergency broadcast I sent and says she's on her way."

"Dear Goddess," Kali muttered, becoming agitated. "Not Weetamoo." Then abruptly, she surprised them all by sitting up and readying to stand.

"Whoa," Reno responded, laying a hand firmly on Kali's shoulder and holding her in a sitting position.

"Kal, stay down," Whit protested.

"Whit, it's nothing, really," Kali replied, sending a sheepish look up at General Medusa.

Medusa's eyes narrowed.

"How can you say that?" Whit demanded. Worried, she ran a hand down Kali's back. "You don't go around fainting. This could be really serious —"

"Serious!" Medusa burst out, her black eyes triumphant. "Of that I have no doubt! If I'm not mistaken, your newly acquired domesticity is about to become serious indeed, Whitaker!" And then the general roared with laughter.

Across the room, Loy commented to no one in particular, "And here I thought she had no sense of humor."

Mika Reno looked some sort of question at Kali, and Kali gave a brief nod, then glanced up at the general again. Kali seemed exasperated.

Completely baffled, Whit frowned. "Am I missing something?"

Medusa managed to control herself long enough to clap Whit on the back and pronounce, "An old-fashioned girl, too! You flyers have all the luck!"

Making a great effort to remain diplomatic when she felt like grabbing the general by the collar and shaking her, Whit gritted her teeth. Quietly, she stated, "I'm not sure I understand what's so funny."

Bursting into laughter once more, Medusa winked at Kali. "I'll leave you to it then. No doubt my barging in on you sent somebody's plans awry." Sobering, Medusa stated, "My sincere apologies, lady."

Still blushing, Kali nodded, then lowered her eyes, studiously avoiding Whit's gaze.

Medusa headed for the door, signaling Reno to follow her. As she passed Loy, the general proposed, "Perhaps your chief of staff can steer us toward chow and bunks."

Loy raised her eyebrows and looked at Whit.

Whit gave a curt nod. *I seem to have no control over this meeting, or anything else. Why the hell should I object to adjourning?*

Pleased, the general finished, "We'll meet you here in the morning — seven sharp."

Medusa continued toward the door, and Hypatia folded her arms across her chest and looked away. Loy hesitated, studying Kali with concern. Smoothly, Reno leaned close to Loy's ear, talking softly. Then, seeming surprised, Loy glanced back at Kali and then flashed Whit a grin of pure wicked delight. With a few quick strides she and Reno joined the general, leaving the office. Hypatia followed behind them.

Feeling vexed, Whit met Kali's eyes. "Would you mind telling me what's going on?"

Just as Kali opened her mouth to reply, Weetamoo came stalking through the door. In her mid-fifties, grizzled and bony and frowning like a fierce tribal grandmother, the healer hurried across the office to Kali's side.

"I'm fine," Kali told her. "I just got a little dizzy."

Using a well-placed elbow to maneuver Whit aside, Weetamoo passed a small bioscanner over Kali, then checked the readouts and sighed. "Let me guess," she answered dryly. "You haven't eaten dinner, and lunch was a long time ago."

"W-well," Kali stammered, "we were just on our way . . ."

Her voice firm, Weetamoo declared, "I warned you about this. There are a great many inconveniences to foregoing the Delphi Clinic."

Puzzled, Whit repeated, "Delphi Clinic . . ."

Ignoring Whit, Weetamoo's dark brows pinched together, further wrinkling her weathered, coppery face. "Carrying a child is not some mystical experiment, Kali Tyler. You have to —"

With a gasp, Whit leaned back, staring at Kali.

"— follow the rules." Eyeing Whit's shocked expression, Weetamoo finished. "And if you weren't such a damn workaholic, Whitaker, your partner would be able to get you alone for an afternoon to tell you the big news."

"A child?!" Whit choked. "But-but . . ."

As Kali watched Whit flounder, a tentative smile broke over her face.

A sudden, loud guffaw escaped Weetamoo. "This is priceless," she told Kali.

"Mother's blood! I can't believe it," Whit managed, as, to her amazement, tears flooded her eyes. Grabbing her partner, she choked, "Ah, Kal." Then she was pulling Kali into an embrace and rocking her in her arms.

Happily, Kali clung to her, laughing.

"Eat something, Kali," Weetamoo ordered, then gathered

her creaking knees under her and stood. "And follow the prenatal guidelines I gave you earlier today. I'm not of an age to be crawling around on the floor treating swooning mothers."

Whit and Kali turned, each calling their thanks, while Weetamoo glanced back at them once, then chuckled all the way to the door.

Shortly afterward, Whit placed a dinner order with the kitchen staff and had a small feast sent up to their bedroom.

Kali snuggled into Whit's side, sighing peacefully. "Dinner in bed . . . What a good idea."

They were in their personal suite, located on the third floor, at the far rear corner of the Leader's House. One huge room contained a fireplace, sofa, and armchairs, with a spacious bedroom area arranged at one end. A low-walled, stone balcony wrapped around the outside of their quarters, providing a place for Kali to pace when she felt too enclosed.

Whit knew Kali's need for open doors and a means of getting outside quickly would probably never diminish. She had learned to accept that Kali would never get over some of the effects of her imprisonment in Elysium.

In their suite now, the lights were low. The two women were lying together on a large bed, propped up by a small mountain of pillows. They were already in their sleeping attire: well-worn gray T-shirts that were the remains of Whit's military uniform days.

Smiling, Whit guided another grape between Kali's lips. "I'm going to pamper you from now on. You need to take it easy."

Kali chewed, then revealed, "I don't intend to change a thing I'm doing." She looked up at Whit. "I'll still be working with the satellite team. And I'll be going ahead with my plans to create a Wiccan Institute, right here in Isis. Which means when I'm not reconfiguring the Border program for the satellites, I'll be up to my elbows in curriculum material."

Whit brought a spoonful of brown rice up, and Kali stopped talking long enough to let Whit feed it to her.

Watching her, Whit sighed. The force of love she felt for this woman shook her down to her marrow.

"As long as you follow those guidelines Weetamoo mentioned," Whit cautioned. Frowning, she remarked, "Keep in mind that this pregnancy is probably going to be a lot harder on you than you think. There's a reason why most Freelanders let their babies grow from embryo to fetus in a Delphi unit."

"Are you all right with this, Whit?" Kali asked. She shifted to better see her lover's face. "I know I kinda went ahead and started this, making a bunch of decisions for both of us, without consulting you. But I wanted to surprise you . . . and . . . well, that's not actually true." Gravely, Kali studied Whit. "I really wanted a baby — and I wanted it this way." Nuzzling Whit's arm, she softly stated, "Can you understand?"

Kissing Kali's forehead, Whit whispered, "I think I do."

Kali confessed, "I've been feeling . . . anxious . . . about the satellites failing, the Border disintegrating . . .the Regs." She stopped and gripped Whit's hand. "I've been remembering the day the Elysians attacked Isis, the day our mothers died. In one afternoon, we lost everything."

*And you lost more than I ever did,* Whit thought. *I was over twenty miles away, in Artemis. You were here. You saw the Regs burn the city and everyone in it. The only reason you survived was because the Reg Tribune who led the raid saw a pretty, fourteen-year-old virgin and decided to take you home as a prize.*

Whit returned the nearly empty bowl of salmon and rice to the tray where the grapes were. Cradling Kali in her arms, she admitted, "I sensed that you were struggling with something. You've been so quiet lately."

Kali said, "After we both had ova harvested and stored in

the Delphi banks last February, I kept thinking about . . . my mother." She reached up and stroked Whit's cheek. "About your mother. I didn't know her well, but I remember Nike Whitaker. Whit, we deserve a family. Even with all the danger Freeland is in right now. It just makes me want this child more."

"Me too," Whit whispered, realizing how much she meant it.

Silently she reflected on the complex science Kali had set in motion. Parthenogenesis was barely fifty years old. Kali's ovum, or egg, had been sliced open by a gossamer laser beam, then an electron microscope had moved chromosomes from one of Whit's ova into Kali's, fertilizing the egg. Once mitosis occurred in a test tube, conception was officially underway. Yet Kali had not left the embryo to the care of the Delphi Unit, the large, artificial womb where just about every embryo in the colony grew from fetus to birth. Kali had obviously asked Weetamoo to implant the embryo on her uterine wall.

"Why a natural gestation, Kal?"

Sleepily, Kali blinked up at Whit. "All the old magic was natural . . . and holistic. Heart, mind, and body. I wanted our little girl to come from that — from my flesh, not a biochemical life-support tank."

Whit smoothed her hand over Kali's thick, blond hair. Grinning, she replied, "Of course. It has nothing to do with the fact that you love doing things the hard way."

Kali snuggled her cheek into Whit's chest. "Do not."

"Do too, my love."

"But you're glad I did it?" Kali asked, her voice soft with exhaustion.

"Great Goddess, yes," Whit returned, then kissed the top of Kali's head.

Barely audible, Kali's last remark drifted up to Whit. "Good. Because, between General Medusa and Loy, it'll be all over Isis by tomorrow."

Whit sighed. *And with the Beltane Ball tomorrow*

*night . . . It seems every rite of passage we have becomes a public event.*

The next morning Loy strolled into Whit's office and deposited a crystal vase filled with yellow roses on Whit's desk.

"Blessed be," she greeted, giving the customary expression with a genuine warmth. "Thought I'd come early and try to catch a moment with you before the great general and her trusty aide arrive," Loy announced with a grin.

Surprised, Whit switched the shuttle-launch project file, which she had been reviewing on her computer, into a temporary security screen. She stood and stepped around the desk. Entranced with their intoxicating scent, Whit bent over the roses.

"Congratulations, Whit," Loy said. "And don't worry, you'll make a wonderful parent."

A small, private smile formed on Whit's lips as she felt Loy's phrase wrap around her. *You'll make a wonderful parent.* Loy knew Whit on a level that few others did. She understood that the very thought of parenthood, with all its unknowns and responsibilities, scared Whit to death.

Impulsively, Whit straightened and turned. She reached out and caught Loy by the shoulders, pulling her into a rough hug.

Instead of returning the embrace, Loy abruptly jerked backward, out of the Whit's grip. Amazed, Whit stared at her.

Loy looked away, her face tense with embarrassed anxiety, unable to meet Whit's questioning gaze.

"S-sorry," Loy whispered. "Can't seem to manage that sort of thing, anymore."

Whit took a step toward Loy, reaching out, wanting to run a soothing hand along Loy's arm.

Again, Loy retreated from her. "Don't," Loy said, her voice tight and quiet.

After a short, strained silence, Whit asked, "Are you still seeing that therapist?"

Shrugging, Loy gave a brittle laugh. "Yeah. She says it's a quite normal reaction to —" She broke off and swallowed.

*To rape*, Whit finished silently. Her cold fury for Arinna briefly resurfaced. *Who would have thought another woman could do this? Could take a strong, vibrant soul and purposefully wound her so badly?*

Despite the scar on her jaw, the combination of Chinese ancestry and pride made Loy breathtaking. Watching her trying to hold her emotions in check, Whit realized that, though her love for her had changed, she still did love Loy. Their adolescent affair had turned into an intense rivalry, and then open animosity. All that had changed, however, since the battle with Arinna Sojourner. The scar Loy wore had been earned in saving Kali's life. Loy was now her chief of staff, her most savvy political advisor and, aside from Kali, her closest friend.

"I'm all right," Loy said quietly. "Really."

"Sure," Whit breathed. She turned and touched one of the rose petals. "Thanks, Loy. For the thought, and for what you did last November — saving Kal."

Looking even more embarrassed, Loy grumbled, "Don't start with that again. It was a team effort." She moved along the front of the desk, away from Whit.

"Okay." Whit studied her. *I don't know how to help you.*

There was a noise behind them, catching Whit's attention. In crisply pressed gray uniforms and shining knee-high boots, General Medusa and Major Reno came through the door.

"Congratulations on your expectant motherhood, Whitaker," General Medusa barked. "Even though you are not the one going the full term, you're still in for quite a ride."

Loy cocked an eyebrow at Whit and one of her trademark smirks tugged at one side of her mouth.

Clasping her hands behind her back, the General revealed, "My partner, Ashanti, carried our first child, as your Kali has chosen to do." A small smile, full of fond remembrance, broke over Medusa's face. "She carried all four of our children, and raised them to be strong, brave women. She was a wonder."

"Was?" Loy asked, the smirk gone.

"Cancer, two years ago," the general stated, her tone quiet. "Like many North Texans, Ashanti enjoyed her tobacco. Grew her own. None of us could get her to give up that damned pipe."

Not knowing what to say, Whit bowed her head. *Goddess, if I ever lost Kali . . .*

Gently, Major Reno inquired, "Shall we begin?"

Whit grabbed the document packets she'd prepared earlier and moved away from the desk. "If you'll follow me," she invited, then guided the group into the conference room next to her office. Loy followed, then lingered at the door, closing and sealing it behind them all by thumbing the crystalline DNA plate embedded in the wall.

Whit handed the documents to Medusa and Reno.

"We've been compiling this data for the past five months," she explained as Medusa and Reno sat down at the rectangular oak table. "I'll let you have some time to look it over before we go into it in detail."

Whit pushed her hands into her pockets and began circling the table. Wordless, Medusa and Reno read, flipping pages occasionally. Loy stood by the door, like a sentry.

Roughly twenty minutes later, Major Reno leaned toward General Medusa and murmured something to her. The general quietly ordered, "Copy it." Reno reached into a pouch on her belt, withdrawing her palm computer. She held the device over a page, preparing to scan the data into her files.

Astonished, Whit shouted, "Stop!"

In a blur of motion Loy was beside the major, wresting the palm computer from her grasp.

Swift as a cat, Reno was on her feet, but Loy sprang back,

pushing the palm computer into her pant pocket as she slipped around to the opposite side of the table. "Don't make me destroy it," Loy warned as Reno made a move to follow her.

"Hecate curse you, Chen!" Medusa threw down the document she held and stood. "Whitaker, is this your idea of a collaborative effort?!"

Whit gave a slight, sardonic laugh. "General, collaboration involves two parties bringing an equal effort to a cause, not one party giving up everything to another and allowing that party to take over the entire operation."

"Do you intend to bargain with me?" Medusa roared, "We're about to go to war, not to some damn market bazaar!"

Furious, Medusa shoved her chair out of her way and strode toward Loy. "Chen, you're every bit as crazy as that psych file made you out to be!"

"You had a psych file done on me?" Loy demanded. "They think I'm crazy?" She snorted, then blustered, "How flattering."

As Medusa came closer, Loy evaded her by hopping up on the long, wide conference table.

Medusa motioned Reno to go after Loy, and the major climbed smoothly up onto the table too.

Her eyes dancing, looking as if she were thoroughly enjoying herself, Loy went into a crouch, ready to fight.

Reno went into a similar stance. A strand of curly, brown hair escaped her French braid and fell along her left cheek. Impatiently, Reno pushed it over her ear.

Going to the edge of the table, Whit muttered to herself, "And the Elysians say women can't govern."

Reno glanced down at Whit. Slowly, she straightened and surveyed Loy. Reno put her hands on her hips and started to laugh. "You *are* crazy," she told Loy.

Loy laughed back at her.

"Has this gone far enough?" Whit asked General Medusa, her voice low and controlled. "Or do we have to have a brawl in here before we can establish a common agenda?"

Silence reigned for a few seconds before Medusa barked, "Sit, Major," and angrily returned to her own seat.

Reno hopped off the table and slid into her chair, but her amused eyes stayed on Loy. A moment later, Loy regally descended.

"Now," Whit said, sitting on the other side of General Medusa, "we have redesigned and assembled a space shuttle. We are about to send it into space, loaded with new satellites. Why, after months of no contact, is the military suddenly so interested in this?"

Loy pulled out a chair next to Reno, across from Whit. As Loy sat down she and Reno exchanged a steady measuring gaze, and Whit was amazed to see a darkening color creep over Loy's face. As if to cover her embarrassment, Loy pulled Reno's palm computer out of her pocket and, with an exaggerated bow, returned it.

"Thank you," Reno murmured, slipping the tiny computer back into the leather pouch on her uniform belt.

General Medusa folded her hands together. "I'm on a fact-finding mission, Whitaker. Despite her youth, Major Reno is an expert in the field of rocket science. Tell Leader Whitaker what you discovered, Major."

Reno met Whit's eyes. "Your launch may fail," she said evenly.

"Speculation," Loy charged quietly.

Reno shifted her regard to Loy. "Between the cargo and the fuel you'll be carrying, there's a lot of weight on board — maybe too much weight for the shuttle to achieve escape velocity."

Loy challenged, "No one knows the exact thrust-potential of cold fusion — it's never been used for a shuttle launch."

"All the same," Reno answered, "you must achieve seven miles per second to leave earth's gravitational field — that's escape velocity."

Loy coolly responded, "We're only going into earth orbit, not space. We don't have to go that fast —"

Her expression earnest, Reno continued, "In trying to launch the shuttle from Isis, you're gambling — admit it." Her eyes swung back to Whit. "The Pacific Northwest is too far north. Even with the benefit of cold fusion's high power-per-liter ratio, you're still forcing the shuttle to carry huge amounts of fuel because you're not involving the natural boost of the earth's rotation. You wouldn't need all that fuel if the launch were made from a latitude closer to the equator."

A thick silence followed Reno's words.

Dryly, Loy suggested, "Such as Lang. What a coincidence that Lang just happens to be General Medusa's home colony. Yours, too, if I'm not mistaken."

Medusa leaned forward and glared at Loy. "Are you accusing me of political patronage?" Furious, Medusa turned to Whit. "I heard she was an impudent maverick, but this is —"

Her eyes flashing, but her expression inscrutable, Reno interrupted her superior. "Beg pardon, General Medusa, but may I debate the point with the chief of staff?"

Medusa growled ominously, "Just get this over with, Major."

Reno faced Loy. "Lang *is* Old Texas territory — Freeland's southernmost city-colony, yes — which makes it an ideal place for a low-latitude launch."

Loy gave a short, humorless laugh.

"However," Reno went on, "in that location a west-to-east launch would also be optimal. So a launch from Lang would have us dropping stages — huge, solid-rocket boosters — all over Tubman and the best agricultural land in Freeland. Clearly Lang is not a logical launch site."

"Then where do you recommend?" Whit asked.

Reno replied immediately. "NASA once launched shuttles southward down the Western Test Range from Vandenberg Air Force Base when that part of the country was southern California." She leaned forward and that same piece of curly, brown hair fell by her cheek. "It was a polar orbit — not as fuel efficient as an equatorial orbit, but the metal debris fell over the southern Pacific. No danger to people or land. NASA was also able to recover its solid-rocket boosters from the ocean. As a known commodity, Vandenberg seems to be the optimal launch site."

Beside her, Loy appeared anxious. "That was my first choice too. But the Regs will know about Vandenberg from archived Pentagon documents. They'll also have access to the later records on how the NASA satellites were used to control the Border. If the Border fails, or even just thins enough to allow our comline transmissions to penetrate, they'll know we'll be trying to get new satellites into space. The Regs will probably head straight for Vandenberg the first chance they get."

Reno grew thoughtful.

Medusa slapped the table. "Hera's sake, Chen! How smart do you think these Elysians are?" She laughed incredulously. "For the most part, they're ignorant savages."

Stubbornly, Loy countered, "In 2083, with only an eight-hour window, two Elysian troop ships and four fighter helijets flew through the northern Border gate."

Medusa snapped, "Don't give *me* a herstory lesson, Chen."

"Why not?" Loy demanded. "They were smart enough then, weren't they?" Loy stood, her voice growing louder as she placed her hands on the table and leaned toward Medusa. "Smart enough to go after Maat Tyler — the woman whose computer program controlled the Border! They knew she was in Isis, and their sneak attack on this city-colony wiped Isis off the face of Freeland for ten years — until Kali and Whit had the guts to come back and refound it."

Reno put a hand on Loy's arm. "Your point is well taken."

Surprised, Loy flinched away from Reno's hand and stared down at her.

Reno folded her hands together. To Whit's observation, Reno seemed to purposefully take no notice of Loy's reaction.

Leveling fierce dark eyes on Loy, Medusa barked, "No one speaks to me like that!"

Still flushed with anger, Loy flicked a look at Whit.

Whit sighed. "Perhaps the tone was objectionable, General." With a shrug, she finished, "But truth is truth."

Seeming satisfied to have had her say, Loy sank back into her seat. Medusa cut Whit a sharp, measuring glance. As if anxious to keep them on the actual topic, Major Reno leaned forward and softly cleared her throat.

"Now . . . suppose we could move up the launch date," Reno proposed. "That would ensure that the Border would remain intact and that there would be no danger of invading Elysian fighter craft."

"How?" asked Loy.

"We'll assign military techs to the shuttle project," Reno answered, "set up around-the-clock shifts."

As Reno paused and looked expectantly at Whit, Whit asked Loy, "What do you think?"

Loy placed her elbows on the table and folded her hands lightly together. "Well . . . lessening the fuel load would make sense. Changing the site would work — as long as the location doesn't endanger the shuttle. We've only got one, you know."

Reno agreed.

"What will a change in launch site involve?" Whit prodded.

Frowning, Loy looked at her hands. She subtly moved them below the table, but not before Whit saw that they were trembling.

"All it would really need," Loy began, "is the construction of a new launch tower at Vandenberg. That would take maybe three weeks. With Cimbri's permission, we could borrow one of those big grain haulers from Artemis, rig a piggyback attachment, and have the grain hauler fly the shuttle down there."

Whit asked, "So you'd be comfortable with reworking your navigational charts?"

Reno spoke up then. "I'd like to do those, if you don't mind."

"A good pilot does her own," Loy stated, sending a glance sideways at Reno.

"Precisely," Reno returned, then lowered her eyes.

As Reno's meaning dawned on her, Loy slowly turned to face the major. "*I'm* the pilot."

General Medusa announced, "I'm sure you'll agree with me, Whitaker. This mission needs a military presence."

Loy shot to her feet. "The hell you say!"

"The mission is too important. I want an officer in charge!" Medusa insisted.

Whit closed her eyes. In Medusa's demands, she was hearing her own words and tone from similar arguments in November, when she had been trying to forestall Kali's dangerous pursuit of Arinna Sojourner.

"Whit!" Loy demanded, her voice cracking. "Don't let them do this! When you needed someone to take on this sprawling mess of scientists and aviation contractors, *I* did it — not them!"

"You're a loose cannon," General Medusa pronounced. "Your behavior in here today has only confirmed my previous opinion of you."

Ignoring her, Loy stared across the table at the Leader of Isis. "I know I've made mistakes in the past. I certainly screwed up by getting involved with Arinna." She took a deep breath and blew it out. "I'm aware that a lot of people still question the fact that you've made me your chief of staff. But this is Freeland's only chance at peace. And I *know* I can do this."

Whit watched her, held by the intensity of Loy's gaze.

"A touching speech," General Medusa commented. "However, I am here to make certain Freeland's best interests are served. The reclamation of your personal honor, Loy Yin Chen, is low on my list of priorities."

Confounded, Loy's gaze swung to General Medusa.

Medusa met her look evenly, then turned back to Whit. "Leader, you no doubt have much to consider. I'll wait here in Isis for the next few days. That will give Major Reno and me the opportunity to tour Cochran Space Center tomorrow, after attending this evening's Beltane Ball."

Medusa rose and motioned Reno to follow her. At the door, they waited for Whit to key the lock-release code into the DNA plate.

As Whit complied, the general finished her ultimatum. "At some point, I'll take my case to the Eight Leaders Council." Meaningfully, Medusa narrowed her eyes. "And given the choice between Major Reno and Loy Yin Chen, I think we both know whom the Council will favor."

The door slid open, and the general crossed Whit's office. Troubled, Whit watched her stroll through the hallway door.

Major Reno lingered a moment, looking from Whit to Loy. "I'm sorry," she said softly, then followed the general.


On the outskirts of Isis, near the great hydroponics sheds that grew the fruits and vegetables that nourished the city-colony, Styx was parking her two-ton truck. All along Etheridge Road stood the burly frames of large warehouses, one alongside another. Cold and dry storage for all of Isis's food, as well as trade goods and mechanical needs, were located here. Among the rough, pinewood and stone structures, Styx's warehouse was a nondescript edifice.

Styx turned off the truck's electric motor. As the comforting purr ended, the young woman seated beside Styx on the front seat, stirred.

Stretching, Tor Yakami shook off the doze she'd fallen into during the drive from the airfield. "All I seem to do is sleep," she remarked unhappily.

"Maybe because you need it," Styx answered.

"Humph," Tor returned, not satisfied by that answer. "The physical therapist says all the strength building and aerobic exercises we've been working on should start to pay off anytime now. Instead, I just sleep more."

"Give it time, Tor," Styx said. "You've only been at it a few months."

Styx climbed out of the truck and greeted the dozen teenagers who tumbled shouting and laughing out of the warehouse door. This was her artifact reclamations class, which met two afternoons a week in a special off-campus arrangement with the Elizabeth Birch School. Both Styx and the school's headmistress believed there was nothing like hands-on education to foster a love of learning. Styx was able to pass on her knowledge of and respect for herstory, while gaining a multitude of enthusiastic, if relatively untrained, assistants.

While the girls raised the back door of the truck and clambered inside, Loy cautioned them to unload the cargo carefully.

"These boxes are filled with books from Old America," she told them. "I spent most of last week with a ruined-structures team, shoring up that big cavern that was once the Seattle Public Library." she told them. "After that, it was days of dirty, dangerous work, finding and carting out what was salvageable." She shook her head, "There was little enough, after so many squatters took refuge in there during the worst of the AGH plague. What books they didn't burn for warmth, many ended up pocketing and taking with them when they tramped off to die. The poor devils seem to have been trying to escape the horror by rereading old favorites."

"Can we read some of these ourselves?" one girl asked as she lifted a box lid and peered inside.

"Once we've catalogued the books, we'll scan them into the comline ancient books files." Styx explained. "You and everyone else in Freeland can read them at will."

Practiced with this sort of drill, the girls formed a bucket-brigade chain, passing the boxes from one to another

Her long black hair lifting in the wind, Tor wandered to the back of the vehicle, as if to join the chain of students. One of the herstory students up in the truck extended a box to her, and Tor obligingly reached for it.

Firmly, Styx called the girl by name and directed her to give the box to the next student in line.

Annoyed, Tor went over to Styx, complaining, "What use am I to you if you won't let me *do* anything. Why did you even ask me to go out to the airfield with you to fetch this junk? Warriors did all the offloading from the Pelican freight plane that flew it here from Old Seattle."

Calmly, Styx put a hand on the back of Tor's black leather jacket. Pressuring Tor forward, Styx walked her farther down the street, away from the youngsters.

Keeping a patient expression on her coppery-brown face, Styx replied, "I want you to help me design catalogs for the comline, catalogs that index the information in these books and maps. I need your brain, not your brawn, Lieutenant Yakami."

"Huh!" Tor answered. "I'm no lieutenant, anymore! I've been on medical leave since December — going on five months, now!" Discouraged, Tor abruptly stopped walking and turned. She stood watching the young women before them as they worked smoothly and energetically, passing the boxes of books from the truck to the warehouse. "I don't know what I am," she confessed.

With a considering gaze, Styx looked over Tor's painfully thin build. "You're a survivor, Tamatori," she pronounced. "My ancestors honored one such as you — one who went into the spirit world and then came back." Unperturbed by the scowl Tor gave her, Styx went on. "Among the Mayan, it would be thought you have been returned for a reason. I think you will discover what that reason is when the time is right."

"That's all anyone ever talks about — about how I supposedly died up there at Hart's Pass —"

Styx interrupted. "You had no heartbeat for over six minutes. Weetamoo told me. You died."

Frustrated, Tor turned on her. "Well I'm tired of this long, miserable recovery from it, okay? Do you know what it's like to have everyone hastening to help you all the time — until you can't go up a flight of stairs without someone hovering by your elbow? Do you know what it's like to have your lover afraid she'll kill you if you get a little wild in bed?"

Styx's dark eyes pinned Tor. "That's the problem?"

Realizing she'd let some of the truth slip, Tor turned away from her. Her shoulders were tense and hunched, and she took a few minutes to regain her self-control.

"Tell me what you're thinking," Styx gently invited.

Heaving a tight sigh, Tor said, "I wonder why she stays with me." She stared at the ground without really seeing it. "Danu's been away so much this year. Eight weeks of basic training way down in Morgan, a half-week of leave here with me, then eight more weeks of flight school in Boudica. That's a lot of time apart. She came up from Boudica a few times to see me, but still . . ." Tor gathered her nerve and finished, "I'm not the woman she fell for last autumn. Sometimes, I'm afraid she stays with me more out of compassion than love."

The girls had finished unloading the truck and were now lounging by the warehouse door, watching them.

Noticing, Styx used her teacher's voice to call, "Go get your computer slates turned on. When I come in, have yesterday's homework ready for me to check."

With a few soft groans, the teenagers all filed inside the warehouse.

"Look at me, Tor," Styx said.

Slowly, Tor turned.

"Danu loves you."

Tears filled Tor's eyes.

"Your loving heart is your strength and worth to us, Tamatori, not all those muscles you once had."

Almost soundlessly, Tor began to weep.

Tenderly, Styx reached out for her, enfolding the frail woman in her big, broad-shouldered frame. "You were given back to Danu when she thought she'd lost you forever, my friend." She laughed softly. "You'll probably never be rid of her now."

When Tor stayed in her arms, struggling to regain her self-control, Styx whispered, "It will get better, Tor. Your body will mend and regain its strength. Meanwhile, try to be patient with Gaea's plan."

Styx lifted her eyes to the blue sky above them, speculating, "There are many ways of being for each of us. Perhaps you have been given this experience as a means of coming to terms with other roles for yourself. You have been a warrior and a martial arts champion. What else can you do, Tor?"

Pushing back, Tor dashed a sleeve across her eyes. "I'm going to find out," she murmured.

"Good," Styx answered.

As they began walking to the warehouse, Styx wagered, "What do you want to bet that half the class doesn't have a slate ready and instead has pulled a book out of one of those boxes?"

With a laugh, Tor answered, "Isn't that what you'd do?"

# Chapter 3

Wrapped in a woolly cardigan, Kali left her room in the Leader's House and walked across the balcony. She shivered, then pushed her hands deep into the pockets of her old khakis. Her day's work with the satellite team had been hectic and draining. Now, studying the horizon, she took a deep, settling breath and tried to center.

Before her, Beltane night was creeping over Isis. In the west, the horizon was iridescent; a vibrant scarlet-and-gold light hovered above the great hills of the fir forest like a glimpse of eternity. Meanwhile, in the east, an ever-deepening royal blue steadily reached across the dome of the sky. The first star glittered over the huge, glaciered peak of Mount Tahoma, and Kali made a fervent wish.

*O Goddess, keep us safe. Give my child a chance to live and grow in this wondrous place.*

Below Kali, Isis was aglow with artificial light. The only completely darkened silhouettes in the Isisian skyline were the four-story office buildings that made up the business district. Farther away, in the residential areas, thousands of warm, yellow windows illuminated the gently sloping hillsides of the city. Closer to Kali, in the streets that led into the vast square that made up the marketplace, Kali could see the earliest revelers passing beneath street lamps. Sounds floated up to her on the evening wind: exuberant exchanges of conversation, gay music, and rollicking laughter.

Through the momentary peace, a disturbing thought surfaced. *Why didn't I know the satellites would fail before the launch? Why did Major Reno have to say it before I knew it was true?*

Frowning, Kali paced the balcony. This past year, she had gradually grown accustomed to living with the strange evolution of the psychic power she carried. Still, any ability at foresight seemed to be a nebulous, hit-or-miss sort of thing. What truly worried her, was something else.

*Is it my imagination, or are my psychic senses — not just the foresight, but the telepathy too, and even my certain knowledge of where Whit is and what she's doing — all getting fuzzy, all just off a little bit?*

"Where is she?" a voice behind her demanded.

Recognizing that voice, Kali turned around.

Through the open French doors, from the depths of the bedroom, she heard Whit say something in reply.

With a firm resolve, Kali set her anxieties aside.

A slender, older woman appeared in the doorway. Dressed in a silken powder-blue jacket and dark blue pants, her silver hair held in a matronly chignon, she presented a striking image.

"Beltane blessings, Lilith," Kali laughed.

Rushing forward, Lilith embraced her. "My little girl — pregnant!"

Unexpectedly, Kali felt tears begin. "I hoped you'd be glad."

Releasing Kali, Lilith stepped back and surveyed her. "Oh, I am, Bean Sprout." Her bright blue eyes shining, Lilith declared, "And I think that somewhere, our Maat is very glad, too."

Kali's throat went desperately tight, and she found herself unable to speak.

Lilith laid her hand affectionately along Kali's cheek, and they regarded each other a moment. Both of them were caught in memories of a loving time when Kali was small, when Lilith and Maat were raising Kali as their child.

Laughing, Lilith went on. "This morning I read the e-mail you sent on the comline, and I was so excited I nearly left the trade conference! I called Styx on her wristcom, and only her calm voice of reason, reminding me that I would see you tonight, kept me away."

"And where is Styx?" Kali inquired, smiling back at her.

"She's downstairs, providing an administrative presence in the ballroom, until Whit, you, and I descend." Drolly, Lilith added, "And loving it, I might add. While our dear colony herstorian pretends to eschew the trappings of pomp and circumstance, she actually adores organizing any sort of ritual."

"Well, my thanks to both of you for dropping by early." Barely suppressing a sudden yawn, Kali confessed, "Gaea, I don't know how I'll ever last until midnight. I'm so *tired* all the time, now."

Knowingly, Lilith smiled. "You'll notice a lot of changes in the next few months, I think." Taking the edges of the thick cardigan Kali wore, Lilith pulled it closer about Kali's chest. "It's cold out here! Why in the Mother's name are you —"

"Let's go in," Kali proposed gracefully, linking arms with Lilith.

Once inside, Kali closed the French doors behind them, then turned and swept her eyes over the room, looking for Whit.

This private suite was Kali's favorite place in the Leader's House. Large and luxuriously appointed, the room she shared with Whit was her safe harbor from the storms of everyday demands.

*Goddess knows that being handfasted to the Leader of Isis is no dance in a meadow*, Kali thought.

Brocaded drapes hung by each set of floor-to-ceiling windows. A thick, blue carpet ran the length of the room. Plush armchairs and two sofas by the fireplace made up a casual entertaining area at the near end, while closets, oaken clothes chests, and a huge bed dominated the space in the distance.

Whit emerged from one of the closer walk-in closets, pulling on a coral-colored, thigh-length jacket. A starched white shirt and black pants completed the outfit. Her shining, shoulder-length dark hair was loose, as usual, and neatly in place, as if she had just brushed it. Kali knew that look would last only until Whit's first nervous moment, when her hand would rake through and leave the tousled arrangement Kali preferred.

Grinning, Whit approached them, still settling the suit jacket on her shoulders.

"Excuse me," Kali murmured, freeing her arm from Lilith.

Whit stopped before them. "How do I look?"

Kali reached out, grasping Whit behind the neck. With a firm tug, Kali pulled her head lower and gave her a lingering kiss.

Beside them, Lilith laughed.

Kali released Whit.

Stumbling back a step, Whit exclaimed, "Wow! What's that about?"

"That's about what you do to me, my wife," Kali answered.

"Really?" Whit remarked, preening a little.

"Really," Kali told her with a smoldering glance, before turning back to Lilith. "And I'm sorry to say, I was admiring the sunset instead of dressing, so I'm not ready."

Lilith laid a hand on Kali's cheek. "I just came by to tell you how happy I am for you." She extended a hand to Whit. "For you both."

"Come down and work the receiving line with me," Whit proposed. "Kal will get squared away and then join us."

Lilith agreed. She placed a kiss on Kali's cheek, and with a grin, Whit mimicked the gesture.

As Lilith took Whit's arm and they walked to the door, Kali overheard Lilith. "So General Medusa has paid us a call."

"That's right," Whit said neutrally. Her free hand immediately dashed through her glossy, dark hair and left behind the roguish appearance Kali loved.

Pleased, Kali couldn't help the soft laugh that escaped her.

Whit and Lilith went on exchanging a series of quick remarks. Then, at the door, as she and Lilith passed into the hallway, Whit looked back at Kali and sent her a wink.

*She's the best thing that's ever happened to me,* Kali decided, sighing. *And she's giving me the next-best thing — our baby.*


Lilith had noted the tension in Whit's shoulders, had seen the distraction in her eyes, even before they had left Kali. She suspected that her protégée had already locked horns with Freeland's most stubborn general.

As Lilith expected, Whit waited until they were alone, walking down the long hallway, before fully venting her feelings.

"Mother's blood, Lilith! Medusa waltzed in here and in the space of twenty-four hours she's damn near taken over!"

Managing to hide a patient smile, Lilith asked for details.

Whit gave her a concise account of the morning meeting, describing how Reno had first lobbied for a change in launch location.

"That request seemed reasonable," Whit stated. "Loy and I were both ready to concede on that point."

"And then . . ." Lilith prompted.

"Then Medusa made it clear that she wanted Reno, not Loy, to pilot the shuttle."

So heated was Whit, that she had begun walking faster as she spoke. As they passed Whit's office, Lilith touched Whit's arm. "Why don't we step inside for a moment and see if we can come up with a few strategies."

Whit checked her chronometer, murmured, "Right. We've got some time," then reached for the DNA lock on the wall.

Before she made contact with the crystalline plate, a voice hailed her. "Leader!"

Lilith and Whit waited as Hypatia jogged down the hall toward them.

Handing over a chip box, Hypatia disclosed, "Chief Chen asked me to make duplications of this afternoon's fuel-test results and deliver one set to you." As Whit accepted the chip box, Hypatia swept a lock of brunette hair behind her ear. "The results include both Cochran Space Center and Vandenberg AFB launch site scenarios. Now we know exactly how much fuel needs to be carried, whichever site is decided upon."

"Thank you, Hypatia," Whit said, bestowing a gracious smile upon the young woman. Glancing at the grimy work jumpsuit, which seemed tailored to the woman's exact proportions, Whit asked, "Will we be seeing you at the ball tonight?"

"Yes ma'am," Hypatia enthusiastically returned. "I'm off to wash up and change into something irresistible, then I'm going to make sure Chief Chen forgets work for a night!"

"Good luck," Lilith said with a rueful smile, thinking of the sixteen-hour days Loy had been putting in lately.

Hypatia jogged back down the hall, as Whit reached out and touched the DNA plate. The door slid open. Whit led the way into her darkened office.

"Lights," Whit instructed the tiny environment-control unit mounted in the high ceiling, and the room was illuminated.

Once the door fully closed, Lilith focused on what seemed to be the important questions. "Who is this Reno? And why is General Medusa so determined that she fly the shuttle?"

Whit went to her desk, opened a secured drawer with a voice command, then dropped the chip box Hypatia had given her inside the unit. Once the drawer was locked again, she verbally keyed her computer. "Whitaker here. Run file on Major Mika Reno."

Behind Whit, a four-foot-by-five-foot wallscreen flickered, and a series of recorded images began to appear. A sweet-faced youngster of about fifteen saluted them, hand over heart. She was dressed in the pale blue flight suit of a warrior cadet, her brown eyes grave as she ran down a preflight checklist with an instructor, then climbed into a Peregrine Falcon. Her mahogany-colored hair blew in the wind for a moment, then disappeared beneath a helmet. Meanwhile, the modulated female voice of the computer was listing Reno's test scores at flight school.

"Great Cerridwen," Lilith couldn't help remarking.

"Yes," Whit agreed. "She's top gun — best marks ever achieved in any flight school in Freeland. She also maintained a 4.0 grade-point average in both astrophysics and avionics at the University of Lang."

Lilith whistled softly to herself. She watched the images on the screen shift, displaying a maturing young woman of increasing military rank. When the screen visual ended with a news-video of Reno's appointment to General Medusa's staff, Lilith raised her eyebrows.

"Only twenty-six," Lilith mused. "Is she Think Tank?"

"No, just naturally brilliant," Whit answered, watching

the wallscreen fade to a dull off-white as the computer program finished. "Store file." Whit's hand rubbed the back of her neck.

Lilith bent her head. *A formidable candidate for the job indeed.*

Whit slouched against her desk, looking disheartened. "And the truth is, I have doubts myself about Loy's ability to carry this off."

Surprised, Lilith studied her. "Why, Whit?"

"As well as Loy has coordinated this entire shuttle project, she seems . . . on edge." Whit pushed a hand through her hair. "She's always cool and in control on the surface, but underneath . . . I don't know how to explain it. She's so tense . . . as if she's suppressing all this emotion."

Lilith chuckled. "You could be describing yourself."

Whit's head snapped up, and her gray eyes widened. Recovering, she said, "Loy's hands shake."

"And you've grown forgetful," Lilith informed her gently. "You make lists of what you're supposed to do, where and when — oh, I've seen you pulling the little scraps of paper out of your pockets in the middle of meetings —"

Whit pushed herself off the desk. "Loy has never fully recovered from the ordeal she went through up in the mountains."

"She's exhausted — and so are you," Lilith returned. "Both of you have been working insane hours, Loy leading all the teams responsible for this shuttle launch, and you leading all the teams preparing Isis for the possibility of an Elysian attack." With a benevolent smile, Lilith laid a hand on Whit's shoulder. "Her hands shake because she's been carrying the world on her shoulders for months, and she's just plain worn out."

Whit looked away, showing Lilith she was unconvinced.

"And when you go home at night to your private suite and Kali, where does Loy go?" Lilith asked.

"Back to that tiny cabin she's leased out on South

Mountain Road," Whit answered, then sighed. "A dismally spartan little place with a computer, a bed, and that's about it."

Lilith let a moment's silence go by before venturing, "Marpe and Samsi tell me that, despite overtures from many different women, including her enchanting assistant Hypatia Rousseau, Loy continues to sleep alone."

Whit grimaced. "Marpe and Samsi are the two biggest gossips in the colony!"

Lilith shrugged and waited.

Finally, Whit grumbled, "Danu's told me the same thing."

"H'm. Will Danu be at the ball this evening?" Lilith asked.

"Yes," Whit replied. "Now that flight school is over, she's got two weeks leave. She's staying with Tor out at the home Kal and I built last spring."

"Almost too bad Danu's so involved with Tor," Lilith remarked. "Something about Danu certainly made Loy hot."

Whit shook her head. "You're outrageous sometimes —"

"The attentions of a good lover might be all Loy needs to cure those shakes," Lilith commented. She cocked her head to one side and inspected Whit. "It certainly has done a lot for you."

To Lilith's delight, Whit blushed scarlet.

Clearing her throat, Whit offered, "Loy has this . . . reluctance . . . to be touched." She passed a hand over her eyes. "Arinna did awful things to her."

Lilith bowed her head. "It may take time and trust, but with the right woman, that too can be surmounted." She looked over at Whit. "You more than anyone else should know the sheer obstinacy of the woman, Whit. Don't underestimate the courage that adversity draws out of her."

Whit sighed. "All right, let's say Loy is up to the task of piloting the shuttle. How in Gaea's name do we convince General Medusa of that?"

Lilith smiled serenely, and Whit laughed.

"Oh, Gaea, I know that look!"

"Does Major Reno have any actual combat experience?" Lilith inquired, her voice exceedingly mild. "After all, she's going to be a long way from home and completely in charge if the ... excrement ... suddenly hits the fan a few hundred miles from earth."

Whit whispered, "Sweet Mother, that's it."

"And we here in Isis are well aware of the mettle of Loy Yin Chen," Lilith elaborated. "She was Arinna's prisoner for months, enduring both physical and psychological torture, yet somehow she succeeded in sabotaging Arinna's entire defense system. Instead of having to penetrate a robotically protected bastion, Kali was freed to face Arinna one-on-one."

Whit shuddered. "And even then, Arinna nearly won."

Moving closer, Lilith slipped an arm around Whit's waist. "Kali won," she emphasized quietly, "because of Loy. Because of you, my dear."

Mute, Whit nodded.

"Freeland needs a woman on that shuttle who knows how to deal with a crisis," Lilith stated. "Someone who has already demonstrated her problem-solving skills." Lilith's bright blue eyes focused directly on Whit. "When confronted with a terrifyingly complex situation, Loy put her life on the line and laid the groundwork for incredible feats."

Whit nodded. "I'm convinced." With several long strides, she led the way to the door. "Now, if I can only make the case to General Medusa as well as you've made it to me."


As she murmured another greeting, Loy sent a restless glance down the line of women who were straggling past her. In the vast hall beyond the arched portico where she stood, Isis's Beltane Ball was unfolding in a loud, joyous eruption of music. From her position by the door, Loy could catch glimpses of beautifully dressed women of all ages and sizes, gathering in ever-changing clusters, exchanging dance cards and looking one another over with delight.

Reproachfully, Loy reminded herself to focus on the receiving line, on making each guest feel welcome. She was the third woman from Whit's side, with only Lilith, the elected deputy leader, between them. As Whit's chief of staff, she knew her placement in both the line and the community had never been more evident. Once, no more than a year ago, standing in this line as third rather than first would have filled her with jealousy and resentment; but a lot had happened to Loy since then. Tonight, she was filled with a stunned wonder.

Loy peered over at Whit. The Leader of Isis was smiling warmly, looking glorious in her coral-colored jacket and dark hair. As Whit shook an elder's hand, the woman dipped her head, looking vaguely overcome. Loy could understand why.

*When everyone else had written me off, Tomyris Whitaker appointed me to the highest post in her administration. I volunteered to fly the shuttle to repay her faith in me, because this mission has to succeed. And I know I can do it.*

Her thoughts were interrupted by a familiar sensation. She looked down at her left hand and saw it quivering like a beached salmon. With a soft curse, she grasped it with her other hand.

She was there again — in the war room of Arinna's stronghold, the ancient Strategic Air Command installation built into the bedrock of the North Cascades.

She was a prisoner, held against her will beneath tons of mountain rock. Her captor, Arinna, was a beautiful, horribly evil woman who nightly delighted in making Loy suffer. Nearby, Danu stood on the floor, three meters below the raised platform, her hands were tied behind her back. A mere meter and a half from Loy, Arinna leaned against her mainframe computer, her eyes on the wallscreen.

On the wallscreen before them, Loy saw Kali and Tor. They were in the large, dimly lit generator room down the hall from the war room, caught by the hidden cameras mounted there. Fighting with mounting desperation, Kali and Tor were paired against two humanoid robots. Arinna's robots were dressed in the green uniforms of Elysian Regulators, and Loy knew by the wide-eyed look on Kali's face that Kali was convinced she was facing her worst nightmare — Regs. With a rapacious smile on her face, Arinna watched one of the robot Regs seize Kali and sling her over its massive shoulder, carrying her toward the door.

Trying to be inconspicuous, Loy edged closer to the computer mainframe that controlled Arinna's voice link with the robots. Loy raised her left hand, fingering Danu's wristcom. It was the wristcom Arinna had taken from Danu when she was captured, the wristcom Loy had stolen from Arinna's bedroom last night. Loy had spent every moment since the theft keeping her intent hidden from Arinna's mind-reading powers. She had masked her thoughts, locking them on a series of chores — mundane sweeping and cleaning, preparing Arinna's victory feast. Arinna's ego had been adequately stroked, and Kali's impending arrival distracted her. Beyond her wildest dreams, Loy's subterfuge was succeeding.

Resolute, she flicked the switch that enabled the nanotech laser Danu had built into the wristcom. Still riveted by the events on the wallscreen, Arinna gave a triumphant yell. Loy fired the weapon. With a sizzling snap, the thin red beam sliced into the metal of the mainframe and, within a second, as the circuits blew, the whole mainframe became a fiery white light. Knocked backward by the explosion, Loy found herself lying flat on the platform.

On the wallscreen, the Reg carrying Kali dropped her. Both robots shuddered, and collapsed like limp dolls.

And then, through the smoke, she saw Arinna coming for her.


"Beltane blessings, Loy," someone said.

Released from the flashback, Loy blinked, disoriented.

As Loy turned toward the voice, something soft brushed over her lips. Instinctively, Loy lurched back.

Major Mika Reno was standing before her.

Astounded, Loy just stared, and for a moment Reno seemed uncharacteristically flustered.

"Beg pardon," Reno offered. "I was aiming for your cheek."

Loy stood there, speechless. She glanced down at her hand. The tremor was gone.

The couple in line behind Reno jostled forward. Reno reached out, took Loy's elbow, and maneuvered them both out of the receiving line.

"I have to talk to you," Reno said.

Feeling dazed, Loy allowed herself to be led into the corner. *Hecate, you've all but stolen my seat on the shuttle. What the hell else do you want?*

"Look," Reno began, running a nervous hand over her gray uniform jacket, "you have every reason to be upset, but" — a pair of earnest, light-brown eyes flashed up at Loy — "I hope you won't hold General Medusa's schemes against me."

Loy took a moment to settle herself, letting Reno fidget. "You're just a helpless pawn, " Loy countered wryly. "Is that it?"

Irritation glimmered in Reno's eyes.

Distracted, Loy glanced over her shoulder at the line of women passing in front of Whit and Lilith. *I ought to get back.*

"She's a general," Reno declared. "I'm a major. I don't get to have a whole lot of say about things, okay?" Suddenly Reno gave a heartfelt sigh. "But, Goddess, I'm sorry."

Struck by the oddity of the situation, of Reno's apologizing for taking her place on the greatest adventure any Freelandian had ever encountered, Loy couldn't help lauging.

"Tell me you're not thrilled," Loy challenged quietly.

The fawn-colored eyes met hers, and Loy saw the undeniable elation there. At the same time she noticed long dark eyelashes and flecks of gold near the iris. Without intention, Loy's gaze lingered, trailing over the smooth, brown complexion, the trace of freckles over her nose, the dark pink lips.

For the first time in months and months, sexual hunger stirred, confounding Loy.

Self-conscious, Loy tore her gaze away; she was looking everywhere, anywhere, except at the lovely young woman before her. As her heart pounded in her ears and she registered her own agitated breathing, she reminded herself of Arinna. *Never again. Never, never again.*

"I'd better get back," Loy said, edging away from her.

Reno, however, stepped forward and boldly reached inside Loy's pale cream-colored jacket. Deftly, she plucked the dance card from Loy's vest pocket.

Loy continued to walk away from her and, unperturbed, Reno followed her, writing on the dance card with the small pencil in her hand. Just as Loy returned to her place in the receiving line, Reno closed the small distance between them and slipped the card back into Loy's vest pocket.

"Where I come from, Missy," Reno told her, laying the Texas twang on thick, "ya gotta have a full dance card."

Loy frowned, perplexed. *Is she flirting with me?* she wondered. *Me? The scar-faced scoundrel her general despises?*

An attractive young woman in the receiving line walked between them, gave Loy a considering gaze, then bestowed a bewitching smile on Major Reno.

Reno ignored her and kept her eyes on Loy.

With a knowing arch of brows, the young woman kept walking.

"I'll be looking for you," Reno said, her voice low. Making a slight bow, she excused herself.

Instead of paying attention to the new group of arrivals going past her, Loy pulled the dance card from her pocket. Diagonally, across all twenty spaces, was scrawled one name: Mika.


Kali hurried into the ballroom, knowing she was late.

Beneath the scintillating lights of the chandeliers, hundreds of colorfully dressed women holding cups of punch or glasses of brew stood together in groups. Beyond the crowded throngs at the outer edges of the room, she could see the dancers whirling past.

From the far side of the ballroom, Lilith and her tall, dark partner, Styx, waved a greeting. Kali waved back and began to walk toward them.

In short, flouncy, pink chiffon, Hypatia Rousseau swept up to her. "I've been looking everywhere!" she complained. "Have you seen Chief Chen?"

Kali barely had time to shake her head no before Hypatia rushed on. "For months I've been trying to get her attention — and she just ignores me!" Glancing around almost angrily, Hypatia finished, "Well, not tonight, damnit! I'm sick of being taken for granted!"

Before Kali could respond, Hypatia made an exasperated noise and walked on.

A few feet away, an older woman turned from her place in a circle of other older women and watched Hypatia disappear into the crowd. Her eyes then moved to Kali, giving her a considering look. The woman held herself stiffly, and there was an ugly, judgmental expression in her eyes. Kali suddenly recognized her as Hel Campanelli, one of the astrophysicists who worked at Cochran Space Center. In a loud, carrying voice, Campanelli began delivering her unsolicited opinion to the group around her.

"Hypatia Rousseau would do better by avoiding that Chen woman than in seeking her out," she pronounced. "No matter what happened during that military strike in the North Cascades, Chen's still a traitor in my book. Too little, too late, I say."

Startled, Kali gazed at the brash woman. Before she could speak, a familiar voice behind her filled the gap.

"What do you know about what happened at Hart's Pass?" Red-haired and resplendent in her new warrior's uniform, Danu Sullivan appeared at Kali's side. "Loy paid in blood for whatever mistakes she made. I saw it."

The women surrounding the astrophysicist all turned. Kali caught two of them murmuring remarks about "That young Think Tank hothead" and "Wasn't there a scandal about Chen and this one?"

Hel Campanelli gazed at Danu and sniffed. "Mistakes? Is that what traitorous acts are called these days?"

Danu took a step closer. "How dare you." The older women all buzzed indignantly. Danu demanded, "Have you ever taken on a psychopath? Ever had your face carved open because you dared to stand up for your friends?"

Tor, Danu's lover, appeared on Danu's other side. Kali heard her uttering gentling words as she grasped an elbow and tried to pull Danu away, but Danu would have none of it.

"It's even more infuriating," Danu snarled, "to hear such crap coming from the mouth of a supposedly enlightened scientist! But then who needs facts to gossip, right Elder Campanelli?"

Kali stepped back, feeling oddly buffeted by the angry emotions swirling around her.

Unwilling to be bested in front of her crowd, Hel dropped her voice. She shot a furious look at Kali as she countered,

"There are still plenty of people unconvinced about Loy Yin Chen's miraculous change of heart — still plenty of people who think Whit is holding a snake at her breast by having Chen be her chief of staff."

Pressing a hand briefly against her head, trying to mute the tumult of thoughts and feelings rushing at her, Kali waited a moment. Then quietly, cordially, she inquired, "And have you had the temerity to make that remark to Tomyris Whitaker, Elder?"

The woman blanched.

Nodding, Kali barely suppressed a grin. "Then perhaps you might want to examine your own credentials in courage a little more closely before you call into question the courage or loyalty of others."

Firmly, Kali grasped Danu's hand and tugged her away. She moved determinedly through the press of women in the ballroom, as Danu tossed over her shoulder, "Gutless wonder!"

From the other side of Danu, Tor's laughter broke free.

Automatically searching the area where she had last seen Lilith and Styx, Kali realized they had moved. By her side, she felt Danu slow. Grinning, Tor moved in front of Kali, blocking her path.

"And now, let's talk about you, little mother!" Tor teased.

Wordless, on the opposite side, Danu was still clasping Kali's hand. She was saying volumes with her delighted smile.

"All right, all right," Kali protested, feeling the heat in her face. "I'm sorry I didn't get to tell you personally." With a mildly exasperated laugh, Kali explained, "You know how gossip travels in this town."

"No!" Tor mocked. "Although, I have heard rumors of my own death a few times this past winter . . ."

"Wow, look at you in that dress," Danu remarked softly, her eyes moving over Kali, fascinated. "Beautiful," she pronounced.

Kali glanced down at the strapless, pale-green gown she

wore. From surveying herself earlier in the mirror, she was well aware that the floor-length fabric accented the still-slender curves of her body. *At least this will give Whit a memory to hang on to in the coming months,* she thought uneasily.

Smiling a sincere thank-you at Danu, Kali reached out and ran a hand over the arm of Danu's new gray uniform. "Now that you've made it through both basic training and flight school, how do you like being a warrior?"

Danu gave a sheepish grin. "Don't much like taking orders all the time, but —"

Beside her, Tor pointed to the lieutenant's insignia on Danu's collar. "Look at this!" Laughing, Tor tousled Danu's short red hair. "Took me years to win those bars, and she got 'em in four months."

"Only because you spent weeks prepping me like a mad professor before I shipped out," Danu returned, grinning at Tor.

Tor tossed her long, black hair over her shoulder and gave a laugh. "I think it's called mentoring."

"You *are* a mentor," Kali remarked, thoughtfully, her eyes drifting over the black, short-waisted jacket and trim black pants Tor wore. While Tor was very thin, a mere shadow of her robust former self, what was even more arresting to Kali was seeing Tor in civilian attire. "If you're interested, once the satellite crisis is over, I'm planning on opening a Wiccan Institute right here in Isis."

Confused, Tor glanced at Danu, then back at Kali.

"You're my first choice, Professor Yakami."

"Me? A professor?" A mixture of disbelief and interest flickered across Tor's face. "What would I teach?"

"What you taught me," Kali said persuasively. "Zen, martial art techniques, channeling ki."

"Wow," Danu exclaimed to Tor. "You'd be great!" She sent Kali a swift look of gratitude.

Seeming bemused, Tor bent her head.

Whit joined the group. Her smoke-gray eyes moved appreciatively over Kali in an incredibly suggestive way.

Without taking her eyes off of Kali, Whit quietly addressed Tor and Danu. "Mind if I dance with my partner, women?"

Tor laughed. Smiling, Danu saluted and moved aside.

Whit had her arm around Kali's waist and was moving them toward the dance floor when Kali chided, "Whit, that was rather rude."

"Oh?"

"I was trying to recruit Tor," Kali explained.

"Recruit her for what?"

Feeling her body respond to the stare Whit leveled on her, Kali elaborated in a breathless voice, "Well, you know that since our encounter with Arinna, Tor's been on extended medical leave. Weetamoo says she may never be physically strong enough to go back to active duty."

Whit watched her, listening. Yet her eyes were tracing Kali's collarbone, then the cleavage displayed by Kali's lime gown. Gently, Whit pulled Kali into her arms and began moving to the music.

Following her, Kali continued. "I want Tor to be one of my professors. She'd be perfect."

"Ah yes," Whit said, her husky voice deeper than usual. "The Wiccan Institute."

"She's already shown her talent," Kali went on, "with Danu and with me . . ."

Whit leaned down; warm breath caressed Kali's ear. "I want to peel that dress right off of you."

A wave of heat engulfed Kali. Speechless, she clung to the firm arms guiding her across the floor, following Whit's motion.

Again, the voice and breath came. "I want to lay you down and run my hands all over you, until you're begging me . . ."

In the distance, a voice barked, "Whitaker!"

Whit straightened. "Damn that woman!"

"Whitaker!" the voice called imperiously, louder and nearer this time.

Stubbornly, Whit kept dancing until General Medusa was right at their elbow.

"Is this some sort of hare-brained plot, Whitaker?!"

Red-faced, Whit finally stopped dancing, circling Kali with her arm. "Perhaps we can discuss this *without* everyone else on the dance floor overhearing us."

Several women moving by them broke into suppressed laughter.

"I can't find Reno anywhere," the general hissed angrily, "and the last time anyone saw her, she was dancing with Chen! I've spent the last half-hour calling Reno on her wristcom — without response! The two of them just up and disappeared, and someone obviously planned the entire thing!"

"Really?" Kali asked, unable to hide her surprise.

"Loy's harmless —" Whit began.

Enraged, Medusa put her face inches away from Whit's nose. "Loy Yin Chen is a legendary womanizer, and everyone from here to Lang knows it!"

Women who were closer to them slowed their steps, some completely abandoning any effort to play out the subterfuge of dancing. All eyes and ears were trained on the stationary discussion in the middle of the floor.

Whit gave a quick, wary glance around, and gestured for Medusa to follow her.

As Kali hurried along beside Whit, Medusa went on talking, though now it was to Whit's back.

"I don't trust Chen," General Medusa declared. "Especially with Reno!"

Whit kept walking, passing by whirling dancers, then through the thick crowds of women on the outskirts of the dance floor. Kali and Medusa hurried to keep up with her as Whit marched past the arched portico at the entrance to the hall and headed for the outside corridor. The two sentries by the door came to attention as Whit led Kali and Medusa across the corridor to the head of security's office.

With a slap of her hand to the small DNA square on the wall by the door, Whit keyed the lock. The panel slid open. Abruptly, she waved both Kali and Medusa in before her, then followed and closed the door.

As Kali finally got a good look at Whit's face, she realized that she had never before seen Whit so angry. And then, almost instantly, both Whit and Medusa were shouting.

"You are impugning the honor of a member of my staff —" Whit roared.

"I want Reno back here right now —" Medusa bellowed.

For a few moments Kali actually lost track of what was being conveyed in spoken words, as the images from each woman's head assaulted her in a psychic barrage. Whit saw herself grabbing Medusa by the front of her gray uniform and then violently shaking her, while Medusa imaged herself boxing Whit's ears.

Startled, Kali clapped her hands over her ears.

"You're not in charge here —"

"I'm taking charge because someone has to —"

Helpless to stop the series of violent telepathic visions, Kali turned away from them. She was breathing hard and felt incredibly dizzy. Her eyes fell on Captain Razia's desk, on the crystal paperweight of a dolphin that sat atop a pile of sentry-shift assignments.

*Goddess, make them stop!* Kali willed with all her might.

The crystal dolphin shot off the desk, whizzing between the two clashing women and hitting the paneled wall above a bookcase. With a loud bang, the five-inch figurine exploded.

Shocked into silence, Whit and the general stared at the shallow dent the dolphin had left in the oaken panel.

Kali moved to the wall. "Uh-oh," she said quietly, more to herself than to the other two.

"What the hell happened?" Medusa asked.

Gingerly, Kali touched her finger to the bits of glass and fine powder on the top of the bookshelf; it was all that remained of Razia's crystal paperweight.

"I think we just found out what pregnancy hormones do to a mage," Kali stated, then bit her lip, amazed.

Whit raked a hand through her hair and muttered, "Oh for Gaea's sake. What next?"

# Chapter 4

Loy rode behind the young major on the motorcycle they shared, her arms encircling Reno's solid form, her torso pressing into Reno's back. Holding on to another woman was something Loy had not done in a long time, and desire was flickering through her entire body like a sweet, hot flame.

*What the hell am I doing*? She knew she was in the grip of a dangerous mood, feeling both exquisitely vulnerable and strangely passive.

*How did I get into this*? She knew how. The memory of the last few hours was already indelibly impressed upon her soul.

Her reception-line duties fulfilled, Loy entered the ballroom. Almost immediately, Reno approached. Something about the way her intense brown eyes held her own was irresistibly intriguing to Loy. Even as she silently warned herself to stay away from the young woman, Loy acquiesced to Reno's request for a dance. Strangely exhilarated by the young woman's steady regard, Loy felt herself being pulled in and let herself drift with the music and the carnival-like spontaneity of Beltane.

She was not surprised to discover that Reno was an excellent partner, capable of following Loy through a series of complex steps, swinging into and out of Loy's arms. All the while, Loy was enjoying Reno's open, bantering flirtation. Despite her mixed emotions about the major's reason for being in Isis, Loy found herself entranced by the woman. Occasionally, Loy attempted to retreat into her usual sardonic reserve, but Reno simply didn't allow it. Eyes sparkling, Reno kept up a constant stream of questions, making Loy talk to her.

Soon, Reno had convinced her to go outside and see the motorcycle she had rented for the evening.


*And now here we are racing into the night . . . to do what?*
The streets of Isis went by in blur. As usual, the cycle had a decibel-squelch device that kept engine noise to a low hum, but Loy could tell by the shuddering vibration against her inner thighs and the wind roaring past Reno, that the cycle was well over the speed limit for the stretch of road.

They reached the western outskirts of the city and passed the row of huge hydroponics sheds, and then the streetlights and illuminations of civilization were gone, left behind. Only the cycle's headlight shone on the roadway before them, as Reno pointed the machine to the darkness beyond the city.

Overhead the stars were shining in that fiery, burnished way they had in this mountain domain. On either side of Loy, the dark silhouette of the land rose up; mountains and more mountains, all of them covered with the fine black outlines of thousands of treetops. They had entered the enormous fir forest that surrounded Isis. Startled, Loy realized they were traveling the South Mountain Road, the road that led to her cabin.

Just as Loy stiffened and tried to create some space between her body and the young major's, the cycle began to decelerate. Reno turned the big bike, jouncing onto a carpet of fragrant pine needles and following a trail all too familiar to Loy. The track wound through the forest, then up and over a ridge. They entered a clearing, and from the windows of Loy's cabin poured a faint but welcoming yellow light. Reno cut the engine and, extending her legs, coasted to a stop before the porch steps.

Loy removed her arms from Reno's waist, straightening slowly. Reno took her helmet off, then turned in the seat and gently helped Loy remove her own.

Suspicious, Loy slipped off the bike and backed away a few steps. She watched Reno knock the kickstand down and fasten the helmets to the handlebars.

*She's brought me home to bed me.*

What was even more alarming was how easily Reno might succeed. All Loy's usual guards had fallen, and she wasn't exactly clear on why or how it had happened.

"Goddess, look at the stars," Reno said quietly.

Loy looked up and felt her soul fall into the well of night above them. Thousands of bright dots were spread across the sky, flickering against an ebony infinity.

*This is what it would look like from space. This is what she's going to see, and soon.*

She felt, rather than saw, Reno come to stand beside her. With a small catch of breath, Reno's smaller body leaned into Loy. Her lips glided with slow deliberateness over the side of Loy's neck; her hands brushed through Loy's hair.

Nervous and tense, Loy tried to step back, but Reno slipped a gentle arm around Loy's waist and checked the retreat.

"I'm not sure we should be —" Loy gasped as Reno's tongue began a subtle flicking motion just under her jaw.

"Loy," Reno whispered. "I have to touch you."

"But —"

"Let me," Reno coaxed.

Her hands were inside Loy's suit jacket, moving over her clothes, exploring with a deft self-assurance that was ensnaring Loy faster than she could believe possible. Dizzily, Loy swayed in Reno's embrace. Reno's lips moved over her face in tiny, teasingly erotic kisses. Reno's busy hands opened the buttons of Loy's vest and shirt. Loy was breathlessly aware of the chill, spring air on her chest. Then, Reno's fingers brushed the sides of her breasts, her nipples, her exposed abdomen. Stooping slightly, Reno took a breast in her mouth, and Loy was shocked to find herself trembling, arching into an increasingly ardent embrace.

"Gaea, I want you," Reno whispered fiercely.

Abruptly, Reno stopped, took Loy by the hand and began pulling her toward the cabin.

Released from the sensual onslaught, Loy ventured, "Does General Medusa have any idea that you're out here with me?"

"I'm on leave tonight," Reno answered cryptically.

"In other words, no," Loy stated.

Reno cast a look back at her, but in the darkness, Loy couldn't see much more as she was led up the steps.

"Open the door," Reno demanded, her voice quiet yet firm. Through the windows of the door, the warm glow from the lamplight inside fell on Reno's face, revealing how flushed and determined she was.

Loy's breath caught. *Everyone believes I'm a disreputable cad, and yet this woman — this goody-goody warrior brat — is chasing me. Why?*

"Did you plan this?" Loy began. Trying her best to appear casual and in control, Loy thumbed the DNA plate mounted by the threshold.

Her eyes incredibly serious, Reno answered, "Sure. I needed a place to stay. The general got the guest quarters in the Leader's House, and I got the closet next door." She laughed slightly, then sobered. "I'd say between the barracks and the Leader's House, you must have three hundred warriors stationed in Isis."

"Four," Loy answered faintly, watching Reno's eyes drift down her body, then rise. "Whit's expecting an air attack if the Border goes . . ."

Not relinquishing Loy's hand, Reno pushed open the door and drew Loy into the cabin.

With a quick, assessing look, Reno took in the rustic pine furniture scattered about. Nearby were an armoire and a chest of drawers. To their left, in the darker part of the cabin, was a small kitchen area with a table and two chairs. To the right was a wide plank of unfinished wood mounted on two steel file cabinets that served as Loy's desk. Piles of printouts and loose chips covered it, and above the keyboard in the center, the small wallscreen glowed.

Focusing on the screen saver, a dancing girl twisting across the luminous blue expanse, Reno commented, "You left in such a hurry you didn't shut the unit down?"

"I was working, and then, well, I was late," she muttered. "Last December, after I moved out here, our security chief, Captain Razia, insisted on making sure the cabin was made secure. The windows are unbreakable Plexiglas; the logs and cedar shingles are coated with a clear plastic sealer that's tougher than diamonds. No one can get in here but me." Loy paused, expelling a nervous breath. "And Goddess knows I wasn't expecting company tonight."

"Your mistake." Reno's eyes moved to the far side of the room, where a wide bed was positioned by a wall of windows.

Shivering, Loy glanced down and noticed her opened shirt. With her free hand, she closed the two sides.

"Get the door," Reno ordered softly.

Hesitating, Loy looked at the thick oak panel, then back at Reno. Scarcely breathing, Reno waited for Loy to decide.

"Maybe we should talk," Loy bargained.

"We can do that," Reno answered.

Loy swallowed. "Okay." With a gentle push, Loy sent the door closed.

She was breathing fast and shallow, feeling almost helpless with the desire to be handled again the way Reno had touched her outside. Reno's hands had been teasingly confident, so devastatingly arousing that a mere few minutes of fondling had left Loy wet and ready.

*What's the matter with me? I'm usually the aggressor!* She felt distracted and agitated.

With a businesslike nod, Reno released Loy's hand. She crossed the room to the bed, sat on the edge, and pulled off her calf-high boots. Opening her gray uniform jacket and slipping it off, she watched Loy expectantly.

"What shall we talk about?" Reno asked quietly.

Reno stood in the glow of the bedstand lamp, opening her starched collar and then the white shirt.

Dry-mouthed, Loy swallowed.

"Perhaps we should talk about why you're so afraid of me," Reno proposed, her direct brown eyes so compelling that Loy nearly gave her the truth.

*No!* The ice-cold will she relied upon rose up, steeling her.

Loy bridled. She crossed the room, glancing about for another place to sit and finding nothing but the bed. She looked over at the kitchen area, tempted to fetch a chair from there.

Reno's eyes followed Loy's search, then settled on Loy. They were filled with a silent dare.

Loy was uncertain what to do. Gathering her nerve, she sank down to sit on the edge of the colorful quilt, unable to make eye contact with Reno.

"You planned this," Loy repeated tersely.

"No," Reno soothed, coming closer. "I was hoping, but . . ."

"Why?" Loy demanded. "You could have had any woman in Isis this Beltane Night. Why me?"

Slowly, as if being careful not to startle her, Reno reached out and passed a finger along the livid line on Loy's cheek. "You're so beautiful."

Incredulous, Loy looked up at the woman standing before her. "I'm not," she protested. "Arinna scarred me — inside and out."

"The scars make you beautiful, Loy." She cupped her hand under Loy's chin, holding Loy's eyes with her own. "I've got a top-level security clearance. I've seen the reports about what happened up at Hart's Pass. You nearly lost your life fighting that madwoman when half of Freeland thought you were a traitor. They still condemn you, using you as a scapegoat for their own blindness to Arinna Sojourner."

"Most of what they say about me is true. I'm no angel."

"So I've heard." Reno's light brown eyes were serious, and she held Loy with her gaze. "Initially, before we'd met, I had misgivings about the depth of your involvement in the shuttle project."

"Which do you doubt — my ability or my integrity?"

"Actually, my misgivings were not caused so much by who you are, as by what had recently happened to you."

"And now that you've met me . . . you've changed your mind?"

"What do you think?"

Loy swallowed helplessly, as the hand caressing her scar slid lower and around the back of her neck.

Slowly, so slowly, Reno bent over Loy, brushed her lips over Loy's mouth. "Don't stop me," Reno whispered.

In a rush, Loy stuttered, "S-sex . . . I-I'm not able to . . . I c-can't . . ." She blew out a harsh breath and her hands fisted at her sides. "Arinna hurt me . . . during sex. I don't know if I can do this anymore."

Heedless, Reno's lips brushed along her jaw.

A convulsive shudder of fear shook through Loy.

"It's all right," Reno whispered near her ear. "I'm just flirting with your body."

Loy closed her eyes. The warmth in Reno's voice was deflecting the terror that had been spiraling through her.

"Do you want me to stop?" Reno asked.

Unsure, Loy waited a moment. "No," she ventured at last.

Reno's lips found Loy's, brushing tremulously across them, once, twice. On the third pass, Loy tentatively kissed back. Reno deepened the kiss until Loy was reaching for her helplessly.

All Loy knew was that she was sick of protecting herself. If she had to create a new body-memory to put the fear behind her, then this might be the woman who could help her do it.

Lightly, Reno's tongue stroked her own, and Loy was caught, wholly suffused with hunger. *Mother of Earth, I want this, I need this.*

Reno's hands moved over Loy, tantalizing her, commanding total capitulation. Loy moaned, pressing reflexively into the bent knee Reno moved against her yoni. A hot, molten rush flooded Loy, and she gasped.

"Ohh."

"Move back," Reno whispered.

Loy put her hands back on the mattress and began inching her hips to the center of the bed.

Reno clambered after her, then captured Loy in a fast, hard kiss. With a minor shift of weight, Reno pressed her down on the quilt. Then she knelt over her, undoing Loy's trousers and tugging them down.

Reno was going for the source. A flurry of panic hit Loy.

"From the moment we met," Reno whispered as her fingers slid inside Loy's underwear, pushing them down, "I've wanted you."

Fingers played at the edge of Loy's clitoris. A tight knot of anxiety in Loy's belly vied for preeminence with surging waves of arousal.

Reno's finger glided between the folds of Loy's labia, dipping into the thick flow and then gliding up to coat Loy's clitoris in an excruciatingly slow stroke. A small, inarticulate cry broke from Loy. She writhed, thrusting her hips up against Reno's hand.

"I've been fantasizing about watching your face while I touched you like this," Reno whispered.

Another cry broke from Loy.

Loy felt crazed with desire, delirious with it. There was no other purpose for her on earth except the need to complete what they had started. Reno was talking to her, telling her what she was going to do, while her mouth and hands sent hot delight through Loy's flesh like electricity through a wire — a steady, sizzling, fluctuating current.

Just when Loy thought she could stand no more, Reno's hand moved to a faster cadence, sliding over her and into her.

"Feels good, doesn't it?" Reno whispered, nuzzling Loy's earlobe.

Dimly, Loy heard herself gasping, "Yes, yes . . ."

She felt herself moving beneath Reno in complete and utter submission. Of its own volition, her voice began crying out raggedly, incoherently. She was blazing with sensation, wet and slick and wide open to anything Reno wanted to do with her. From deep within, a pure, scintillating bliss was gathering, compounding. Then she was wailing, helpless against a force that owned her completely.

Perspiring and shaking, Loy's taut body finally went limp. She was hoarse and bleary-eyed with exhaustion. Reno pulled an edge of the quilt free, covering them both, then gathered Loy close to her.

"Thank you," Loy managed, breathing hard.

Reno's hands still moved over her, gentle and cherishing. "My pleasure," Reno stated. "My honor."

Blinking sleepily, Loy gazed up at Reno and wondered about this stranger. Though women had often flirted with Loy, or let her know in every way imaginable that they were interested and available, Loy had always been the initiator. She had never been sought out, pursued, and seduced like this. Even in the avalanche of afterglow, the role felt decidedly odd.

A long, satiated sigh escaped Loy. *Well, my ego may not like it, but my body certainly does.*

Above her, Reno leaned on an elbow, watching her with a pleased smile.

Summoning the last of her strength, Loy reached for her, but Reno laughed and pushed her back down.

"I can wait," she assured Loy. "Rest awhile. Let me hold you."

"Mmm," Loy managed to reply, allowing herself to relax in Reno's comforting arms.

Outside, the night wind whispered across the tops of the firs, and from deep in the forest came the ghostly call of wolves. For a moment, Loy studied the face above her. In the golden glow of lamplight, Reno's sculpted cheekbones and twinkling dark eyes seemed almost magical.

"Can you sleep?" Reno asked quietly.

As if in answer, Loy's eyes closed. With all her might, she fought to open them again, but could not. The bed seemed to absorb her, pulling her down and down, deeper and deeper, into a sleep unlike any she had had in months.

* * * * *

Beneath the bright lampposts that lined Cammermeyer Street, Danu tried to match Whit's long stride. Behind them, Tor and Kali walked together. Danu could hear a few phrases now and then, and surmised they were deep in discussion about Kali's plans for a Wiccan Institute.

As their small group moved along, throngs of women streamed continuously around them. Some of them were singing rowdy warrior songs, some were laughing in the incredibly hearty and infectious way that marked a free woman. Others in the crowd appeared dreamy and silent, leaning slightly against the woman beside them. Those couples had a way of staring at each other every so often that made Danu realize they were on their way somewhere, to be together for the night.

Danu noticed Whit examining the faces passing by them. Occasionally someone would recognize Whit and call Beltane blessings, and Whit would nod back and smile. For the most part, though, she was anonymous in the crowd and seemed to like it that way.

Projecting her voice slightly, to be heard over the noise, Danu asked, "What are you thinking about?"

Whit gave a sheepish grin. "It's been a rough year." She made a sweeping gesture at the women with them in the street. "It isn't often that I've seen so many so happy."

Danu turned and looked at the jubilant women all around her, internally acknowledging the truth of it. She, like many other young women, had left civilian life this year and joined the warriors. Eight grueling weeks of basic training in Morgan had been followed by eight weeks of an accelerated flight school in Boudica. In many ways it had been overwhelming, and yet the blessing was that it had been so all consuming it had kept at bay the memories of what she'd endured as Arinna's captive.

She shook her head and wondered how Loy dealt with the nightmares. In her dreams, Danu still found herself back in the North Cascades about once every other week.

These days she often felt as if she were reeling with all the new material and skills she had acquired, and she knew it was the same for most Freelanders. They were all frantically readying for the conflict they knew was coming. For the first time in any of their lives, the Border was in danger of falling. Within months, Freeland could be at war.

A hand touched her shoulder. "Just wanted to let you know how glad I am that Warrior Command stationed you here," Whit told her, the gray eyes soft. "I've missed seeing you, little sister."

Smiling, Danu felt her face get hot and she dropped her gaze. She was an adult now, an award-winning architect, an officer, and an expert pilot. Still, Whit could turn her into a tongue-tied schoolgirl with an affectionate remark.

They had reached Tor's motorcycle, parked in a long line of other bikes on the edge of the square. In the daylight, the broad expanse was the marketplace; when morning came it would be filled with booths selling vegetables, bread, and craft goods. Now, however, it was an impromptu dance area where women moved to the music and a rock band held court from a large, center stage.

Whit and Kali hugged Danu and Tor and said good night, then wandered back toward the Leader's House hand-in-hand. Tor got the bike started, and Danu climbed on behind her. They wove slowly along the side streets, waving at friends, and made their way to the road that led out to the high country.

The night air was bracing, and Danu shivered as she gripped Tor tighter. Gradually, the city fell behind them. Tor opened up the throttle, following the North Mountain Road through the woods. They were alone in the darkness, two beings flying behind a headlight. The bike zoomed up and over the ridge that separated the meadowlands above from Isis, and Danu felt a rush of joy to be going home with the woman in her arms.

A short time later they turned into a long dirt driveway, then rode up to the big, stone house. They had left a few lights on, and now, as the cycle decelerated, Danu admired the lines of the two-story structure. While Tor pushed the bike toward a shed behind the house, Danu headed inside, intent on arranging the setting for her first proper Beltane.

Only a few small candles were lit and placed about the upstairs bedroom. Danu wanted the star shine from the skylight above the bed to set the mood. Hurriedly, she brushed her teeth and shed her uniform.

Tor was only moments behind her, her boots echoing on the stairs as she came closer. Danu slipped under the covers, elated with anticipation.

Tor walked in, grinning. She undressed in the habitual, meticulous way Danu had first observed last autumn, when they were barracks roommates. Every article of clothing was taken off in a certain order, then neatly hung up, folded, or put away. Danu noticed again, for the hundredth time, how spare Tor's body appeared compared to the muscled form Danu knew from last November. Tor had been hit with one of Arinna's death spells during the Battle of the North Cascades and had barely survived. She had not regained her robust physical strength.

*Thank Gaea, Kali's come up with the idea of a professor's position at the Wiccan Institute. This long medical leave of absence from the warriors is withering Tor's soul as much as that spell withered her body. Working with Styx on that old-books catalogue is okay for now, but Tor needs something long-term, something she can invest herself in. With a fierce burst of pride and love, Danu decided: . . . Tor needs to contribute. She needs to be needed.*

When Tor climbed in next to her, for a moment all Danu could do was hold her. In a moment of clarity, she realized that for most of her life, she had kept her distance from the people around her. She had become adept at relying only upon herself. As a known Think Tank creation, a genetically engineered human, she'd been shunned by some, or viewed as obscenely different by others. She had always been an outsider. It had been natural to start protecting herself, to never let anyone get close. Things had changed irrevocably since she had come to Isis. Whit, Kali, Lilith, Styx, even Loy had all become her friends, the first she'd ever known.

As Danu hugged Tor to her, she realized that what she had managed to find with Tor was another level of trust altogether. *She makes me feel like I'm . . . something precious. I love her so much.*

After a bit, Tor gently disentangled herself.

Flashing a knowing smile, Tor inquired, "This is the first Beltane you've celebrated in bed with someone, isn't it?"

Not sure what to expect, Danu gave a slight nod.

In a sensuous brush of warm skin, Tor climbed on top of Danu. "This is a special night, then," Tor said, her voice low.

"In the old days, centuries ago," Tor began, "Beltane was a rite of spring, a celebration of the return of life to the land."

Smiling, Danu realized Tor was telling a story, which she often did as a beginning to their lovemaking. It was a means of teasing Danu. Tor knew Danu's avid intellect would be trying to listen to the story while Tor's inciting hands distracted her, caressing the length of her body.

"Beltane was a night when the villagers built bonfires, and drank too much mead." She tongued the rim of Danu's ear and Danu shivered. "They danced around the Maypole, which, by the way, was a means of revering the phallus."

Slowly, sinuously, Tor moved her hips against Danu. Instantly gripped by body memory, as Tor wanted her to be, Danu gave a small moan and rocked back, trying to hold Tor against her. With a pleased chuckle, Tor slipped away, sending her hands skimming over Danu. Breathless, Danu felt electricity sizzling in the wake of Tor's hands.

Her voice low, Tor finished, "And after the drunken dancing, they all slipped off into the woods and hayfields, where they worshiped the Goddess by" — she licked Danu's ear again, deeper this time, then whispered — "fucking."

Tense with arousal, Danu ran a hand down Tor's side, trying to reach the wet heat Danu felt against her leg. Rising up, Tor captured both of Danu's hands, then slid her grip along Danu's arms, stretching them out before pinning them down on the sheets.

"No, no, no," Tor informed her. "You are first tonight."

Danu trembled, feeling at odds with herself. One part of her worried about Tor's fragile health, wanting to stop her, wanting to spare her the exertion of what she so obviously planned. At the same time, Danu craved body and soul what she read in Tor's eyes. With a wolfish smile, Tor moved lower, kissing her stomach, her legs, keeping her lips lightly on Danu's skin in a constant, sweeping pass of lips. An occasional flutter of tongue joined the tease as Tor's mouth moved over Danu's inner thighs.

Soon, Danu was begging her. "Oh, Tor . . . oh, Tor . . . please, please."

*So much has changed, but not this*, Danu thought. *She takes me apart. And Gaea help me, I love it.*

Finally, Tor tasted her. Deftly Danu's arousal ascended to another plane, and then another, until Danu was unreservedly lost in the revel, and the caprice of her lover was all she knew.


Whit carefully arranged the wood in the fireplace, then leaned over and picked up the microlaser. She aimed at the layer of kindling underneath the smaller logs on the bottom, shot a short, fanlike blast, and grinned with satisfaction as the first small flames licked around the wood.

The sweet scent of herbs filled Whit's nose, and then Kali was kneeling next to her, her brown eyes fastened on the fire.

She set two mugs of hot herbal tea on the hearth. Carefully arranging the long folds of her pale-green dress, she sat down beside Whit.

Just looking at her sent desire through Whit.

Kali seemed to feel the heat in her gaze, for she glanced over, smiling.

Whit laughed, "Thank Gaea you finally persuaded General Medusa that it would be a horrendous breach of etiquette to try and track down Loy and Major Reno on Beltane night." She shook her head, then confessed, "I think I've been waiting for this moment all evening long."

"Me too," Kali returned.

Appreciatively, Whit moved her eyes over the woman.

As Kali scooted closer, Whit glanced down at the hooked rug before the hearth and quickly proposed, "Let's use the sofa — it'll be softer for you."

Kali threaded her fingers through Whit's thick hair, giving her a look that warned Whit that things were going to move very fast now. "Are you going to turn into one of those overprotective partners?"

"Of course not," Whit answered distractedly. Kali's hands were at her shirt buttons, nimbly opening, then stripping the cloth from Whit's shoulders. "It's just that, you know, we get kinda carried away sometimes and —"

With the power of knowing what ruled Whit, Kali leaned forward, pressing against her. Whit flattened out with a low, soft moan.

"You'll keep me comfortable," Kali whispered in Whit's ear. "Won't you, love?"

"Yes," Whit told her, cradling Kali gently in her arms.

"I'm not suddenly made of glass," Kali informed her. "I want you to . . . do me . . . same as ever. All right?"

Cautiously, Whit sent her hands roaming over Kali's slender form. After a moment, her heart pounded and her body tingled with steadily increasing hunger. Her breath

86

quickening, Whit moved her lips across Kali's cheek, searching for her mouth.

With a quiet, willing sound, Kali gave Whit what she wanted, and they kissed deeply. Methodically, Whit glided through Kali's singular, exquisitely fired triggers until Kali's hips were rippling into her and Kali was gasping, completely under Whit's control.

They had come to know each other's bodies so well that sex was often fast and furious. Even when Whit was trying for slow and teasing, the consummation itself seemed to get away from her. Kali seemed to surrender so completely to her that the entire experience became electrifying for both of them. A few minutes of foreplay usually had Kali on the brink and Whit not far behind.

*But not this time*, Whit resolved, slowing her hands. *Tonight is Beltane.*

She coasted her hands up over the pale-green dress, pushing Kali into a sitting position. Kali was straddling Whit's hips, still undulating slightly, her eyes half-lidded with desire.

"What?" she gasped, mildly frustrated. "What are you doing?"

"Take off your clothes," Whit urged. "Then go sit on the sofa."

Kali gave a slight, negating shake of the head. "Whit!"

"Kal," Whit replied firmly, sitting up so that she was a mere few inches from Kali, holding her off with her hands on Kali's shoulders. "Do as I ask."

Something in her voice must have alerted Kali, for the dark brown eyes flared with an instinctive understanding. *Or else she's reading my mind, again*, Whit realized.

Trying to shield some of what she intended, Whit instead focused on the woman who stood up and moved away from her.

Gracefully, Kali unfastened the catches along her left side, then slowly pulled off the form-fitting dress. In the firelight,

Whit watched first slip, then sheer underclothes, then fair skin emerge. With a practical efficiency, Kali gathered the clothing and laid it aside on an armchair.

Whit breathed, "Sit, Kal," her husky voice suddenly deep and raspy.

Kali sent her a look, and Whit saw the laughter in her eyes before she went to the sofa and sat there, waiting.

Cursing softly, Whit couldn't restrain herself. She went quickly to Kali, kneeling before her, running her hands over Kali's lithe body. Moments later, any semblance of Kali's laughter was gone. She was flushed, her deep brown eyes were half-closed with longing. Feeling tremendously powerful, Whit leaned forward and savored first one breast, then the other. Kali moaned and arched, her head falling back and her long, blond hair cascading over her shoulders.

Whit's hands lingered on the small pooch of Kali's stomach, the first and only real sign of the baby. "Hello, little one," Whit called softly. Then Kali grasped Whit's right hand and guided it lower.

Whit gently resisted, breaking free of Kali and positioning a hand on either one of Kali's thighs. Whispering, "Beltane blessings, love of my life," Whit trailed kisses down the slope of Kali's abdomen.

Reading Whit's intentions, Kali hissed with a sudden intake of breath. Her body tensed as Whit slipped her hands under Kali's thighs and tugged that exquisite pelvis forward. Bending lower, Whit cradled Kali's hips in her arms, maneuvering Kali to her lips.

Kali was whimpering as Whit hovered just beyond touch, smelling her lover's arousal, drinking in the ardent anticipation that telegraphed itself from Kali's shivering body. At last she lowered her mouth. Whit's uncontrollable breath caused Kali's first cry, though the cries that followed were the work of a supple, tormenting tongue.

By the end, the fire was not throwing off nearly enough heat or light anymore. Whit lifted a much more compliant woman in her arms and carried her across the darkened room to their bed.

"Goddess, you're dependable," Kali sighed, as she was lowered to the sheets.

Whit broke into laughter. "Is that a compliment?"

"The best a woman can give," Kali remarked archly, "when she's talking about a lover."

"Oh?"

Hurriedly, Whit completed the undressing Kali had begun a short while ago, then slid in beside her. Whit took Kali in her arms again, and Kali's hands began coasting all over Whit's flesh, causing a riot of goose bumps.

Feeling noble and protective, Whit said, "I'm okay, Kal." She kissed Kali's forehead. "You're tired. Just hold me and we'll go to sleep now."

"You can't fool me, Tomyris Whitaker," Kali answered, delving between Whit's legs with an exploring hand. "You're so wet my telepathic brain can taste it . . ."

Deliberately casual, Kali caressed that particular square inch of Whit's yoni where Whit was erotically hot-wired. Rigid, Whit cried out, and her hips bucked like a spanked mustang. Groaning, defenseless against Kali's teasing touch, Whit was suddenly on her back, feverish with want.

Leaning over her, Kali whispered, "I'm going to take you, Tomyris. Take you until you've got nothing left to give me."

Whit gasped. Her body was moving like a river under a strong wind, rising and falling with each pass of Kali's commanding hands. Finally, Kali returned to the spot that made Whit wild.

"Is this what you want?" Kali asked softly.

Whit was incapable of speech, and she knew Kali was well aware of it. Her hips were answering for her, snapping in response to each graze of Kali's fingers.

"Here?" Kali asked, teasing over the hot, dripping entrance.

Whit heard herself moan, and then those fingers slid in

deep, adroitly relieving Whit of any control she had left. Orgasm ripped through her like a great white light, so good, so sweet, eclipsing everything. Suspended in a timeless state, her body opened beneath the sun that was Kali, erupting with absolute rapture. Quivering, Whit collapsed back on the bed. Her breath was coming in rasping sobs as Kali pulled her in close, nuzzling her neck.

"Dearest Cerridwen, you are so hot," Kali stated, her eyes ablaze. "So damned hot. I can't stop touching you when you're like this."

Still quivering, Whit felt Kali's hands beginning the seduction again. Whit's breath became a series of low, needful cries as Kali leaned over her, nibbling Whit's breasts, stroking her to full readiness.

Slower this time, but just as adeptly, Kali led Whit into ecstasy once more.

Afterward, Kali lay against Whit's chest, murmuring memories. "Two years, Tomyris. You know you nearly crushed me when you jumped on top of me in that muddy Elysian ditch."

"I was evading Regs," Whit informed her. "Crushing you was completely unintentional, I assure you."

"And then you started bossing me," Kali mumbled, "I thought you were the most arrogant, most obnoxious woman I'd ever met."

"Sweet Mother, I love you," Whit answered. "I love you more each day."

Barely audible, Kali replied. "Is that possible?"

"Yes," Whit said with certainty.

Through the partially open door to the balcony came a woman's voice, sounding very drunk and yet still melodious. Smiling wearily, Whit knew it was one of the revelers, no doubt wandering home from a night of carousing, singing a song about women-loving-women as she went.

Kali was quiet. Her breathing had shifted into a slower,

more relaxed pattern, and Whit knew she had abruptly fallen asleep.

Whit smoothed the loose blond hair beneath her hand and whispered, "By the Mother, I swear I'll die before a Reg ever lays a hand on you again."

# Chapter 5

The next afternoon, Whit chose to personally pilot General Medusa and Major Reno to the shuttle launch site. Elated to be out of the office and at the controls of her Swallow, Whit sent the small, tilt-rotor jet over the Cascade foothills toward a mountain valley roughly ten kilometers southwest of Isis.

Flying was always a rush for Whit, a visceral exultation that swept all other cares and concerns aside. Flying over the glorious Pacific Northwest was sheer nirvana. Like a thick, dark-green carpet, the forest rose and fell below them. Only the high, gray-granite ridges and aqua-colored glacial rivers were free of the unending presence of trees. Within minutes, Whit was wearing a carefree grin.

"Your attitude baffles me, Whitaker," Medusa growled

beside her. "You must know that I won't hesitate to call your bluff."

Whit flicked a glance at her, but kept her grin firmly in place. "I wasn't aware we were playing a game."

"Since you have not set aside Chen as the shuttle pilot, I've requested an emergency meeting of the Eight Leaders Council." Her dark eyes hard, Medusa finished, "I learned just before our takeoff that the meeting is scheduled for tonight. I have no doubt that it will be televised. Every citizen in Freeland will be glued to the comline, while you and I present our individual plans in a debate format."

Her mood effectively punctured, Whit sobered. *Mother's blood, this woman is ruthless!* Deliberately, she avoided looking at Medusa, unwilling to give the woman the satisfaction of seeing how rattled she was.

The tilt-rotor jet swept over the last ridge and Whit banked the craft, circling the valley and the newly constructed facility below them.

"Jackie Cochran Space Center," Whit announced.

Behind her, Whit heard Reno stir. "Wow!"

Obviously still angry with Reno for her unexplained disappearance the night before, Medusa sent a quick, glowering glance over her shoulder. "Impressive, yes, for civilians." With an edge in her voice, Medusa remarked, "We shall no doubt find things that need sorting out." Narrowing her eyes, Medusa sat back and folded her arms.

A sudden apprehension came over Whit, an apprehension concerning Loy. As the chief of this project, and the surprising focus of Reno's interest, Loy was going to be an enticing target for the general.

Frowning, Whit engaged the foot pedal that triggered the Swallow's landing sequence. On each wing, the rotors began to slowly shift on the mounts, causing the craft to drift smoothly from a fast forward glide to a hovering position above a white painted circle on the landing zone.

As the plane touched down softly, Medusa gruffly

commented, "Well done, Whitaker. You still fly like a seasoned vet."

Mildly exasperated, Whit shut down the engines. "General, I became a civilian last year to run for public office. I didn't forget how to fly."

"Humph," Medusa returned. "You exchanged a distinguished career as a Freeland warrior for a political dog-and-pony show."

*Is that what's behind this animosity?* "I was needed in Isis," Whit began tersely. "I thought I could contribute more to my country out of uniform than in it —"

"You met a lovely woman and suddenly *her* goals were your goals," Medusa stated brusquely. "Isis could have gotten along just fine without you."

On the brink of fury, Whit clenched her teeth together. *If I reply to that, this conversation is going to turn into a political incident — which is probably just what she wants.*

Whit took a deep breath and made herself review her postflight checklist. She had nearly completed the tasks when someone rapped sharply on the Plexiglas that formed the entire front of the Swallow. Looking up, Whit found Loy before the craft, clad in buff mechanic's coveralls and an open bomber jacket. Her cheeks were ruddy and her dark hair was blowing in the wind.

Stunned, Whit thought, *She looks relaxed, rested. Damn, she looks wonderful.*

As if aware of Whit's perceptive evaluation, Loy's color went deeper. Abruptly, Loy motioned toward a troop transport parked across the tarmac.

"Let's move," General Medusa barked, unbuckling her seat belt and climbing out of her chair.

Hurrying to follow, Whit noticed that Major Reno beat them all to the door. The young woman made quick work of the pressure locks, then nimbly climbed down the steps.

General Medusa was concentrating on her stiff knees as she maneuvered her husky bulk down the steel staircase, but

Whit stood just inside the doorway and saw Reno and Loy face each other.

Reno's gaze was incendiary, and Loy seemed helpless to look away.

*Sweet Mother. Kali's right. They* did *spend the night together.*

Medusa turned, straightening her tunic, and caught the stare Reno and Loy were sharing. As Whit hopped down to join them, Loy collected herself and launched into a short welcoming speech. Meanwhile, Medusa glared at Loy like she was an enemy hologram in the cross hairs of a missile-targeting system.

At Whit's quiet request, Loy took charge, directing them all to the troop transport for a tour of Cochran Space Center. During the next twenty minutes, Loy drove them around the vast tarmac-covered base, pointing out various hangars and relating their function.

Concisely, Loy described how each team involved in the shuttle project had coordinated it's segment of the shuttle restoration. Using the modular computer design Loy had developed with Danu in early December, Loy explained how the refitting had gone forward like a precisely planned battle campaign.

Listening to her, Whit realized again how simple and efficient Loy and Danu's computer-graphics approach had been. All the adjustments to the craft that involved newly manufactured parts had been made to exact specifications, with hairline allowances. The computer program had been the place where all the creating and subsequent errors had occurred. When the actual parts were manufactured, they fit and performed their conceived function perfectly. As a result, Danu and Loy's system had greatly reduced the clock hours necessary for the project and effectively eliminated the need for test flights.

Then Loy drove them by the towering Vehicle Assembly Building, where the orbiter, external tank, and solid rocket boosters were all housed, waiting to be joined together for the blastoff. From the VAB stretched what was obviously a wide road, marked out with bright yellow paint on each side. With a nod, Loy explained that the crawler-transporter would use the road to move both the mobile launch platform and the spacecraft to the launch site a half-mile away.

Despite her cool appraisal, Whit knew by Medusa's silence that she was impressed. Loy, however, was busy turning the big troop transport onto the marked road and seemed unaware of the way Medusa watched her. Smoothly, Loy changed gears, and the transport accelerated in a new direction.

Looking at the hand just leaving the gearshift, Whit thought, *No sign of the shakes today*.

In the backseat with Whit, Reno's eyes, too, were on Loy.

*Why?* Whit wondered. *Is she trying to take Loy out of contention for shuttle pilot? Maybe she senses how wounded Loy is right now. Maybe, before Medusa, or the Eight Leaders Council, or anyone else does the dirty deed for her, she herself intends to knock Loy out of the running.* Whit's jaw clenched. *Or was Loy just conveniently at hand — a challenging Beltane seduction?*

Feeling Whit's regard, Reno glanced over at her. Their eyes locked. Whit knew her gaze was unforgiving and hard but didn't change it. *This is my best friend you're toying with, little girl. You'd better not hurt her.*

Reno seemed to get the unspoken message, for she lowered her eyes self-consciously.

"And here's the launch pad," Loy was saying.

With a soft gasp, Medusa leaned forward to peer up through the windshield. "Stop the transport," she ordered.

Loy braked, then threw a concerned look back at Whit as Medusa opened the door and jumped out. Hands on her hips, the general scrutinized the sprawling one-hundred-and-sixty-meter-high metal framework before her.

Reno leaned forward and squeezed Loy's shoulder. "I think you've actually succeeded in surprising her," she whispered.

"Major Reno," Medusa called. "Is this bigger than the one at Vandenberg, or is it my imagination?"

Without a word, Reno opened the back door and slid out of the transport.

For a moment, Loy and Whit blinked at each other.

Recovering, Whit shoved open her transport door. As Loy jumped out of the other side of the vehicle and hurried to join her, Whit was demanding, "You've already built a launch pad in the ruins of that old Air Force base?"

Medusa gave Whit a slightly smug smile. "It was readymade, Whitaker. As Reno mentioned yesterday, back in the last century, Vandenberg was the Kennedy Center's alternative launch site. The shuttles with equatorial orbits originated from Cape Canaveral, Florida, while the shots that involved polar orbits were launched southward down the Western Test Range from Vandenberg in California."

Appearing beside Whit, Reno stated softly, "There was a modest orbiter-processing facility already in place, still in pretty good shape due to the desert climate. No Vehicle Assembly Building, but they left the erection cranes in sealed hangars. In those days, they used cranes to get the orbiter, tank, and solid boosters hooked up outdoors." She glanced at Loy's stricken face and fell silent.

Loy swallowed hard, then shook her head. "I think we've been back-doored," she observed to Whit.

Medusa stepped closer to Loy. "We're all ready to go at Vandenberg because it's a simpler operation. We've refurbished our own external tank and two solid rocket boosters, and now that we've learned the exact calculation of your cold-fusion fuel formula, all we need is the shuttle itself."

At a loss, Loy turned and looked at Reno. "You know the formula? But I only isolated it yesterday. How could you . . . ?"

Medusa laughed. "There are always loose tongues and, shall we say, inept security measures among civilians on a Beltane night. That's why this should have been a military project all along." Turning, the general gestured toward the scientists and construction workers hurrying to and from the launch pad in the distance. "Which devoted Isisian had too much wine and gave away your treasured formula?"

Then Medusa fixed her attention on Loy and asked softly, "Or was it you, Chen?" Laughing softly, Medusa stated, "Anyway, you know that's what everyone here will think. That you gave Reno the key to the whole program while you were in bed with her."

Loy's startled, bewildered dark eyes moved from General Medusa to Reno to Whit.

"You're not fit to pilot anything, let alone the shuttle," Medusa finished.

"That's enough!" Whit told the general.

Frowning, Whit asked, "What's she talking about, Loy?"

"It's not what it sounds like —," Reno began.

Loy abruptly turned and walked away from them. Whit called her name, but Loy broke into a run.

Reno took several steps after her before Medusa barked, "No, Major! Stay! I'll need your expertise."

Reno stopped, her shoulders rigid, her eyes riveted on Loy's retreating figure. Arms and legs churning, Loy had accelerated into a full sprint, racing down the road toward the VAB.

Whit turned and met Medusa's level stare. It shook Whit to see how devoid of emotion the woman's face was. "This mission must succeed, Whitaker. There will be no ne'er-do-well maverick at the controls, despite her personal friendship with you."

"Did you set her up?" Whit demanded.

Medusa gave her a mildly exasperated glance before saying, "The fact that you even have to ask the question speaks volumes, does it not?"

Uncertain of Loy and hating herself for it, Whit looked at Reno for some sort of answer. Reno, however, was staring at the woman who continued to run into the distance.

"Now," General Medusa said, her eyes on the VAB, "let's have a look at the ship, shall we?"


It was early evening when Whit marched down the third-floor hallway of the Leader's House, her boot heels clicking on the shining, hardwood floors. Reaching the door of her private suite, she slapped her hand across the DNA plate.

As the door glided open, Whit snarled at the sentry stationed there. "Cook's sending my dinner up. That will be the only reason you disturb me. Clear?"

Eyes forward, the straight-backed young sentry saluted and answered, "Yes, ma'am. Clear, ma'am."

*Mother of Earth*, Whit realized, *I'm behaving just like Medusa.*

She sighed and rubbed the back of her neck, wishing her pounding headache would just go away. "Sorry, Corporal. I don't mean to take out my tough day on you."

Eyebrows raised, the woman slid her a glance. "Ma'am?"

Whit moved closer. "I mean . . . thanks for looking out for Kal and me. Is she in there?"

"Yes, ma'am," the corporal replied, still impossibly straight-backed but making eye contact now. "She's not feeling well, ma'am."

Instantly alarmed, Whit asked, "Has a healer been by?"

"No, ma'am," the Corporal stated. "But Deputy Leader Lilith has been here since late afternoon, and she had some broth sent up a short while ago."

"Thanks," Whit said, then quickly strode into the suite she shared with Kali.

Lilith was at the far end of the room, sitting before the fire. As Whit came closer, she saw that Lilith's chair was beside the sofa. Reclining on the sofa and covered by a blanket, was Kali.

Glancing behind her and seeing Whit's anxiety, Lilith quickly began explaining. "It's nothing serious, dear. Just a little morning sickness."

"But it's nearly seven o'clock at night!" Whit protested, annoyed to hear her voice crack. "Isn't it called morning sickness because it's a morning thing?"

Standing, Lilith moved to Whit's side. "Some women have the same effects, but they have them in the evening."

On the sofa, Kali opened her eyes and laughed weakly. "Is that panic I hear? You're going to be a wreck if this is the way you react to every new development of this pregnancy."

Whit clutched her aching forehead and retorted, "Well, first you faint and now you're sick . . . What else is going to happen? Prepare me a little, and maybe I won't feel like I've fallen into a time warp back to the days when their biology enslaved women."

Lilith pursed her lips and shook her head, but Whit already knew by the outraged look on Kali's face that she had gone too far.

"I thought you understood!" Kali asserted, thrusting the blanket aside and struggling to sit up.

Whit hurried to justify herself. "I do. I do understand. I just have this headache, and I'm a damn bear."

Kali was nearly crying. "I don't want my baby going from a petri dish to a biochemical hatchery the way I did!" She swung her legs over the side of the sofa, and Whit took in the rumpled clothes she must have been wearing when she'd gotten ill and come home. "Your mother carried *you*, Whit!" Kali declared. "Don't you see? I want this baby to be like *you*!"

And then Kali covered her face with her hands and doubled over, sobbing.

Whit turned a desperate look on Lilith, who gave her a wry smile and whispered, "Most expectant mothers are also a little emotional."

Lilith stood on tiptoe and kissed Whit's cheek, then headed for the door.

Aghast, Whit began to follow her. "Wait! I don't know what to do!" she hissed.

"Just hold her and tell her how much you love her," Lilith answered. "Same as you've always done." Then, relenting at Whit's dismayed expression, Lilith came back to Whit and smoothed a hand over her cheek. "I'm sorry about your headache, dear. It might be a good idea if you both go to bed early tonight." Lilith's lips quirked up as if she knew a delightful secret.

Wearily, Whit asked, "Haven't you heard? There's an Eight Leaders Council tonight — in an hour to be exact."

Guiltily, Lilith glanced at her chronometer. "I was paged on the comline sometime earlier, but Kali was so dreadfully ill that I simply stored the message. I'm afraid I forgot about it."

Shrugging, Whit said, "The general's outflanked me. She's going to make a strong case to take the shuttle down to Vandenberg and have Reno pilot an all-military crew."

"Oh no," Lilith responded, her blue eyes betraying her apprehension. A slender hand crept over her heart. "But didn't Loy tell her that the Elysians will have all that archival Pentagon information at their fingertips? That if the Border falls, Vandenberg will be the first place the Elysians strike?"

Tired beyond words, Whit muttered, "Medusa is convinced the Regs are too ignorant to understand that the satellites control the Border. She even thinks they won't know that Vandenberg was the backup launch site for Canaveral a hundred years ago." Whit rubbed her eyes. "Can you believe it? She's relying upon the assumption that the Regs won't put any of it together. That they won't figure out we're racing to prevent the loss of the only thing separating Freeland from Elysium."

Apprehension clear on her face, Lilith surmised, "She's gambling — same as she accused you of doing with the extra fuel necessary for an Isis launch."

Her throat tight, Whit could only nod.

"Go to Kali, dear," Lilith urged quietly. "I'll meet you soon at the comline studio downstairs."

Feeling suddenly guilty about her divided attention, Whit turned and studied Kali as Lilith moved away.

The sobs had grown quieter, as if Kali were struggling for self-control, but the sound still made Whit's heart ache. *I haven't seen her cry since . . . Mother's blood, I can't stand this!*

Whit moved closer, then cautiously sat down beside Kali.

Kali's tears were interrupted by a series of hiccups.

Tentatively, Whit reached an arm around her, whispering, "I'm sorry, Kal."

Kali moved her hands away from her face, sniffling steadily. Her eyes were swollen, her cheeks were pink, and her nose was running. Pierced through the heart at the sight of her, Whit pulled a kerchief out of her back pocket. Kali didn't look at her or utter a word of thanks, but she accepted the offering and made use of it.

Sighing, Whit tried again. "I'm not used to feeling so completely out of my depth. All this baby stuff — it scares me, a little." Whit swallowed, ashamed of herself. "Guess I'm not being a very good partner."

In answer, Kali leaned into her, burrowing into Whit's arms like a small child. "Oh, shut up and hold me," she pleaded. "Just hold me."

Closing her eyes, Whit embraced her more fully. "It'll be all right," she soothed. "I'll do better — I promise." Silently she resolved, *And I will, damnit.*


"Places, ladies," the senior comline technician called.

Lilith felt Styx squeeze her hand, and she looked up at the weathered, red-brown face beside her.

"Don't worry, Lil," Styx murmured. "Whit's always at her best under fire."

Lilith was worried. She leaned forward slightly, peering past the various women walking back and forth across the comline studio. General Medusa sat at a small table with her three aides. Their heads were all bent together as they reviewed the General's prepared speech.

*I've known you a long time, General,* Lilith thought. *I've seen you connive funding and mission assignments. I've seen you bully colony councils, reducing competent public servants to confused pawns. For years, now, you've steamrolled over anyone who got in your way.* Lilith took a long breath and held it. *But you are not going to steamroll over Whit. Not while I'm Deputy Leader.*

Feeling incredibly tense, Lilith exhaled. After fifteen years as Leader of Artemis, she wasn't used to being second in command. Much as she attempted to act as a mentor for Whit, there were still times when she had an overwhelming urge to assert herself. Times when she yearned to subtly slip the reins of power into her own hands again and take full command of a situation. This was one of those times.

She turned to Styx for a brief good-luck kiss, then went to the table where Whit was arranging her palm computer and a file of handwritten notes. They sat down together, and Lilith pointedly eyed the empty chair on the other side of Whit, where Loy was supposed to be sitting.

"I'm not sure she'll come," Whit said. Sending a hard stare to the women gathered roughly six meters away from them. "General Medusa and Major Reno have done everything but kick her in the teeth."

Nearby, Medusa and Reno were sitting before a similar table. The two junior military aides accompanying Medusa moved away, and the comline techs made last-minute adjustments to the miniature cameras and microphones suspended from the ceiling on roboticized mounts.

"Two minutes to broadcast," the senior tech announced.

Lilith saw Whit close her eyes and bend her head, perhaps sending a prayer, perhaps just collecting her thoughts.

Nervously, Lilith looked for Styx. Her eyes caught on the tall, square-shouldered frame in the corner. Fingering the end of her silvered black braid, Styx met Lilith's gaze and mouthed *Good luck*. Lilith tried to smile in reply.

*We* have *to win this referendum*, Lilith thought. *Everything — our freedom, our very lives — depends upon it.*

"One minute to broadcast," a tech announced.

The door on Lilith's right opened and closed. There was a murmuring noise as women reacted to the entrance of the person striding toward them. Lilith did not need to turn and look. She knew who it was.

As the woman passed behind Lilith on her way to Whit, Lilith turned and said quietly, "Good for you!"

At the other table, Lilith saw Reno suddenly stand. Medusa grabbed her by the arm before she could do more, and then a fiercely whispered exchange erupted between them.

Pale and hesitant, Loy stopped beside her chair. She seemed unwilling to meet Whit's eyes. "I don't know if I should be here or not." She pulled out a chip box and handed it to Whit. "All the data you need is in here. I've updated what I gave you this morning."

Quietly, Whit asked, "Why shouldn't you be here?"

"I've . . . I've become a liability to you."

Whit stood and pulled out the chair for Loy. "Not so. You're my chief of staff. As ever, I need you." Whit's gray eyes bored into Loy's.

The senior tech interjected, "Mother of Earth! Twenty seconds to broadcast." Pointing at Loy and Whit, and then at Reno and Medusa across the room, she finished, "Quiet! For Gaea's sake, quiet!"

Seeming both overwhelmed and slightly embarrassed, Loy

gave Whit a brief nod. Lilith reached over and squeezed Whit's hand. Whit shook her head and broke into an ornery grin.

*I know that look!* Lilith thought with a burst of excitement. *She's decided to give a three-star general the fight of her life — on a national comline link, yet!*

Somewhere in the shadows, the harried comline tech counted, "Ten, nine, eight, seven, six . . ."

Across from them, the large wallscreen flickered. Techs scurried to find chairs at the far sides of the room. Except for the beams focused on the women at each of the two tables, the room lights slowly dimmed. On the wallscreen opposite the two tables, the Delphi symbol appeared: a purple six-pointed star with a leaping dolphin in the center. The Freelandian national anthem began to play in a stirring, melodic flow of music.

Everyone stood, silent now, her attention focused on the wallscreen. Lilith noticed a movement out of the corner of her eye. Reno had stepped back, just behind Medusa, and she was blatantly staring at Loy, as if trying to compel Loy to look at her. The national anthem was drawing to a close when Lilith saw Loy's head turn toward Reno. Though Lilith could not see the expression on Loy's face, Reno's eyes burned with some deep, anguished emotion.

*Good Gaea*, Lilith thought. *If I didn't know better, I'd swear Reno's in love with her.* Frowning, Lilith considered the possibility. *Could it be that her pursuit of Loy is genuine — unrelated to Medusa's desire to take over the shuttle program?*

The anthem ended, and everyone sat. From the wallscreen speakers, a woman's voice announced, "Good evening, Freeland. The Eight Leaders Council is called into emergency session."

The wallscreen filled with seven separate boxlike images. Lilith knew that throughout Freeland, other wallscreens were projecting nine images, because everywhere else the debate coverage would include the groups at the two separate tables in this room. Where individual Leaders sat alone in various comline studios, the wallscreen would be devoid of their own images. In each city-colony, a skilled staff of technicians was coordinating the broadcast about to commence.

Lilith's attention snapped back. The announcer was introducing the elected Leaders of Freeland, their areas of governance separated by hundreds, and sometimes thousands of miles. This was traditionally how the Eight Leaders Council met — via the satellite-dependent comline.

*Yet another reason we need the satellites to stay operational*, Lilith realized. *Without the satellites, we'll be reduced to radio signals. And if the Regs ever do come through the Border, radio signals won't be fast enough. By the time the alarm has been passed, some poor colony will be enduring a punishing attack.*

Lilith watched the Leaders acknowledge their introductions, beginning with the southwestern contingent. Devi Stone from Tubman, her numerous black braids specially beaded for the occasion. Shekina Rosenberg from Susan B. Anthony, adjusting her shawl and looking imperious. Kore Martinez from Lang, the dark brown eyes flashing as she grinned. On the other side of the Toxic Zone from the rest of Freeland, close to the Border, these women represented the city-colonies most likely to be attacked first when the Border fell. Loy knew these women would be easily swayed by Medusa's claim that Vandenberg Air Force Base would provide an earlier launch date and the greatest probability of success.

From Old California territory, there was Jefferson Chamberlain of Harvey. Harvey was still primarily a gay male colony, and gray-haired, distinguished Chamberlain was the only male on the Council. Coatlicue Rodriguez was there representing Morgan, her youthful face markedly grave. Chamberlain and Rodriguez would be closest to Vandenberg, and whatever arguments Whit had to make about the Regs knowing about the viability of that site would be directed to those two. If another hydrogen bomb was dropped, as the Regs had unbelievably dared to do over Las Vegas in 2013, most of Old California territory would be left irreversibly toxic for a thousand generations to come.

The announcer moved onto the three Pacific Northwest Leaders. The well-respected elder Kybele Pagano of Boudica raised her hand as she settled her generous frame more comfortably in her chair. Cimbri Braun's lovely, dark face smiled from Artemis. Then Tomyris Whitaker of Isis was introduced, and beside Lilith, Whit formally nodded at the camera.

Lilith drew a deep breath. She knew that all over Freeland the people were sitting before wallscreens and comline units, observing everything.

In most ballots, every adult citizen in the land had a vote, except in cases such as this one, where national security was involved. In matters of national security, only the Eight Leaders voted. Tonight this select group was going to publicly decide for the nation where the shuttle would be launched, and who was going to be her crew.

The announcer outlined the topic, then presented the two teams of debaters. Moments later, the debate was officially opened.

Medusa stood and strode before her table.

She spent the next half-hour making her case for Vandenberg and a completely military operation. Familiar by now with Medusa's ideas, Lilith only half listened. Instead, as Medusa spoke, Lilith found herself scrutinizing Medusa's insistently fervent manner. Once or twice, she mentioned the contributions of "the civilian task force in Isis," but for the most part she kept her remarks to a minimum about the solid preparation involved to date in the shuttle program. Medusa's theme seemed to be that national security mandated that the experts take charge.

Near the end, Medusa had Major Reno stand. The general ran through a dizzying list of accolades and accomplishments while Reno gazed into the cameras, her face carefully devoid of expression. From Reno's ramrod straight posture and the set line of her mouth, Lilith could detect no sign of pride or heartache.

As Reno sat down again, Medusa stared into the comline camera before her. "In conclusion, let me say that we are warriors and that we are ready to serve. Give us this mission and we will succeed. Give it to the citizens of Isis and . . . well, civilians are amateurs when it comes to defense. Our security and welfare should not be left to people unfamiliar with risk."

A gasp of outrage came from the Isisian technicians standing by in the shadows. Lilith had an instant to wonder if the sensitive microphones had picked up their audible reaction. Seconds later, she saw frowns on the faces of Kore Martinez and Jefferson Chamberlain, and knew that they, too, disapproved of what the general had just said.

The announcer invited Whit to present the opposition point of view. Obligingly, Whit rose, took a few steps forward, then motioned for Loy to join her before the table. Loy reluctantly stood and joined Whit.

In a clear voice, Whit introduced Loy as her chief of staff in administrative functions and chief of operations for the shuttle project. Whit asked Loy to update everyone on how the shuttle project had begun.

Loy nodded, walked over to the comline computer that was built into the back wall, and inserted her palm computer into a port, causing the palm to interface with the larger unit. As video images of Jackie Cochran Space Center superseded the comline studio camera feed, Loy began giving a brief outline of the development of Isis's shuttle project.

Whit gave Lilith a wink, then returned her attention to Loy.

*Brilliant*, Lilith thought, warmed by a rush of pride in her protégée. *In having Loy explain things, Whit is also making it unmistakably clear that Loy has organized and run the*

*entire operation from beginning to near end — until a certain*
*general got military entitlement into her head.*

The computer video displayed Cochran Space Center when
it had been nothing but rolling, brown grass meadows at the
edge of the Cascade foothills. With a flicker, the strength of
daylight changed, indicating a later film time. There were
suddenly bulldozers working in the December drizzle. Metal
blades bit inexorably into damp, dark earth, pushing mounds
of glacial till along, and leveling it. Then thick, black tarmac
was being laid and various buildings were going up; finally,
the launch tower rose like a steel cathedral spire. Mud-covered
workers clambered off of construction machines and waved
proudly at the camera.

Almost immediately, the film segued to inside shots.
Women gathered before wallscreens, discussing the diagram of
a booster rocket. Women working on shining white spacesuits
that were suspended on special racks; women inside the tight
cockpit of the shuttle refitting the consoles with twenty-first
century technology. Women standing at a control board; a
woman in a spacesuit and helmet giving a thumbs-up before
going through a door. A sign by the door proclaiming SHUTTLE
SIMULATOR/AUTHORIZED PERSONNEL ONLY. Women inside
the huge VAB scampering like ants around and over the wings
of the prone FS *Independence*. One young scientist passing by
the camera turning and calling, "Ain't she a beaut?"

The video feed ended there, and the studio camera focused
on Loy standing in the comline studio. A spontaneous
eruption of applause from the normally staid studio
technicians cut into Loy's first sentence, surprising her. Whit,
with a grin, waved the techs quiet, and Loy began again.

"Now that we have the fuel requirements worked out, all
we need to do is fine-tune the controls for the robotic arm
that's anchored within the orbiter's cargo bay. The robot will
be responsible for seeding the skies over North America with
twenty brand-new telecommunications satellites."

As if still a military officer herself, Loy unconsciously clasped her hands behind her back and shifted to a more relaxed parade-rest stance.

Whit paused before asking, "How long have you been a pilot, Warrior Reserve Captain Chen?"

At her table, General Medusa half rose, looking as if she were ready to protest.

Loy glanced at Medusa before answering, "Sixteen years, Leader Whitaker."

"And have you trained to fly the shuttle?" Whit asked.

"Yes," Loy admitted. "After Danu Sullivan's successful design of the Peregrine simulator for Isis's Artificial Reality Centrum, we asked her to create a shuttle simulator." Loy swung her hand toward the comline computer and used a small remote to key the palm still affixed there. As she spoke, external images of a huge metal unit were displayed. "As you can see, the shuttle simulator is the largest building — besides the VAB — at Cochran." The wallscreen video footage shifted to interior scenes of a flight deck crammed with technical equipment and four flight chairs. "Five other volunteer crew members and I have been working out in it for three hours or more every morning since February."

Medusa stood up and interjected, "May I point out that flying a simulator is still only flying a simulator."

Baffled, Loy regarded Medusa. "Do you know of anyone alive who has actually flown a shuttle?"

"Chen," Medusa hissed. "You are wasting our time. No one cares that you can fly a shuttle simulator."

Loy bit her lip, as if debating whether or not to say what was on her mind. Then, in a measured tone she replied. "Last December, when we here in Isis started this project, you and the rest of Freeland's highest ranking officers told us we were wasting both time and precious tax money on a pipe dream." Her cheeks went a shade ruddier and the scar along her jaw stood out as Loy elaborated. "I heard through the grapevine that you, in particular, lampooned us regularly, calling our effort 'Project Sally Ride,' as if we were a bunch of schoolgirls playing at being astronauts. You didn't give a royal — Well, you didn't care to know much about what we were doing up here until we were damn near ready to pull it off."

Scowling, Medusa allowed, "Your team saw the need and recognized the shuttle's potential in meeting it long before those of us among Freeland's top brass, that's true." She turned toward the camera, "However, what is the point of anything they have done, if the mission is not successfully carried out to its conclusion? This launch and the events of the flight must be planned and executed with the precision of a military campaign. There is no margin for error. It only makes sense that the military should be in charge of the project."

"Excuse me, General Medusa," Whit stated quietly. "This time period is my segment of the debate, and I'll thank you not to interrupt my chief aide again."

Medusa aimed a simmering look on Whit. With exaggerated dignity, the general lowered herself into her chair.

Still looking angry, Loy said to Whit, "I've said my piece. Why don't you wrap it up."

Whit nodded, then turned toward the camera, gracefully accepting that the close of the debate had now fallen to her.

"An element of risk exists in each of the options we are discussing this evening. True, a launch from Isis will need to carry much more fuel than a launch from Vandenberg. Still, the launch from Isis can be done." Her gray eyes narrowing, Whit made a slight gesture with her hand. "Also, the Regs, no matter how technologically devolved we assume them to be, may well know about Vandenberg. And if the Border falls before *Independence* is launched, they will bomb our best chance for a bloodless defense." She let the quiet drag out a moment, allowing the thought to be absorbed, before adding, "Freeland will be left facing a Holy War."

Whit moved closer to Loy, who turned to look at her. "As for my selection for shuttle pilot . . . well, I, too, was looking for a brave, skilled woman who could produce results." Gently, Whit laid a finger on Loy's face and turned the scar toward the camera. "Some badges of honor are bestowed not by generals, but by enemies." Whit's hand came up to stroke that cheek. "This woman I would trust with my life."

A glimmer of tears shone in Loy's eyes, and Lilith saw her swallowing hard, trying to keep her composure.

Whit looked at the camera once more. "If there is one thing we here in Isis know about, it is risk. Two years ago our colony was a blackened ruin, an abandoned outpost of anguished memories." Whit lifted her head, her dark gray eyes fierce. "Let no one forget that the first citizens of Isis died, most of them burned or raped or beaten to death by Elysian Regs. It will *never* happen again. Not while *we* have anything to say about it."

Lilith's hands clenched into fists.

From the shadows, the comline techs burst into a roar of noise, temporarily drowning out everything.

Whit made a small bow toward the camera, then turned and moved back to her chair. Loy followed her, dashing away tears.

Pitching her voice above the continued cheers and outbursts of support from the techs, the announcer closed the debate. "Thank you, General Medusa and Leader Whitaker. Citizens of Freeland, your Leaders are now withdrawing from the all-access channel to conduct a private meeting of the Eight Leaders Council and further discuss the issues presented tonight."

A few voices hissed, "Quiet! We're still on the link!" and the women in the studio managed to bring their noise down to a low murmur.

The announcer concluded, "The Eight Leaders Council will return to the comline all-access channel when they have reached a decision. Thank you and good night."

The red signal light on the cameras went off, and the senior tech yelled, "End broadcast."

Women broke into whoops of victory. Whit slung one arm around Loy and the other around Lilith, hugging them both.

Over the heads of the women who pressed in, surrounding them, Lilith saw Whit spy someone near the door. Grinning sheepishly, Whit began freeing herself from the congratulating crowd. Moments later, she had made it to Kali, who was laughing as Whit caught her up in an exuberant embrace.

Across the room, Medusa was berating Reno, but Lilith could not hear the conversation. Reno was obviously not listening to the general. Instead, Reno was glumly watching Loy fend off the persistent attentions of Hypatia Rousseau and the other women Whit had left in her wake.

Looking flushed and embarrassed, Loy was soon making excuses and fleeing the comline station right behind Whit and Kali.

Styx had a sardonic smile when she came to Lilith's side. "Told you so," she cracked.

# Chapter 6

The next evening, Whit and Kali walked up the flagstone path to their first home in Isis. Before them, the great stone house rose against the vivid aquamarines and royal blues of a twilight sky. Welcoming, amber light poured from the downstairs windows, while the last birdsong echoed across the mountain meadow. On an impulse, Whit stopped, surveying the scene.

As if she read Whit's somber mood, Kali moved into her arms.

"I still can't believe we lost," Whit said. "That the Eight Leaders Council actually gave the whole project to Medusa."

Kali nodded. "Sometimes, I think nothing is predictable." She turned toward the lovely country manor before them.

"Who would have thought last spring, when we built this place, that we wouldn't even be living here now?" She looked up at Whit. "That in a year's time, you'd be Leader and I'd be pregnant? And Tor and Danu would end up renting our house while we were stuck in the city?"

"So much changes so fast," Whit responded wistfully. "It frightens me sometimes."

Kali studied Whit more closely, as if amazed to hear this confession of vulnerability.

Before Kali could say anything, Tor opened the front door and walked out to stand on the porch. "The gang's all here," she called softly.

Kali took Whit's hand, and they moved up the porch steps. With a rueful grin, Tor led the way through the wide doorway and into the lamplight.

Upon entering, Whit sent a nostalgic glance at the gleaming madrone floorboards, flooring that she had spent weeks laying and polishing herself.

Kali squeezed her hand. "One day we'll be back, love," she whispered.

Whit frowned, but nodded her head.

Then, they were in the living room, greeting their friends. Lilith and Styx came forward to give comforting hugs. Danu, dressed in casual civilian clothes, commented sadly, "When I sent those invitations earlier today, I thought this would be a victory celebration."

"This is still probably just what we all need," Kali told her. "An evening to unwind with friends."

Beyond Danu, Whit spotted Loy standing near the broad, colonial-style fireplace. Hands in her pockets, Loy's shoulders were hunched, and she looked away self-consciously. Determined to set the record straight, Whit moved to her side.

"Loy —"

"I'm sorry," Loy whispered.

"It wasn't you." Whit stated, trying to keep her voice low.

"Who, then? You?" Barely suppressed emotion strained

Loy's voice. "I'm like those icicles hanging on *Challenger*'s solid rocket boosters a hundred years ago. Anyone who knows anything knows doom when they see it."

Lilith was suddenly beside them. "Loy, why don't we all sit down? Since this afternoon's announcement I've been checking my sources, trying to discover what played out behind the scenes, and I think much of what I've learned will surprise everyone."

"What?" Styx mocked, slapping a hand dramatically to her chest. "Subterfuge and chicanery in Freeland?"

Lilith threw her a weary look. "Yes, like anywhere else human beings govern, political connections sometimes have more power than even the most persuasive arguments."

Loy moved away from Whit to the opposite side of the room, where she began pacing by the windows. Kali settled with Danu and Tor on the sofa before the fire. With a troubled frown, Whit parked herself on the plush, rounded arm of the sofa next to Kali, but her eyes kept straying to Loy.

Styx sank into an armchair and gestured impatiently. "So what did you learn?"

Lilith lingered before the fireplace, turning slightly to allow the fire to warm her back. A regretful expression crossed her face. She rubbed her forehead with her hand, her lips becoming a tight, straight line. "I'm afraid I've done something rather unforgivable."

Intrigued, the others all stilled, their full attention on Lilith.

Lilith dropped her hand. She gave a nervous half-smile, then addressed Styx. "Do you remember who Medusa was involved with before she settled down with Ashanti?"

For a moment, Styx's head cocked sideways, as she regarded Lilith, perplexed. "No," she said at last. "I wasn't moving in elite circles with you movers and shakers in those days."

"Oh, that's right," Lilith recalled, "you were still studying with Baubo then, in that cabin out beyond Cady Stanton

Pass." Facing Kali, Lilith rolled her eyes and commented, "Why do Wiccans have to hibernate in the wilderness to learn basic herbology?"

"I was also finding my inner goddess," Styx informed her, lifting her chin and striking a humorously haughty pose.

"Well, Nature Child," Lilith returned, "while you were roaming the Cascades picking berries, Medusa had a fiery, three-year on-again, off-again relationship with Kybele Pagano."

Whit suddenly ended her surreptitious watch on Loy and straightened.

Lilith noted Whit's interest and addressed her next remarks directly to her. "That was how I first met Medusa — kept running into her at the Boudica airfield because she was flying in and out of there on every leave pass she could wrangle."

Danu leaned forward. "You can't mean . . ."

After a small shrug, Lilith elaborated, "And before that, during her school days in Tubman, Medusa was deeply involved with Shekina Rosenberg —"

"But they're Leaders. Freelandian Leaders!" Danu turned to Whit and sought the intense, dark-gray eyes that were still aimed at Lilith. "Whit, they wouldn't let old love affairs affect how they cast their votes on an issue this important, would they?"

Whit merely waited for the rest of the story.

Quietly, Lilith explained. "Last night I did something I've never done before." Guilt flooded her face. "I overreached my authority as a deputy leader. I had our security officer, Captain Razia, run a standard utilization check on the comline, specifically on the unit in General Medusa's guest quarters in the Leader's House."

"Shit," Kali breathed.

"Not quite illegal, but completely unethical — I know," Lilith replied, her serious blue eyes moving from Whit to Kali. "I had Razia compile a log, monitoring whom Medusa contacted and the length of each interaction. It's not exactly a wiretap, because I did not ask Razia to access the actual content of the conversations. However, checking on whom another citizen speaks to is *still* ethically an infringement of rights." Lilith frowned. "I still can't quite believe I've let myself stoop so low."

"My little spy!" Styx joked.

From the back of the room Loy's surprisingly calm voice inquired, "What you're saying is . . . Medusa was twisting arms?"

With a nod, Lilith answered, "She spoke with Kybele Pagano and Shekina Rosenberg for over an hour each. Then she contacted the other Leaders, one by one. The sole exception was Cimbri Braun in Artemis." Inclining her head at Whit, Lilith remarked, "No doubt Medusa feels that your past herstory with Cimbri would weigh in more heavily than any argument she could make."

"No doubt," Kali echoed quietly. Whit responded with a slight push and an even quieter, "Stop."

Lilith walked toward Loy as she spoke. "I believe General Medusa spent the evening calling in every favor and personal reckoning owed her — and in a career of forty-plus years, she probably had plenty to call in." Pausing beside Loy, Lilith finished. "The vote went five to three against us because Medusa lobbied the Leaders after the debate. I think it had nothing at all to do with you."

Thoughtfully, as if still unsure, Loy questioned, "So this decision was based more on the loyalty of Medusa's exes than on doubts about my ability?"

Lilith gave a soft laugh. "I believe so, yes. Come here." She opened her arms, reaching out to Loy.

Loy allowed herself to be pulled into a solid, maternal hug.

Whit murmured, "I'm still in shock that Jefferson Chamberlain voted with Cimbri and me against all the others."

Tugging the end of her silver-and-black braid, Styx countered, "Chamberlain's from Harvey, not too far from ground zero if the Regs go for Vandenberg. What's your surprise there?"

"He's a male," Whit answered. "Guess I'm used to underestimating their intelligence."

"Careful, dear, your prejudice is showing," Kali said.

Uncomfortable under everyone's scrutiny, Whit shrugged.

Lilith remarked, "I know it's leftover from what you went through during your undercover work in Elysium, Whit, but you really do have to get over your . . ." Unsure how to express herself, Lilith hesitated.

". . . low expectations," Danu supplied, then ran her hand through her short red-gold hair and offered Whit a penitent smile.

Taking Whit's hand, Kali stated softly, "All men are not like the Regs, Whit."

With a noncommittal *humph*, Whit shrugged.

"What do we do now?" Tor asked, gazing expectantly at her.

Standing, Whit rubbed the back of her neck. "This afternoon, before I left the office, I received an encoded transmission on the comline from the Eight Leaders Council. We've been ordered to deliver the shuttle and all necessary flight material to Vandenberg Air Force Base within the coming week."

Kali let go of Whit's hand, commenting, "And compliance with that order will have to be absolute. Medusa made sure it's a military directive."

As Loy stepped away from Lilith, she seemed to brace herself. "And?"

Her hands clasped behind her back, Whit answered, "And you are in charge of the move."

Loy's surprise showed on her face.

"General Medusa requested that you coordinate it," Whit

announced. "She wants you to report with the orbiter, and then stay at Vandenberg to assist with the project. She says she will need you for a while as a consultant."

In the silence that followed, Danu and Tor traded a disgusted glance. Kali turned toward Loy, her deep brown eyes filled with compassion. Styx muttered, "The old battle-ax." Setting her lips in a firm line, Lilith's hand gently rubbed Loy's arm.

"I'll get right on it," Loy said.

Loy's gaze swept the faces of her friends. "Excuse me for leaving early, but . . . there's a lot to be done. Thank you for your support — tonight and always." She crossed the room and entered the hall, grabbing her bomber jacket from a row of pegs on the wall. Eyes down, she returned to stand in the threshold as she shoved an arm in a leather sleeve. "You're great friends." Her jacket on, she half turned as she spoke, as if to hide the shine of tears in her eyes. "I'll check in with you tomorrow, Whit, with a transport plan." Swallowing, she ended with a "Good night" that was hardly more than a whisper.

Abruptly, she headed down the hall. They heard the front door open and shut, and then the muffled sound of her boots on the porch stairs.

Danu stood. "Damn, that's not like her," she declared. "The old Loy would have had a fit. Someone should go after her."

"No," Whit said wearily. "Leave her be."

A log in the fire popped, sending up a spray of sparks.

To no one in particular Whit commented, "The old Loy is gone, shed like old skin." She shook her head slightly, still amazed. "Seems she's a leader, now. She put the welfare of her countrywomen first."

\* \* \* \* \*

Four days later, Loy stood beside her assistant, Hypatia Rousseau, watching two cranes maneuver the orbiter toward the broad back of a grain transport. Into the tiny microphone of the communications headset she wore, Loy remarked, "Okay, even her up."

Loy was squinting against the light rain that was falling, watching the impossibly huge, bulky form of the shuttle dangling by what appeared to be delicate cables. In actuality, each of the two cables was three feet across, and the bundles of braided steel were specifically designed for the task at hand. Moving slowly, the cables adjusted the orbiter to the horizontal line of the immense grain transport sitting on the tarmac below it. Then, just as slowly, the cables began lowering the orbiter to where it would be mounted.

Loy looked back down at the computer slate she held in her hand. Colored diagnostics readouts told her that the trajectory of the shuttle was perfectly aligned for the mounting brackets on the back of the grain transport.

"You're right on target, crane operator," she said into the headset microphone.

Beside her, Hypatia pulled the hood of her raincoat aside as she turned toward Loy. "If you've nothing further for me, I need to tie up some loose ends with General Medusa."

Aware of the brusque tone Hypatia used with her now, Loy murmured, "You're free to go."

Hypatia marched away through the shallow puddles. Loy returned her attention to the color diagnostics on her computer slate.

"Lookin' good," she commented to the microphone.

Nearby, someone remarked, "Same could be said about this shuttle project —*finally*!"

Unable to stop herself, Loy turned to see who had spoken. One of the senior astrophysicists on the project, Hel Campanelli, was walking by with several other scientists.

They carried boxes that Loy knew were filled with the contents of their desks.

"It's about time," Hel went on, her eyes on Loy, though she appeared to be speaking to her two companions. "About time this project got the caliber of leadership it deserves."

Silent, Loy watched her, feeling the droplets of cold rain running down her face. She wondered where Hel's animosity was coming from when she barely knew the woman.

As Hel stalked away, the word *traitor* came floating back.

A strange mix of anger, shame, and despair washed over Loy.

The headset crackled. "Are still good to go, Chief?"

Loy fought down her feelings and checked the computer slate. "Yes. Good to go."

In the periphery of her vision, Loy noticed someone else approaching. This time she didn't dare shift her attention. Her eyes stayed fixed on the digitized readouts, as she evaluated the smooth transit of the shuttle.

"Hey," a low voice greeted, the slight Texas inflection unmistakable.

Despite all the internal shields she had spent the past few days erecting, Loy winced. She switched off her mike. "Go away, Major."

"Not before we talk," Reno answered fervently. "You've been avoiding me —"

Loy turned on Reno angrily. "Look, I agreed to be the general's flunky, but I didn't agree to be harassed!"

Reno was bareheaded. In the light rain falling on them, her hair was soaked and her earnest face shone with moisture. "Is that what you think I'm doing?"

"What do *you* call it? Or should I just ask what state secrets you want now?"

"Loy, I didn't steal the fuel requirements from you."

Loy laughed cynically. "They were on my desk, and after the postorgasmic stupor you left me in, what am I supposed to believe? I never even heard you leave." She stared down at Reno, daring her to brazen out what was so obviously a lie. "You . . . you didn't use that little palm computer you carry around all the time to scan those documents and steal my hard work?"

"No, I didn't," Reno declared angrily.

A series of transmissions came through the headset, as the orbiter came within a few feet of the grain transport. Frowning impatiently, Loy muttered to Reno, "You got what you wanted, Major. Just stay the hell away from me."

The voice in the headset called urgently, "Permission to land the package, Chief?"

Fumbling with the switch, Loy turned the microphone back on. On her computer slate, the readouts all gave the green for proceeding. "Granted," Loy answered. "Lower away."

"I did not get what I wanted," Reno said. "And like it or not, I'm assigned as copilot for the flight down to Vandenberg. I'll be right beside you when that grain transport takes off. Deal with it."

Reno spun on her heel and trudged away. Unsettled, Loy watched her for a moment, her heart twisting within her.

Then, gritting her teeth, Loy made herself turn back to the shuttle. Across the tarmac, the big ship slowly settled without a flaw on the back of the larger grain transport.

"Lock her down," Loy ordered. "We piggyback the package to Vandenberg at dawn tomorrow."


That same day, in Isis, Danu hopped off the electrobus at the intersection of South Mountain and Etheridge Roads. The rain fell steadily, but Danu had her billed warrior cap on, and she knew the well-cut gray uniform she wore was made to withstand bad weather. A burly warehouse woman smiled and winked at Danu as she went by her to the bus. Feeling her face heat up with a blush, Danu began walking along Etheridge Road, intent on getting to Styx's warehouse.

As she walked along the street, two women approached from the opposite direction, coming from the hydroponics sheds. They looked her over, grinning, before one of them was bold enough to ask, "Buy you a drink, Lieutenant?"

Danu blushed a deeper shade, laughed, and shook her head, no. While the other two waved good-naturedly and headed toward the Rough and Ready Tavern two blocks away, Danu wondered if it was the imminence of war or some additive in the water supply that had everyone's libido turned up a notch.

She reached Styx's warehouse, rang the bell by the entrance, and opened the big, pinewood door. Crossing through the well-lit interior, Danu noted the stacks of boxes on the floor. Behind the boxes were high, reinforced-steel shelves that stood seven by two meters, row upon row, stretching to the distant rear of the warehouse.

The shelves were filled with all sorts of strange things from another time. Some were recognizable to Danu from the comline herstory files, like the cubes of plastic and glass called "televisions," or the screen units called "monitors" that were the predecessors of wallscreens. Near them were the rectangular metal drive boxes that always accompanied monitors as part of a "desktop PC." The comline had replaced those individual drive units, providing information and access sites on everything anyone ever needed. She strolled by another set of shelves, peering at other artifacts that were complete unknowns to Danu. She found herself slowing as she passed one shelf, eyeing in wonderment the small, glass globes mounted on colorfully painted metal stands. As she moved closer to them, a voice from above, a voice she recognized as Tor's, called her name.

Danu turned and looked above her. Tor was leaning on the steel handrail of the deck that surrounded Styx's office loft.

"What are these things?" Danu asked, pointing.

"Bubble gum machines."

"What are —"

Tor cut her off. "Later. Get up here!" She gestured impatiently, waving for Danu to come join her upstairs.

There was a huge warehouse elevator on the far side of the building for moving artifacts to the second or third floors. Styx's office, however, was on a loft platform built into the southwest corner against the first-floor ceiling. It was about ten meters off the ground floor, and could be reached by a dark, steel-mesh staircase.

Danu jogged upstairs, and Tor gathered her into a warm embrace as soon as she stepped onto the deck. They kissed, and as their hello kisses still tended to do, the exchange became ardent. Conscious of where they were, Danu gently disengaged and stepped around Tor, heading for the office.

"Where's Styx?"

"Went out to get us some lunch," Tor answered, then caught up to Danu and slipped an arm through hers. "But aren't you here to see me?"

Danu opened the office door and went inside, saying, "Yes. There's something I need to talk about with you."

Her dark brows rose up and down in a clowning reaction. "Sounds serious."

Danu took off her cap, folded it, and slipped it into the back pocket of her pants. Extremely nervous, she ran her hand repeatedly through the short strands of her red-gold hair.

As if recognizing what Danu's body language was conveying, Tor grew serious and moved closer. "What is it, Little Red. You can tell me anything, you know."

As Danu was taller than Tor by at least three inches, it

always made Danu smile when Tor called her that. Now, with the smile quickly fading, Danu blurted out, "I'm going to volunteer for a hazardous-duty assignment."

Tor's dark, slanted eyes widened, but she seemed to restrain any other sign of alarm. "What is it?"

"Whit's asked for a Scramble Squadron. It's a group of pilots willing to take off in Peregrines at a moment's notice in case the Elysians mount an attack."

Nodding thoughtfully, Tor remarked, "You'd be on standby duty, stationed at the Isis barracks."

"I'd be able to come home sometimes. We'll get some leave passes . . . until the Border deteriorates."

Tor tilted her head and reached for Danu, pulling her in close.

"Has it ever struck you," Tor asked softly, "how we've completely exchanged roles?"

"What?"

Tor elaborated, "You're the dashing warrior now, not me."

Giving a snort, Danu laughed. "No I'm not!"

Moving back from her a bit, Tor gazed at her fixedly, without a trace of amusement on her face. "You don't see how much you've changed, Danu. Last autumn you were a reserved, intense scholar who lived her life hunched over a computer keyboard. You never dared look another woman in the eye. If I hadn't seen the torch you bore for Whit shining in those baby blues, I would not even have been sure you were lesbian."

Lightly, Danu swatted Tor's arm, "Hey, quit psychoanalyzing me."

A fleeting smile tugged at one corner of Tor's mouth. She reached out a hand and ran it along the sleeve of Danu's uniform. "Do you have any idea how you look in this getup? You look strong and brave and . . . bewitching. You look like you could save all of Freeland and make a woman weep with your lovemaking." Tor gave her head a slight shake. "In that set of grays . . . you are *hot*."

Feeling flattered but not sure how to reply, Danu just watched her, and waited. She sensed that Tor was working through something deeply personal.

Tor motioned toward the tables that surrounded them. The tables were covered with books of all sizes. Some books were open, some were closed. Books that had already been scanned and catalogued were sealed in vacuum packages and set aside, to be stored in the vaults on the floors above them.

"This is my work now," Tor said. "Bending over a keyboard each afternoon, speed-reading pages in order to index the contents, entering each book in Styx's computer catalogue, referencing, cross-referencing. I'm lost in my head for hours."

"I thought you said you liked it," Danu countered. "It's important work, Tor. And you don't *have* to do it if you don't want to."

"I know," Tor murmured, moving away from her, shrugging. "It's just so strange the way we've changed places."

Danu reached for a book on a table that was close to her. Idly, she flipped through some of the pages. Photographs of a mountainous land filled her eyes. From an aircraft, flying over a dense green deciduous forest a hundred years ago, someone had snapped a photographic record, and here it was, caught for all time. Danu closed the book and looked for the title.

"I would love this job," she said softly. "Learning all about Old West Virginia territory. Wonder if it still looks like this . . ."

Danu went back to turning pages, her keen eyes moving over the maps and topography charts with a hungry interest.

"Knowing that whiz-kid brain of yours," Tor commented, "you're probably storing away that whole text for future reference."

"Photographic memory," Danu mumbled, feeling instantly ill at ease. "Courtesy of the Think Tank, of course."

Tor moved close, nestling against her. "Doesn't matter

where or how a gift is given, as long as you make good use of it."

Danu returned the book on West Virginia to the table, her arms going impulsively around Tor and holding her tight. "You feel bigger," Danu remarked.

"What?" Tor asked, half laughing.

"Your torso," Danu answered, then reached for Tor's arms and placed a hand on each of Tor's biceps. "Your arms, too. I think you're gaining weight."

Her eyes hopeful, Tor admitted, "Maybe the strength-training program is finally kicking in. And that protein supplement Neith gave me to add to my meals better be worth it — because it tastes awful!"

"So," Danu said, "I should expect my beautiful scholar to turn into a beefcake any day now?"

Tor took hold of the hair on the back of Danu's head. "Watch yourself, Little Red." With a sanguine ease, she pulled Danu's head down and captured her mouth.

"I love you so much," Danu whispered.

"Show me," Tor whispered back.

They were still deep-kissing when Styx, and the delectable aromas of lunch, interrupted them.


The next day, a thick fog had gathered over Cochran Space Center. The dawn lent the mist hanging over the tarmac an eerie glow. Shivering against the chill morning air, Loy flipped up the collar of her bomber jacket and jammed her hands deep in her trouser pockets. On the grain-transport wing, two young women muscled a cold-fusion hose onto the tank's metal mouth, then efficiently coupled the hose's nozzle to it. Moments later, they began fueling.

From the rear of the transport, a dark form came through the ethereal white cloud, approaching Loy and the ramp crew.

Loy swallowed hard and watched her come, unable to look away.

"Brought you some tea," Reno called, extending a cup in her hand as she came closer. "Lots of honey, right?"

Loy took the cup, murmuring, "Thanks." *She remembered.* She realized almost immediately that this was the sort of thing that Reno did to advance her career. She found out what people in charge liked, then used the information in subtle campaigns of ingratiation.

Looking at Reno now, even with the bitterness of her betrayal, Loy felt as if she were a thirsty woman finally being allowed a drink of sweet, cool water.

"We need to talk, Loy," Reno said.

Loy sighed and turned away, making herself focus on the ramp crew again. "Why?"

"Because we have to work together" — she touched Loy's elbow — "and because I haven't done anything wrong. The general wanted you to jump to conclusions. She wanted to drive a wedge between us. Can't you see that?"

"What do you want, now?"

Reno went perfectly still.

"If you want to fly the transport down to Vandenberg, just ask me." With a sigh, Loy took a sip from the cup she held, savoring the taste. "You don't have to bring me tea the way I like it."

Glancing at Reno from under her lashes, Loy saw the stunned look on her face, and regretted her words. "I'm sorry. I promised myself I wouldn't —" Loy swallowed hard. "The only way I can get through this is if we stick to business. Just business, okay?" Her voice was strained.

"Okay," Reno whispered.

They stood silent in the fog for the next ten minutes. *If there is a hell,* Loy thought, *then this is probably it — standing beside an ex-lover for time interminable, with nothing left to say to each other.*

Reno finally spoke up. "Why is it taking so long to fuel this thing?" She pulled her palm computer out of the pouch on her belt and ran a fuel-requirements program. "A grain transport is a huge craft, but the liquid is delivered at a pressurized rate, and we're only going to Vandenberg, not Mars, for Gaea's sake!"

"I'm taking enough fuel for a two-way trip," Loy answered.

Reno shut down the palm and slipped it back in its pouch. "Ah yes, I'm traveling with the overly cautious Ms. Chen."

"It's just in case," Loy said. "Better to have it and not need it than —" Loy stopped, feeling suddenly very foolish.

Reno slid her a sideways look. "You're right. We're on the verge of war. Better to be prepared."

"Ready to go aboard?" Loy asked, trying for a solicitous tone. "The cargo got loaded last night. Once the fuel crew is done, we can just go through the preflight checklist and head out."

"Sure," Reno said, her face expressionless. "Lead on, Chief Chen."

Loy moved to the side of the transport and the metal ladder that hung there. *Keeping things 'just business' isn't helping. How am I ever going to do this?*

Roughly four hours later, Loy stood on the tarmac at Vandenberg. The *Independence* had made the trip successfully and was still mounted on the broad back of the grain transport she and Reno had flown down from Isis. The white shuttle craft glittered in the mid-May sunshine of Old California territory, while the dull gray grain transport looked like what it was, a serviceable mule, beneath her.

From the area where several giant cranes stretched into the clear blue desert sky, a small Buzzer came toward Loy. A sardonic laugh escaped her. *Of course, Medusa would have a Buzzer.*

Buzzers were one of the newest pieces of Freelandian apparatus: small hovercraft engines mounted on all four sides of a rectangular metal car frame had yielded the electronic equivalent of what was once called a "jeep." Top brass personalities like General Medusa favored the new vehicle both for its speed and the global positioning gadgetry on board.

As the Buzzer glided up, desert sand puffing out from beneath it in a fine beige cloud, Major Reno appeared at Loy's side. "The crew asked me to tell you that they're standing by. Say the word and they'll begin transfer of the hold cargo from the transport to the base trucks," Reno announced evenly.

Loy nodded, allowing her eyes to travel over Reno. In the stronger southern sunlight, her hair was shot through with golden threads. Surprisingly, Loy saw no triumph or excitement on her face. Instead, Reno looked grim and slightly depressed.

General Medusa descended from her Buzzer seconds after it lowered to rest on the tarmac. "Wait here, Captain," she said to the capped woman in uniform beside the driver. Squaring her broad shoulders, Medusa faced Loy. "No trouble finding the place?" she quipped, looking pleased with herself. She walked closer, focusing on Reno. "Major, what was that nonsense I overheard on the radio during the approach?"

"I ordered precautionary radar sweeps," Reno replied. "The airfield radar wasn't online until I asked for it. With the Border in such an unreliable state —"

Medusa cut her off. "Hecate's drawers, Major, we are thousands of miles deep into Freeland and a century ahead of the Elysians in jet design." With a contemptuous laugh, she pronounced, "The Elysians are no threat to this project."

Loy spoke up. "What harm can there be in taking a few precautions, General?"

Reno glanced at Loy, as if surprised by this unexpected defense.

Medusa regarded Loy. "I wouldn't expect a bureaucrat to grasp the complicated issues of a military endeavor, Chen." She looked about to drop the topic, then made a disdainful face. "Suffice it to say that Vandenberg Air Force Base has been nonoperational for about eighty years. We've set up a campaign bivouac, so things are a bit primitive. As yet, we have no power-plant link or cell grids supplying electricity. All our electricity is coming from the twelve crystal-drive generators by the flight tower." She turned her suddenly fierce glare on Major Reno. "And I'm not about to waste precious resources on needless radar sweeps."

Loy saw Reno stiffen. An unexpected wave of empathy washed over Loy, forcing the words to her lips.

"In a military operation, taking precautions is sometimes the difference between success and failure."

"How dare you preach strategy to me, Chen," the general snapped. "The radar has been shut down, again. On my order."

Beside Loy, Reno stayed at attention, staring beyond the general. Only the twitch of a muscle in her jaw betrayed her anger.

General Medusa faced the captain still seated in the Buzzer. "Commence unloading the grain transport. Once all flight gear and related material are inventoried, Chen will review the launch plan with our unit and assist in finalizing our design." Medusa swung back to Loy, as if to monitor her reaction to this announcement.

Loy willed herself to appear serene and made no reply.

Satisfied, Medusa climbed back into the Buzzer, while Medusa's captain barked a series of orders into the comline unit on her wrist. With four small puffs of dust, the Buzzer lifted and began moving away from them.

Loy turned and watched the answering scurry of activity as a truckload of warriors rolled up to the grain transport. The tailgate was lowered and women in gray coveralls began hopping down from the back of the vehicle.

"Thanks," Reno said.

"For what?" Loy asked, all the while knowing the answer and not daring to turn and look into her fawn-colored eyes.

"For speaking up for me," Reno said, the edge in her voice relaying how much she hated the evasions Loy was using.

Loy grunted, unable to say more.

"This may be the last time we're alone, together," Reno went on, "and I have to say this." She stepped in front of Loy. "I know this is the last thing you want to hear, but . . . I'm in love with you."

Loy stepped away, trying to leave, but Reno's arm shot out. She grasped Loy's wrist to prevent escape. "No. Listen to me. I've been crazy about you since you hopped up on the conference table in Whit's office, ready to fight the whole world alone if you had to, ready to laugh in my face if I dared take you on. I've never felt like this before, and the fact that you hate me . . . well it's all gone so *wrong*."

Loy's throat tightened, and unwelcome tears sprang into her eyes. *Why did you betray me?* she wondered.

Sighing heavily, Reno let Loy go. "That's it." She shook her head, closed her eyes, then turned.

She walked away from Loy, toward the tower on the other side of the airfield. Loy watched the wind catch Reno's lustrous brown braid, lifting it, as Reno hurried across the tarmac.

"Damn," Loy gasped, crushed by the wave of desolation that seemed to engulf her. Her throat ached, her lungs could not seem to fill, and unchecked tears streamed down her face.

In the recesses of her mind, she was back in the soft lamplight of that glorious night, gazing fearfully and wonderingly up into Reno's face again. Her body was aflame with the memory of being loved; her lacerated soul was being soothed and cherished by a healing touch.

Loy allowed herself to linger there. For several long minutes, she lost track of the present.

Then, a loud siren split the air.

Startled, Loy stared uncomprehendingly at the tower. A continuous chorus of incomprehensible shouts began in the distance. Loy registered the figures and vehicles racing across the airfield, moving in myriad directions with only one thing in common: Every person and vehicle appeared to be going at full speed. And the warriors were armed — some with small hand weapons, some with missile-targeting systems. A few were carrying small rocket launchers on their shoulders.

Loy's eyes suddenly caught a distinctive form — Reno, tearing toward the shuttle. Loy ran a diagonal path, trying to catch up with the major.

Closer to the grain transport, Loy saw the warriors who had just been unloading launch computers and hardware quickly returning the material to the cargo hold of the plane. Off to the left a sergeant was shouting, "Faster! Faster!"

As Reno dashed by the sergeant, Loy heard her yell, "I'm taking off in one minute. Whatever is not on board by then, leave it and get your women to cover!"

The sergeant saluted, then began bawling orders at her unit. Reno raced up the ramp that formed the rear hatch of the transport, jostling by warriors and weaving around forklifts. Loy plunged into the crowd, keeping her eyes on Reno, trying to close the distance between them.

Inside the cavernous transport, the wail of the air-raid siren echoed off metal walls, reverberating through Loy's bones. Loy briefly wondered if that was what the banshee sounded like, then she was abruptly through the worst of the tangle of cargo, machines, and humans. She sprinted the last twenty-five yards and got to the cockpit door just as Reno keyed the lock and opened it.

As Loy pushed by her, crossed the cabin, and lunged into the pilot seat, Reno hung back, too stunned to speak. Loy donned the radio headset and began flipping switches. Reno slipped into the copilot seat.

Loy glanced at her. "The *Independence* is my baby. I gave Whit my word I'd keep her safe. Okay?"

"Okay," Reno replied. She went through the motions of strapping herself in, then held her own headset in one hand. She was visibly shivering.

Loy barked a permission-to-take-off message, and the tower radioed back, "Go! Go! Go!"

Loy switched on the outside broadcast speakers, ordering, "All personnel, leave the area at once. Jet engines will engage in ten seconds."

Reno pulled her headset into place, then doubled over, as if in physical pain.

"What happened?" Loy whispered.

"Lang is gone," Reno answered, her voice quavering. "My home, my family . . . gone . . ."

Feeling as if she had been punched in the stomach, Loy could only stare.

In the same stricken tone, Reno continued. "A large section of the Border near Old Louisiana territory went off the satellite feed about three hours ago. The system never registered the failure." Reno covered her eyes with her hand. "No one in Freeland even knew until Elysian jets were penetrating air space near Tubman. Their radar triggered a full scramble, and our Peregrines went up to dogfight the Elysians to a standstill. The casualties in Tubman, and later in Susan B. Anthony, were extensive. But Lang . . ." Reno's voice faltered. "One jet made it that far. It dropped some sort of small thermonuclear weapon."

Loy shook her head in disbelief.

The voice from the tower squawked through the radio again. "Mayday, Chief Chen, Mayday! Bogeys incoming from the southeast! Get outta here!"

"Shit, shit, shit!" Loy responded, her hands flying through the ignition sequence, then reaching for the lever that controlled the jet thrusters. "How much time do I have, Tower?"

"Two minutes," came the harried answer. "Maybe less."

Concentrating on turning the lumbering bulk of the transport, Loy took a quick look at the airfield through the huge windshield that compassed the front of the craft. Before her, women were still running, taking up positions at hastily assembled batteries. On the eastern end of the airfield, three Peregrines were firing their jet engines. Meanwhile, Loy watched a fourth Peregrine flash by in a burst of flaming power, hustling to get ahead of her on the long strip of tarmac.

"Tower, who's the hot dog?" Loy demanded angrily.

Through the radio, a familiar voice replied, "Think you can outrun those rabid dogs all by yourself, Chen?"

Shocked, Loy could only manage, "General Medusa?"

The jet sped down the runway, the blue-green flame that marked a cold-fusion engine flickering from its tail. Then Loy hurried to pull her own power-bar back, and the transport trembled as it rolled forward faster and faster.

Medusa's voice came again. "No way was I gonna stay grounded after what they did to Lang." A strangled laugh came, and the next sentence was choked with tears. "I want some payback."

Loy watched as the Peregrine piloted by General Medusa lifted up and blasted skyward at a near forty-five-degree angle.

Focusing on gathering the speed necessary to gain altitude, Loy did not spare the General another thought. She knew the transport was laboring under the heavy load of the piggyback shuttle and all the related equipment onboard in the cargo bay. Anxiously, Loy kept glancing from the runway down to the speedometer, waiting for her craft to acquire the necessary kilometers per hour.

The tower controller shouted through the radio, "Chief Chen, two bogeys at four o'clock."

Finally, the speedometer registered the speed Loy needed, and with both hands she steadily pulled the stick toward her. Like a huge, fat fly, lazy with the end of summer, the grain transport left the runway, and slowly began gaining altitude.

"Chief, you've been spotted!" the controller announced. "They're heading straight for you!"

Almost immediately, Medusa commanded. "Chen, bank right."

Loy let the right wing dip a little, and the transport shook as something long and thin, shining silver in the sunlight, slid past them on the left side. Seconds later, the ground below them erupted in an inferno, then the transport outflew the explosion.

"Floor it, Chen!" Medusa ordered. "Get our package back where it belongs!"

As Loy rolled the transport back to center, she shot a look at Reno.

Reno switched off her microphone. "She means Isis! She's probably afraid that the Elysians are monitoring our frequency."

Loy nodded and kept her gaze fixed on the bright blue California sky above her. Her arms were trembling with the strain of pulling on the stick. In desperation, she was murmuring, "Get up, get up," but in reality she knew the transport was already climbing at its top speed.

"Come on, you old grain bucket!" Reno pleaded.

"Rear visuals," Loy gasped to Reno, willing her arms to hold out a little longer.

Reno keyed the onboard computer, and the two-foot-square screen mounted on a panel between Loy and Major Reno flickered to life. On the screen, they could see the runway stretched out behind them, and the remaining three

Peregrines rising from it. They could also see Medusa's Peregrine dogfighting with two ancient Elysian jets, which were trying to pursue the transport and its piggyback shuttle.

"F-24s," Reno muttered. "Flying antiques nearly a century old, and still capable of blowing this shuttle project to hell."

"Not if Medusa has anything to say about it," Loy responded. "Look at her!"

Medusa's Peregrine was baiting the F-24s away from the transport, then slipping down and sideways to escape the heat-seeking missiles launched at her craft. The missiles exploded harmlessly on the desert floor, targeting only cactus and tumbleweeds.

Then, as if understanding Medusa's gambit, one of the jets peeled away from Medusa, streaking after the transport. While the other three Peregrines raced after the F-24 closest to them, Medusa's Peregrine pursued the antiquated jet closing on Loy and Reno.

"You've got trouble on your butt, Chen," Medusa radioed.

"What else is new?" Loy called back, trying to adjust her flaps to level off a bit. What she needed now was speed, not altitude. Suddenly, altitude could wait.

"Hey, Chief," the General's querulous voice stated, "I've rolled the dice on this one, and by the looks of things . . . well, I've been a horse's ass." Silence interrupted for a moment, as if that admission had cost her. "But . . . what I did, I did for my country. Now, by the Goddess, you and Whit started this thing and you're gonna have to finish it."

"Roger, flygirl," Loy answered, not quite believing she was hearing what seemed to be an apology. "Love you, too. Meet you where the sun doesn't shine."

"I take it that's code for *Meet me in Isis*," Reno murmured. "Everyone in Freeland knows it rains or snows nine months out of the year in Isis."

Reno was staring at the rear visuals. Loy followed her gaze and saw the Elysian F-24 rapidly gaining on them. Just in back of and below the F-24, Loy could see Medusa's Peregrine. With a sinking heart, Loy realized that there was still one heat-seeking missile mounted on the F-24's right wing, and Medusa's Peregrine wasn't carrying any missiles at all.

The radio crackled. "Time for a little one-on-one . . ."

"No!" Reno cried out.

Medusa's Peregrine suddenly sped up, heading straight for the underside of the F-24.

A silent fireball erupted, filling the screen.

Speechless, Loy and Reno stared at the orange-yellow explosion, watching as they left it farther and farther behind them. The fireball and its meager scattering of debris began drifting toward the ground.

Reno ground the heels of her palms into her eyes, as if trying to wipe away what she had just seen.

"Chief Chen! This is the Tower," the radio blared. "We just downed the Elysian F-24 that was still over Vandenberg. Our two Peregrines are heading your way." The controller seemed to take a deep breath. "We saw an explosion in the northern sky. Are you there? Over."

"Chen, here," Loy stated.

"Thank the Goddess," the tower voice uttered, a background swell of cheers carried across the air.

"Thank General Medusa," Loy answered quietly. "She made a kamikaze run at the Elysian jet on my tail." More quietly, Loy said, "The old battle-ax died saving us."

"Roger," the tower managed.

Beside her, Reno started to cry. Impulsively, Loy reached out a hand and smoothed it tenderly over Reno's hair.

"What now?" the controller asked, sounding more than a little lost.

"Send an emergency comline to Leader Whitaker," Loy ordered. "State the following message: 'The big fat goose is coming home to lay an egg.'"

"Right away," the controller said.

"Over and out," Loy concluded.

She slid her hand down to Reno's wet cheek and cupped it. "I'm so sorry, Mika."

Bending her head to her knees, Reno gave herself over to grief. For most of the two-and-a-half-hour trip back to Isis, Reno wept. Loy felt helpless. She sat there listening, wishing with all her might that she could take this pain from Reno, while knowing she could not.

# Chapter 7

Feeling numb, Whit sat in the Cedar House, only half listening to the Seven Leaders Council telecast being relayed on the giant wallscreen across the room. Around her, the sixty-four elected representatives of the Isis Council were seated along the continuous ribbon of a wooden oval table. Whit saw her own shock and dismay mirrored on their faces.

All of them were intently aware that since the last telecast just over a week ago, one Leader, indeed, one entire city-colony, had perished. Dashing Kore Martinez was lost to them forever, along with all the other inhabitants of Lang.

*If I hadn't seen the film from surveillance craft flyover, I probably still wouldn't believe it*, Whit thought.

Taken from several miles above the radioactive site, the

telephoto laser pictures were burned into her memory. Nothing but charred earth remained where Lang had once sprawled in the Texas spring sunshine. The only indication that a city had once been there was the mass of twisted, blackened metal left near what had been the most urban part of the colony.

Whit gripped the edges of the armrests and breathed in the sharp, soothing scent of the cedar logs that composed most of this structure. Based on the council lodges of the Native Americans who had originally peopled the lands, the Cedar House was where the Isisian legislature met. It was richly appointed and outfitted with intricate mosaic floors and carpentry that marked the expert craftwomanship of the builders.

Whit consciously tried to sink into the tranquil beauty of the place. Her glance swept upward, to the pine crossbeams that vaulted overhead. She sighed, and her eyes fell back to the women within the rectangular hall. Seated around the gleaming, red-brown ribbon of desk were the best minds in Isis, and all of the women were grim-faced and cheerless.

In her capacity as deputy leader, Lilith sat on Whit's right. Her gaze was turned inward, and had the burning intensity of deep grief.

From the wallscreen, Shekina Rosenberg's voice pronounced, "And so it is a unanimous vote. As the shuttle has safely returned to Jackie Cochran Space Center, the Seven Leaders Council rules that the launch shall go forward from that site, restored to its status as a civilian project."

In the Cedar House, a sound like a strong wind in the fir forest rose, as many in the hall realized that Isis would now become Elysium's primary target.

Whit knew all too well that they were right to be afraid. If the Elysians were capable of finding out about Vandenberg, they were capable of finding out about Isis. Some military strategists were speculating that the Border had thinned to the point that it was allowing stray Freelandian comline transmissions to be monitored. During the past several weeks, while the debate about the two possible launch sites played out, the strategists had surmised that Elysian Regulators may have been preparing to launch their attack as soon as a Border failure allowed it. Other military minds said the wealth of NASA material about Vandenberg AFB in the old Pentagon files would have made Vandenberg the most likely site for a shuttle launch anyway. In either case, nobody really knew the truth. They only knew that the Freelandian top brass had grievously underestimated the reach and capability of Elysian air power.

Shekina Rosenberg inquired, "Would the Leader of Isis honor us with a response?"

Whit stood, feeling oddly disoriented.

She glanced at Lilith, hoping for some sort of guidance, but Lilith was in the grip of her own thoughts.

All around Whit, members of the Isis Council stirred in their chairs, turning uneasily toward her. An array of faces swam in her vision. All races, all ages; the many variations of women that made up her city-colony. Although they were attempting to hide it, they all looked afraid.

Whit called out, "What say you, free women of Isis?"

A full minute passed.

Suddenly, a full-figured elder across from Whit stood. "Aye," she shouted. "The shuttle goes up from here. Just like we planned."

"Aye!" another woman agreed, leaping to her feet. "Let the damn Regs just try and stop us."

Cooler heads whispered among themselves. Then, one by one, the Council stood, echoing the sentiment, until the last voice sounded.

Beside Whit, Lilith said, "We know our duty."

Whit looked down at her.

Lilith at last met her gaze. To Whit, she looked stricken,

wounded, older than Whit had ever seen her. Yet beneath Whit's scrutiny, her face shifted, adopting an austere power. "Tell them, Whit."

Whit gazed up at the wallscreen, into Shekina Rosenberg's dark, haunted eyes. "We accept the mission. The Freelandian Ship *Independence* will launch as soon as we can safely manage it."

"Our thanks, Leader Whitaker," Shekina Rosenberg stated solemnly, then placed a hand on her heart, in the traditional salute of a Freeland warrior. Neither of them were active duty, but given as it was from one retired warrior to another, it was a gesture filled with respect. Freeland was already at war.

Shekina spoke again, her rich voice filling the hall. "Please relay to your partner, Kali Tyler, and to your entire satellite team our humble gratitude. Their ability to restore the Border has given Freeland some time to recover and prepare. Without their contribution, I fear we all might have suffered Lang's fate."

Knowing it was true, Whit nodded. Her eyes were brimming. Tears trickled down the side of her face, and she swallowed hard, unable to assert the control to stop them. She had been on her feet and in command since the first reports of Elysian attacks had come over the comline forty-eight hours ago. Fatigue and anguish had steadily eroded the facade of composure she wore.

With a striking dearth of formality, the Seven Leaders Council quickly adjourned. The wallscreen had been blank for only a few minutes before the Isis Council session summarily ended and women headed for the exits.

Whit knew most of the women were on emergency action committees. They were all on their way to some task, some duty having to do with either the launch from Cochran Space Center or the defense of Isis.

Left alone with Lilith in the vast, silent hall, Whit turned to her. "Are you all right, Lil?"

With great dignity, Lilith rose and smoothed her hands

over the navy knee-length coat she wore. "I feel I must apologize to you, my dear."

"What? Why?"

"During the past few weeks, you have been engaged in a complicated and challenging test of wills." Nervously, she rubbed her forehead. "It was a political duel that far exceeded your experience or training. You did well in some respects, but not so well in others. That is to be expected. Leadership is a skill learned more thoroughly by mistakes than by successes. However, there is no excuse for my performance. As both your mentor and your friend, I failed you."

Whit was shocked by the resigned guilt on Lilith's face. "You didn't —"

Making an abrupt, chopping gesture with her hand, Lilith cut her off before she could say more. "I failed you," she repeated. "When General Medusa arrived here, full of her own ideas for the final phase of the shuttle project, we did not handle her opposition well."

Lilith began pacing back and forth before Whit. "Rather than hashing out with her the strengths and weaknesses of the Vandenberg launch site, you and I closed ranks against her. Rather than proposing a compromise, of trying to use both Major Reno and Chief Chen on the shuttle flight, we dug in and fought to advance our own agenda. Early on, each side was locked into backing their own woman to the exclusion of the other."

Lilith stopped pacing and faced Whit. "General Medusa wanted what was best for Freeland. In her direct, somewhat obnoxious manner, she was pressuring us, yes, but she only wanted the shuttle project to succeed."

Whit couldn't help countering. "Succeed *her* way."

"Whose way of succeeding is of little consequence!" Lilith snapped.

Whit stiffened.

Lilith softened her tone. "Don't get stubborn on me, Whit. A good Leader takes the methods and ideas of numerous individuals and melds them into a singular, powerful program of accomplishment."

Whit considered the concept. "As you did in Artemis."

"As I tried to do, yes," Lilith said. "It is not the easiest work."

Whit found herself thinking of General Medusa's last words, "What I did, I did for my country." Loy had relayed them to Whit in a tone of bafflement, looking impressed, despite how much the general had ill used her.

Feeling a heavy weight in her chest, Whit bent her head. *In many ways, I suppose I did misjudge Medusa. Like some female dog, I got so busy protecting my turf that I never even heard most of what she was saying.* Sighing, Whit realized, *We disagreed, but Medusa believed in what she was doing . . . believed in it so much she was willing to die for it.*

Lilith's voice was quiet yet firm. "I served as Leader of Artemis for fifteen years. During that time, I endured power plays by headstrong, abrasive opponents." She blew out a breath, as if exasperated with herself. "I knew better than to get drawn into one with Medusa. Instead, under the guise of political preparedness, I had Captain Razia monitor whom the general spoke with on the comline after the national debate. It was cheap. And perfidious."

"You're being too hard on yourself. We were fighting for an Isis launch —"

"It was infighting, Whit!" Lilith persisted, her voice rising. "We indulged in the worst kind of self-serving political posturing and chicanery — all of us!" Lilith finished in a lower tone. "For a while, securing Freeland became a distant second to an egotistical insistence on getting our own way. We do our democracy no service by pretending such behavior is necessary."

Whit bent her head.

"In our struggle with General Medusa, we could have taken the high road," Lilith said.

Whit waited, sensing that Lilith was readying to end her lesson with meaning.

"But I did not think of that, let alone advise it," Lilith admitted. "More fool I." She went to her chair, picked up her computer slate, and slid it into a carryall. "I shall regret for a long time the way I misread and responded to the general's tactics. I shall regret, even more, the fact that I did not lend you proper counsel when you needed it most."

Lilith slipped the long carryall strap over her shoulder. "We have suffered staggering losses. Lang, with all her colonists, has been obliterated. And now, when we need her most, we have also lost our foremost military strategist, a woman of unsparing determination and courage. It is a lot to bear all at once." Gently, she reached out and stroked Whit's cheek. "I do not mean to be harsh with you, Whit, or in any way increase your burden. We just need to do better. Both of us."

Whit pulled her into an embrace. "There is too much at stake for you to coddle me, Lilith. Thank you for loving me enough to expect my best, and for letting me know when it's not delivered."

Lilith stepped out of Whit's arms, wiping tears from her eyes. Her hand squeezed Whit's arm, as if in silent encouragement. Then, adopting a brisk pace, she set out across the room. The big oaken door at the far end closed behind her with an echoing thud.

*As ever, she's right,* Whit realized. *I screwed up. Will I ever get any of this right? Gaea, I stink at being Leader! I should've just stayed a warrior grunt. That way nobody would ever end up getting killed because of something I did or didn't do . . .*

She unleashed a vicious kick into a thick wooden leg of the Leader's chair, then grabbed her booted foot, cursing. She limped off the sharp pain. "Stupid."

Wearily, Whit rubbed a hand across her face. *I need to sleep or I won't be worth shit to anyone.* She cast a glance to the far end of the Council Room. *If I'm feeling beaten into the ground, then what must Kali be feeling?*

Decisively, Whit lifted the leaf in the table that acted as a gate to allow entrance into the center of the room. She crossed the distance to the crest of the oval shape, then used another leaf to exit. Near the back wall, she entered a small hallway.

This corridor led the way to what was still called Maat's lab. Slowing her steps, Whit brushed the lab door's DNA plate with one hand and stepped into the dim light.

She moved past the tables, the cabinets, the wallscreen, and found the door that led downstairs. She keyed another, far more selective, DNA plate. Secreted in the subterranean facilities beneath the laboratory was the complex of computer banks that regulated Maat's Border program. Only three DNA samples in Freeland could open this door. Kali's, Lilith's, and her own.

In a fluid rush, Whit descended the cement staircase. Bright lights temporarily blinded her, and the low hum of computers was the only sound. She was surrounded on all sides by sleek, metal machines that stood twelve feet high and ran in long, regimental rows, almost like bookshelves in a vast, archaic library. Few people in Freeland, let alone in Isis, had ever seen the room.

These were the computers that ran the Border program, Maat's wondrous self-regulating invention. The complex software system sent data to the old NASA satellites orbiting the Earth, and the satellites translated the data into pinpoint emissions of energy. The Border that separated Freeland and Elysium for most of the twenty-first century was the projection of a huge photomagnetic force field. No one in Freeland understood the numerous possible reconfigurations of the Border program data as well as Kali did.

*For the love of Sappho, she's been working the same insane hours that I have, and she's pregnant!*

Pricked by a guilty conscience, Whit hurriedly moved through the stacks, looking for her lover.

Beyond the last row she found Kali, sitting at a work station, hunched over the keyboard, staring intently at a wallscreen. Empty chip boxes, drained water bottles, and discarded sandwich wrappers overflowed from a knee-high metal trash can onto the floor around her. She clutched a palm computer in one hand, and papers with math calculations and formulas were scattered over the desk. Kali's face tipped up as Whit walked closer, and Whit saw the fevered exhaustion in her eyes.

"I got it back up, Whit," Kali announced hoarsely. "It's held now for twelve hours."

"I know," Whit soothed. "We all know."

She slipped her hands beneath Kali's arms and pulled Kali from the desk chair. Kali's rigid body at first resisted, but after a tight sigh she relaxed into the pull and fell against Whit. A half-smothered sob alerted Whit to the fact that Kali was at long last breaking.

"I don't know how long it will hold," Kali confessed. "Too many satellites have virtually no functioning circuitry. I think I've reprogrammed the software about as far as it can go."

Whit smoothed a hand over bright yellow hair. "Shh," she soothed. "You've been here for over two days. The rest of the satellite team are taking shifts in the Leader's House, monitoring your latest upload from the link in the Watch Room. It's time you got some rest."

Kali choked, "I catnapped sometimes . . . I had to."

"It's not enough. Come home."

"I can't. What if the system crashes again? What if —"

"Think of the baby."

"The baby," Kali echoed, wiping a sleeve over her eyes.

"Are you ready to go?" Whit asked, taking gentle charge of her. "Do you need any of this?" She gestured at the papers and palm computer on the desk.

Kali grabbed the palm computer and slipped it into the cargo pocket of her trousers. "Ready," she said softly, then sniffed like a tired child.

Filled with a sudden, overwhelming need, Whit stooped and found Kali's lips. Pulling Kali closer, Whit kissed her, losing herself in the staggeringly sensual feel of her.

Whit's lips moved down Kali's neck, and Kali clung to her, trembling. "Whit, Whit . . . I love you so much. I'm so afraid of losing you."

"You won't lose me," Whit whispered. Her hands moved over Kali, knowing what she desired.

"All those people in Lang . . . None of them knew it was their last day . . . None of them knew their last kiss when it came . . ."

In answer, Whit gathered Kali in her arms and lifted her. "You're all worn out, love. Time I took you home, all right?"

Kali sighed and leaned into Whit's shoulder, displaying her exhaustion more completely than she knew.

Feeling stalwart and solicitous, Whit carried her, cradling Kali against her as she walked across the vast room. One by one, they passed the rows of humming machines that still managed to serve as Maat's sentinels of freedom. Whit eyed them, feeling a new reverence for Maat and her legendary creations.

Kali stirred and insisted that Whit let her walk up the concrete flight of stairs. Whit kept her in the circle of her supporting arm as they walked wearily to Whit's motorcycle.

After a hastily assembled dinner of oatmeal and fruit an hour later, Whit put Kali to bed. Then, though her eyes were burning, Whit sat in a rocking chair by the hearth fire, reviewing reports on her colony's readiness to combat an all-out air assault. Sometime in the quietest part of the night, against her will, she drifted to sleep.

She dreamed of antique Elysian jets, dropping from the sky like slow, nasty wasps on a late summer's day, the kind of wasps that, unprovoked, sting anyway.

\* \* \* \* \*

The next three weeks passed in a surrealistic blur for Loy. From the moment she set the grain transport down on the tarmac at Cochran, her life had gone into light speed. Each day of intense, fast-paced work blended into the next, with only the hours of exhausted, deathlike sleep to separate them.

Extra warrior crews had been assigned to Cochran, and the new three-shift, twenty-four-hour schedule cut their projected preparation time in half. Still, it amazed Loy when, four weeks after General Medusa's arrival in Isis, the project was ready to attempt its noble goal: a space shot.

*We go tomorrow. June 2, 2095.*

Loy shrugged her shoulders, adjusting her body to the weight of the cumbersome white spacesuit she wore. At least the new suit Danu had assisted them in designing and building was lighter and more maneuverable than the extravehicular mobility units — EMUs — the twentieth-century astronauts had been forced to use. The cooling and ventilation garment underneath was made of a much lighter filament, and plastic tubing woven into the mesh carried cool water. The gossamer undersuit removed excess body heat with twice the efficiency of the earlier models.

Taking a deep breath, Loy took the helmet from Major Reno. Reno looked back at her, before settling her own helmet onto the metal collar that ringed her shoulders. Loy pulled her helmet on, then made certain she properly secured the hookups for oxygen and communications. Nearby, the support crew was leaving the mock cargo bay of the shuttle simulator. When the hatch shut, a light above it went red, signaling that the air was being pumped out of the simulator. For the next few minutes, Loy and Reno practiced moving and communicating in the airless compartment.

Finally, they handled a few sample satellites. They went through the motions of retrieving the round, three-foot-wide units from the cargo-bay storage compartments, staggering under a weight that would be insubstantial in space. Carefully, they rehearsed manual implementation of the small rocket engines mounted on the metal cradles that circled each satellite. Once they were in space, the rocket engines would engage when the satellite floated clear of the shuttle, boosting the satellite a mile or so higher, into a preset orbit.

In Loy's mind, even though they were still anchored by earth's gravity, the drill was instructive. The sense of containment and the restricted motion they would face while in the bulky EMUs made Loy feel nauseous and slightly panicky. Someone safely in a control booth kept speaking through Loy's earpiece, telling Loy her heart rate was too high, coaching her to breathe slower and deeper. Loy concentrated on compliance. She had come too far to let claustrophobia get in the way. If the computerized robot arm in *Independence*'s cargo bay failed to function, this drill was exactly what would happen. Loy knew she and Reno would by necessity become nothing more than elaborately dressed stevedores.

After the exercise, once they were safely out of the vacuum chamber and climbing out of the EMUs, Loy looked at Reno. Her physique was clearly outlined in the clinging mesh of the cooling undersuit. Helplessly caught by her beauty, Loy stared, remembered the feel of Reno's soft, warm body lying in her arms on Beltane night.

Pivoting, Reno met Loy's eyes. Reno's face carried sadness now, sadness for her family and for the friends she'd left behind in Lang. Sadness for General Medusa, whom she'd served faithfully. A lovely eyebrow arched up in question.

Loy turned away, a powerful surge of emotion rushing through her, vibrating from her chest out to her tingling fingers and toes. *Sweet Mother, I love her.* The sudden certainty of it shocked and frightened Loy.

*I don't want to be in love with her! There's so much depending on this mission, on her, on me. I don't need this stupid shit making me crazy! Besides, I don't ever want to love anyone again! It always goes wrong — always.* Loy stripped off undersuit and donned the powder-blue jumpsuit one of the support crew handed to her. *Well, I'll just have to tough it out, won't I?* Roughly, Loy secured the snaps.

Because the extra fuel they needed to carry was now top priority, all the other flight-crew positions had been eliminated. A satellite deployment mission such as theirs would normally entail at least five to six people: a flight commander, a pilot, a mission specialist, and several payload specialists. This flight, however, would have only two crew members. With the aid of enhanced computer software programs, Reno was to be flight commander and payload specialist. Loy, was to be pilot and mission specialist.

The grasp of detail necessary to do these complex tasks was a crushing weight. In addition, Loy was worried about the emotional toll the journey was going to take. Being enclosed for a week in a small, inescapable metal ship with someone she longed to make love to, and had vowed to leave alone, was surely going to make her a stark lunatic.

*This is an assignment of the highest national security,* she reminded herself. *The future and well-being of Freeland rests on both our shoulders. We need to be concentrating on accomplishing our work, and on nothing else.*

One of the launch support warriors, a colonel this time, waved Loy and Reno into a side office. Moments later the three of them were embroiled in a last-minute review of the flight plan and timetable. Finally, as both Loy and Reno were observed trying to stifle monstrous yawns, the colonel dismissed them to their separate quarters in the barracks beside the VAB. Dutifully, they each went off to sleep their last night on the planet's surface, alone.

Loy lay awake, staring into the darkness above her for a long time before exhaustion dragged her down into oblivion. Her dreams, like her waking thoughts, were filled with a mocha-skinned woman with beguiling, light-brown eyes. Only in her dreams, Loy took Reno in her arms and loved her thoroughly.

* * * * *

That same evening, Tor stood before the Isis warriors' barracks, checking her chronometer. It was late, after eleven o'clock at night. Because the FS *Independence* was launching the next day, the warriors were on full alert. Danu, and all the other Scramble Team members were inside the large, clapboard structure, bedded down for the night. The slightest sign of trouble would trigger the air-raid sirens mounted on tall wooden poles throughout the city-colony. The Scramble Team would tumble into the big troop transport parked by the curb, and race out to the airfield.

Purposefully, Tor marched up the steps of the barracks. A craggy-looking older sergeant was standing sentry at the door. The veteran seemed to recognize her, for she saluted, even though Tor wasn't in uniform.

"Permission to go inside?" Tor asked, feeling tentative. She grasped the small box she held in her hand a little more tightly.

The sentry caught sight of the box and said, "I'm not supposed to let anyone in after the nine curfew, ma'am."

Disappointed, Tor started to leave. She was at the top of the steps when she heard the sergeant say, "But the hero of Hart's Pass can go anywhere she damn well wants, any time she wants."

Slowly, Tor turned. She exchanged a long, meaningful look with the elder campaigner, then crossed the porch. The sergeant saluted again and opened the door.

Tor walked up the wooden stairs in the half-light of third watch. She was lost in memories of last autumn, when she and Danu had shared a room on the first floor. Danu was now assigned a bunk on the second story, and Tor made her way there as quietly as possible on the gleaming hardwood floors.

She came to the room she wanted and knocked lightly in the call segment of the shave-and-a-haircut pattern they used to signal one another.

The door was flung open and Danu was squinting at her, half awake and grinning. Her red hair was sticking up in the back, and the long underwear she wore as pajamas clung to her firm, young body.

"Miss me?" Danu asked hopefully.

Overwhelmed with sentiment, Tor nodded.

Danu's roommate pushed by Danu, a blanket around her shoulders. "I'm going to Levin's room," she said in a quiet voice, as she padded down the hall in bare feet.

"You don't have to —" But the woman shushed them.

"I owe you for last week, Sullivan," the woman whispered. She opened another door farther along the corridor and disappeared into the black interior.

Tor faced Danu. "Still loaning out your room to lovers?"

Danu smiled sleepily. "Only now I have a honey too, so I get paybacks." She leaned forward and placed a soft kiss on Tor's lips. "I'm so glad you came," she whispered.

Danu took Tor's hand and drew her into the dark room.

"I'm just here to give you something," Tor explained, "and then I really should go, 'cause you're on duty . . ."

"Oh no," Danu crooned, pulling Tor against her as she closed the door. "Just lie down with me a little while. I miss you beside me."

"Well, I don't want to get you in trouble . . ."

Unable to see much in the starlight coming through the long, rectangular window ahead of them, Tor allowed Danu to maneuver her toward the narrow cot in the corner.

Danu laid her down, then rolled against her. They were kissing and touching, when Danu felt the box in Tor's hand.

"What's that?" she asked.

"I brought you a present," Tor answered, laughing as Danu gave a small squeal of joy and grabbed the box from her. "What is it?"

"Put a light on for a minute."

Danu rolled away from her and reached for the little lamp beside the bed. In the warm, golden light, Danu sat up and opened the box, gasping as she gazed upon the contents.

"Oh, Tor," she whispered.

"It's a crescent moon, a symbol —"

"Of Isis," Danu said with her. "Oh, Tor, this looks expensive!"

A field of deep blue sapphires surrounded the little gold crescent. The jeweled square was only two by two centimeters, but it had an elegance of fine artistry to it. The gold necklace that threaded through it would be long enough to drop the charm between Danu's breasts.

"I saw it at a booth in the marketplace a few weeks back, and I've been earning money beyond my warrior's stipend while working for Styx . . ." Tor stopped and met Danu's eyes, trying to convey all she felt. "I wanted to give you something to take into battle with you," she offered. "If you have to go, I want you to have a charm. Something that comes from our Isis, and my love for you."

"Oh, Tor," Danu whispered again, this time crying.

"Let me help you put it on."

Gently, she eased the long underwear top over Danu's head and reached for the necklace. With slow care, she lifted the chain over Danu's coppery hair. The flashing blue sapphires and the gold crescent embraced, adorning Danu's freckled, creamy skin just as Tor had imagined they would.

"You are so glorious," Tor breathed.

Danu pulled her down, then. With the light on, they made love in a manner that was different from anything that had ever passed between them. It was at once fiery and abandoned, yet their passion was filled with an emotion that verged on tears — as if they would never be together again, as if they would never be apart.

Sometime before the first birdsong, when Danu had fallen into a deep, satiated sleep, Tor rose and dressed. She crept along the hall and down the staircase. When she opened the front door, a new sentry saluted her.

"Was informed a notable was with us, tonight," the young private said, keeping her voice low.

"I hope it's no trouble," Tor replied, glancing around guiltily. "I don't want anyone ending up pulling extra guard duty."

The sentry waved a dismissing hand, "Nah. You're bringin' us luck, Lieutenant Yakami." She gave a cocky grin. "A warrior can always use a little more luck."

Tor smiled and said good night. She hurried down the barracks steps to where her motorcycle was parked in a line of other cycles, farther down Cammermeyer Street.

She rode along in the half-dark, traveling through the sleeping city-colony. As she went up and over the ridges into the high meadows, the brilliant, rose-colored glow in the east intensified. She rode down the driveway to Whit and Kali's country home just as the sun crept over the horizon. Her heart was full to overflowing. The entire way home, she'd been thanking the Goddess for the luck she'd had in finding Danu.


Later that morning, Reno sat on Loy's left, gripping her cue cards, her eyes fixed on the launch-and-ascent checklist. Loy watched as Reno anxiously wriggled deeper into the flight commander's chair and one of the support staff stepped over, adjusting the straps of Reno's seat belt. On the right side of the small flight deck, Loy tried to appear calm in the pilot's chair. Occasionally, she leaned forward to flip a switch or read a display, each action on schedule. Like quiet worker bees, the handover/ingress team squeezed in and around each other, moving about the cabin, assisting them in the last-minute preliminaries. Abruptly, launch control broadcast the order for the handover/ingress team to leave, and the women disappeared down the access ladder.

Loy's mouth was dry. They had been there for nearly two hours. The forced jokes and nervous laughter were behind them. Loy and Reno were both clad in gunmetal-gray launch/entry suits. Their flight helmets were on and secure. The *Independence* was upright, and the external tank was filled with the cold-fusion propellant that would feed through the three main engines and thrust them into the sky.

The same calm voice she had been hearing in her helmet earpiece all morning informed Loy that the handover/ingress team was crossing the orbiter-access arm and that the side hatch was closed. Automatically, Loy began a cabin leak check, then water-boiler preactivation.

"Ground crew secure. Over."

Loy knew she responded, but she was in a haze of incredulity, acting reflexively on hours and hours of study and preparation. Immersed in the details of preflight execution, none of it seemed real. She reached for the computer keyboard and typed the command that loaded the flight plan. Some time later, she keyed the main propulsion system, then shortly afterward, switched the event timer to start. She heard launch control advise her that the crew-access arm had retracted, and she rogered back. Minutes passed, then she was ordering Reno to prestart the auxiliary power units, the APUs.

They spent a nervous few minutes watching various pump pressure gauges before Loy ordered Reno to start the APUs. The computers switched the orbiter to internal power. Control announced to Loy that the main engines had swiveled to launch positions.

"You are go for launch, *Independence*," the voice in Loy's

ear stated. "Crystal drives activating. Cold fusion in T minus one. Over."

"Copy that," Loy answered. She knew the orbiter's computers were now directing the sequence, leaving her free to think about other things. Trying to keep her voice nonchalant, she asked, "Any sign of bogeys?"

Reno's graceful hands froze over the instrument panel.

"That's a negative, Chief Chen," the voice answered. "Radar is clear. Special flybys report the Border is firm and holding."

"Blessed be," Reno breathed.

"Got someone here who wants to say a few words to the pilot," control said, the tone light and chipper.

*Probably attempting to keep our minds off what happened to the* Challenger *back in 1986*, Loy thought.

Then a voice she recognized cut through her cynicism. "Hey, buddy."

"Whit," Loy responded, a genuine smile overcoming her.

"No stunts up there. You be safe," Whit instructed firmly. Then softly she added, "We need you to come back, you know."

Loy's throat suddenly closed. "Right," she uttered. With great effort, she quipped, "Should be no problem. Got the best here with me." She turned her helmet so that she could see Reno.

Reno looked up and laughed, then returned to her former posture. Her helmet was bent slightly over folded hands. Surprised, Loy realized she was praying.

"We'll be okay," Loy finished.

In quick sequence, the three main engines below them roared to life. Loy heard them, felt them. The entire crew compartment was shaking, and the deep rumbling shuddered through her flesh like thunder in the midst of the fiercest storm. For some incomprehensible reason, she found herself singing under her breath.

Reno must have heard the magnified transmission

through her own earpiece, for her smooth, warm alto joined Loy's. Loy automatically checked the main engine pressure. The timer was winding down on the solid rocket boosters, then the SRBs ignited.

Loy felt herself shoved back against the chair.

They were still singing when the unmistakable sensation of liftoff shivered through the cabin.

From mission control, on a promontory a half-mile from the launch tower, Whit watched the *Independence* rise steadily above the blue-green flare of fire and the billowing, white smoke. On either side of her, Lilith and Kali gripped her hands. Through the huge, Plexiglas windows of mission control, Whit could see Styx, their colony herstorian, out on the steel-mesh balcony. She was personally supervising the film crews getting this momentous event on permanent record.

Near Whit, a launch-control technician began laughing. As Whit turned toward her, she called, "Listen to this!" and flipped a switch.

Untrained and breathy with excitement, the voices of two women singing came over the speakers mounted in the computer console. Whit recognized the Freeland Anthem and lent her voice to the song. By the time the shuttle rolled to its preprogrammed head-down position, everyone in mission control was singing, most of them with tears of pride and joy in their eyes.

As they continued to roar into the sky at 2800 kph, Loy gripped the chair armrests, her body shaking with the bone-jolting ride upward. Solid-rocket-booster separation occurred just over two minutes into their ascent. Loy swore she heard the charges go off, knocking the two smaller SRBs on either side of the *Independence* into a free fall over the Pacific Ocean. The ride was suddenly smoother, but the weight of gravity pressing against her chest steadily increased. At about seven and a half minutes, the main engines throttled down to keep the acceleration at less than 3 Gs. Loy gulped air, relieved to be able to breathe freely again. At eight and half minutes, the automatic cutoff on the main engine shut down all three engines.

For an instant, the silence was overwhelming. Loy and Reno looked at each other, too overwhelmed to speak. Sixteen seconds later, a sudden vibration signaled external tank separation, and the big, fat tank the *Independence* had ridden into space peeled away.

"*Independence*," launch control radioed. "Ground computers read your ascension as A-OK. You are go for OMS-one burn. Over."

"Roger," Reno answered, reaching for the ADI altitude switch. "OMS-one. Out."

*Orbital maneuvering system burn. This is the first shove, the one that gets us into a low, elliptical orbit.* Loy shook her head, feeling dazed.

Before her, through the forward windows of the crew compartment, Loy saw the royal blue rim of the upper stratosphere arcing against the deep black of true space. In another thirty-five minutes, having traveled half an orbit, the OMS engines would fire again. The *Independence* would be driven into a higher, circular orbit roughly 400 kilometers, or 250 miles above the earth.

The soft wonderment in Reno's voice broke Loy's reverie. "We made it."

Loy gazed at her.

Her eyes sparkling through the helmet glass, Reno said, "Congratulations, Chief Chen."

Suddenly, the undeniable love Loy felt for Reno shook her so much that words were impossible. *If I had any guts at all*

*I'd unstrap this seat belt, get rid of these damn helmets, and kiss you senseless.* Loy smiled.

Her eyes must have betrayed her, though, for Reno stared back at her, just as intensely.

# Chapter 8

Two days later, Whit looked across the holomap grid and repeated the instructions she had just given Lilith and Captain Razia. "I do not want Kali to know."

Unable to believe her ears, Lilith placed her hands on the wooden edge of the holomap grid and leaned forward. "Whit, she has every right to know. And if the situation were reversed, you'd be furious if she did not tell you!"

"These are only cursory arrangements," Whit said coolly. "After all, an attack may or may not occur. I don't want her needlessly worried." She reached for the computer keyboard and activated the holomap. A three-dimensional hologram model of Isis appeared on the flat surface of the grid. "Now, about the ground-to-air missile emplacements on the east side of the colony —"

Lilith interrupted, "How in Hera's name do you intend to keep it from her? Kali is psychic — and reads you better than anyone!"

"That is my concern," Whit answered, her lips tightening. "Simply agree not to blurt out the truth to her, Lilith — that's all I ask."

Seething, Lilith drew herself up to her full height, gazing across the holomap at Whit. "You have no place on a scramble team! You're not even warrior reserve anymore!" Her words were clipped, frostily betraying her anger. "Your job is here, at this desk, leading your people — not in a Peregrine in the midst of a dogfight!"

Whit's voice cracked with frustration. "We don't have enough pilots, Lil!" She turned away. "Tell her, Razia."

Captain Razia made worried eye contact with Lilith. "We have only nineteen scramble team members left. Since the *Independence* successfully launched two days ago, anyone with aircraft proficiency has been summoned back to their home colony."

Flustered, Lilith stated, "I knew Warrior Headquarters down in Boudica was in an uproar, and a lot of somewhat panicky reassigning was going on, but we still have plenty of warriors, here —"

"Who do not fly, Deputy Leader," Razia quietly clarified.

"If the Regs come again, Lil, we're in for an air assault," Whit said, gazing out the window at a city that looked gilded in the amber June sunshine falling over Isis. "We either engage them and blow them out of the sky before they get near Isis, or they'll bomb us. The Regs will do everything they can to reduce this city-colony to ashes."

Razia pulled her high uniform jacket collar away from her neck. "I agree with Leader Whitaker's analysis. We are the colony that organized the building and launching of the

*Independence*. As we speak, the *Independence* is seeding space with new satellites, the components that will guarantee the Border stays in place for ages to come. Any acts of vengeance the Regs can manage will most likely be directed at us."

Whit pushed her hands in her pockets and moved back to where Lilith stood. "Our only defense is to have every available pilot ready to report for scramble when the alert sounds." With a glint in her gray eyes, Whit finished. "And that includes me."

For a moment, Lilith fought tears. *Oh, Sweet Hera, have mercy. I could lose you*. Raising her chin, Lilith stated, "I'm a pilot too."

With a rueful smile, Whit shook her head. "We'll need you here to take up the reins," she said simply.

"Damn you, Tomyris," Lilith whispered as her eyes filled.

Gently, Whit grasped Lilith's shoulders. "Don't worry. Danu is my wingwoman, and she's the best of our homegrown talent." A ghost of a smile crossed her face, then she leaned down and kissed Lilith's cheek.

Lilith bent her head. "Danu is a rookie, Whit. She only has six months in as a warrior."

"And like the rest of us, she's been training like a madwoman on the Peregrine simulator," Whit returned, her voice soothing. "Did you know she's racked up the second highest battle score on the unit?"

"For a first-year pilot," Lilith reflected, "that's incredible."

Razia commented, "She's Think Tank — genetically engineered to be a superior human."

Whit shot Razia a narrow glance. "She also works her ass off."

"That, too," Razia allowed.

"Who has the highest battle score on the unit?" Lilith asked.

Whit colored, then gave an uncomfortable shrug.

Smirking, Razia helpfully supplied the information.

"Someone who never signs herself in on the list of flyers — almost as if she doesn't have a commanding officer reviewing her scores."

Whit seemed at once both proud and embarrassed. "Can't keep a damn thing private, anymore," she muttered.

As if to divert their attention, she gestured at the holomap before them. Colorful and detailed, a three-dimensional hologram of Isis covered the length and breadth of the four-meter-square table.

"This is our backup plan, in case the Reg F-24s get by our Peregrines." With the cool poise of a warrior, Whit proceeded to detail this worst-case battle plan she had developed for the defense of Isis. She had only covered the deployment of warriors to various strategically placed batteries when the Leader's office comline announced a security squad sergeant.

Captain Razia excused herself, keyed the DNA plate, and went outside.

Looking tired and a bit irritated, Whit slouched against the polished wood cabinet that flanked the grid.

Lilith gazed at her, memorizing her loose white linen shirt, sleek black pants, and ankle-high black boots. *I know there's no dissuading you. You're going to be in the thick of the fight. And I have such a dark feeling about that.*

Razia came back, securing the door behind her and moving to Whit's side. She murmured something in Whit's ear.

"Captain Razia's security squad has discovered how General Medusa got hold of the shuttle's fuel requirements," Whit said to Lilith. Then to Razia Whit said, "As deputy leader, Lilith needs to know the source of this leak too. We cannot tolerate sensitive information like this being disclosed without authorization."

Captain Razia gave a curt nod. "As you know, it was thought that Major Mika Reno scanned documents left on a desk in Chief Chen's private quarters after an . . . interlude . . . they shared on Beltane night. Chief Chen advised me that this was how the information was inadvertently made available and I had no reason to believe otherwise at first. Until I began to hear barracks' rumors. One of Chen's shuttle-team members suddenly had a great deal of money."

Amazed and disheartened, Lilith sighed. "Couldn't there be a reasonable explanation? Maybe just getting lucky at cards, or a Beltane gift from family?"

"Sorry," Razia stated. "Checked into that. No gambling, no gifts. Besides which, another telling development occurred soon after the shuttle project was reclassified as a military mission. When Chief Chen and the entire Isis shuttle team were directed to accompany the *Independence* down to Vandenberg, the suspect went too. However, upon arrival, she was transferred to Medusa's staff and given the title *civilian liaison*. She was Medusa's, not ours."

Confused, Lilith shook her head. "Who would betray us?"

"Hypatia Rousseau," Captain Razia said.

Shocked, Lilith protested, "She's Loy's principal assistant! Surely not!"

"This morning, when she was questioned about her finances and her sudden attachment to a civilian position on Medusa's military staff, Rousseau confessed." Razia shrugged. "It was actually more a self-righteous listing of justifications, but it was a confession nonetheless."

Looking dazed, Whit asked, "Why? What reason . . . ?"

Razia's hands locked behind her back. "Seems she had an ax to grind. She'd spent the winter attempting to charm Chief Chen." A sardonic smile escaped Razia, along with a quick rise and fall of her brows. "Then Hypatia saw Major Reno get more intimate with Chief Chen in just a few days than Hypatia had managed in months."

"Jealousy," Whit surmised.

"And vindictiveness," Lilith declared angrily.

Razia cleared her throat. "When information necessary to city-colony security is exchanged for money or favors, it is treason." The captain looked from Lilith to Whit. "Hypatia has been arrested and, with your consent, will face a jury trial on that charge."

Silent, Whit frowned and looked away.

Almost instinctively, Lilith glanced skyward, then said, "Whit! You have to get word of this to Loy."

Whit gazed back at her, enlightenment dawning in her eyes. "You're right." She moved to her desk, thought a moment, and jotted a note. She folded the paper, then handed it to Razia.

Razia opened the door and handed the message to the security squad warrior who had interrupted them earlier. "Encode this and have it relayed immediately to Chief Chen on the FS *Independence*."

The warrior saluted and left.

Lilith smiled, but Whit guffawed. Having secured the door, Razia gave them a perplexed look as she returned to the desk.

"An unlooked-for opportunity for a scientific study," Lilith sallied. "Perhaps titled *The Effect of Microgravity on Human Responsiveness*!"

Whit returned, "Subtitled *Sex in Space*." Then she was overcome with laughter.


Gently, Loy used the controls to adjust the camera riding on the wrist of the robot arm. As payload specialist, Reno was operating the remote manipulator system, coordinating the motion of the arm itself. She stood just a few feet away from Loy at the aft flight-deck station, gripping both the RMS translation hand-controller and the rotational hand-controller. Reno watched the arm on the closed-circuit television monitor mounted in the wall above her, a keen concentration in her eyes. With a dexterity acquired by painstaking practice, Reno was using the image Loy's camera provided to direct the remote robot arm that carried the satellite.

Her voice low, Reno announced, "Ten seconds to release of satellite number fourteen of twenty."

"Check," Loy responded.

"Payload assist module looks good," Reno stated.

Loy dropped her gaze to the computer readout on the panel before her, double-checking Reno's visual analysis with the instrumentation. The computer readout showed all systems on green for go. That meant the metal cradle fitted around the circumference of the satellite was spinning, making the satellite itself spin. The constant motion protected the satellite from the heat of the direct sunlight in the cargo bay.

"PAM is go," Loy echoed.

Reno said, "Releasing satellite," at the same time the small metal unit drifted out of the end effector of the robot arm. There was a brief flicker of light, signaling that the tiny rocket boosters built into the spinning cradle had fired. In silence, the satellite began its climb to a higher, preset orbit.

Reno was already working the RMS, bringing the robot arm back to pick up another load. With her camera duties temporarily ended, Loy moved effortlessly in the microgravity to the overhead aft window. She floated there, peering through the three panes of pressurized glass. The satellite they had just deployed was already gone. It was traveling in the opposite direction from where Loy was facing, into an orbit several kilometers higher on the edge of true space. Because the *Independence* was performing the deployment while inverted, Loy was perched near the roof of the shuttle flight deck. Entranced, Loy stared out at the glowing blue-white rim of planet Earth.

*I don't think I've ever felt more insignificant.*

"Damn," Reno said.

Alerted by the tone, which seemed at once both distressed and annoyed, Loy turned and looked at Reno. "What's wrong?"

"Problem with RMS," Reno said, wiggling the translation hand-controller. "The arm partially retracted toward the cargo bay, then for some reason got stuck."

Smoothly, Loy used her hands to walk from the overhead aft window, coming to rest beside Reno's position at the controller. Reno's face was close to one of the two smaller windows on the aft bulkhead. Mimicking Reno's upright position, Loy slipped her socked feet into the grips mounted before the work station and looked through the other window into the *Independence*'s open cargo bay, where the robot arm was anchored near the external aft wall.

The arm had failed to retract more than halfway toward the position required to pluck the next satellite and its attached metal cradle from the line of six units still stowed by the inside wall. Bathed in the strong sunlight pouring into the cargo bay through the open doors, the arm appeared to have no visible obstruction. Yet the arm was not responding to Reno's working the controls that operated the manipulator arm. Her face tense, Reno jiggled first the translation hand-controller, then the rotational hand-controller. At last, frustrated, she stopped.

"RMS is down," Reno breathed.

"Can it be fixed?" Loy asked.

Minutes ticked by while Reno inspected the internal RMS circuitry. When that proved okay, she used the newly installed diagnostic software to check the arm's external dynamics and finally isolated a site-specific problem.

"It seems to be on the elbow joint," Reno informed Loy. "The yaw control is gone, and all the other mobility commands are locked out because of that," Reno informed Loy.

"Okay," Loy said, steeling herself. "Let's suit up, go outside, and unload the rest of the units ourselves, like we practiced."

"Negative," Reno said quietly. "Remember, extravehicular activity has firm parameters. The *Independence* has EMUs. In fact, it's geared for three two-person, six-hour EVAs. But you have to go through the twelve-hour preparation process before —"

"Quit the space jargon," Loy ordered. She had stopped listening on the word *negative*. She guessed by Reno's overly calm expression that Reno was preparing to do something heroic or stupid, or possibly both. Loy moved closer to her. "What do you mean *negative?*"

Lowering her eyes, Reno turned her brown face away. "I mean we'll have to drop the cabin pressure and oxygen level for twelve hours before we put the suits on, or we'll end up with the bends."

"Shit," Loy whispered. "That's right." Discouraged and tired, Loy recalled that particular training session. *If we go directly from an oxygen-nitrogen cabin atmosphere, to pure oxygen reduced-pressure suits, nitrogen gas dissolved in our blood will bubble out into our joints. And that means excruciating pain — and possible crippling or death.*

"I'm changing the cabin settings." Reno announced, moving past Loy to the other side of the flight deck. She hovered over the flight commander's left-hand console, touching the appropriate parts of the instrument panel. "Why don't you go and get some sleep, Chief."

Frowning, Loy replied, "Let's clarify our plan first. We'll both be doing the space walk together, right?"

"I'm the payload specialist on this mission," Reno said firmly. "Before we take on the cumbersome and time-consuming job of manually releasing the rest of the satellites, why not let me try to repair the robot arm? If I can't start it from in here, I'll go outside to have a look at it. There's no sense in both of us doing an EVA for that," she said in a casual, businesslike tone.

Gracefully, Loy floated backward, heading for the access ladder. "As mission specialist, I overrule you. A solo, unscheduled EVA is too dangerous. I can't let you go out there alone, Mika."

171

For an instant, Loy read the relief in Reno's eyes, then Reno turned away from her.

Her voice very quiet, Loy continued. "If we have to stand by for twelve hours, getting some sleep is probably a great idea — for both of us. Don't you think?"

"Okay," Reno answered. "I've lowered the cabin pressure from 14.7 to 10.2 psi. I'm going to report our problem to ground control, then I'll come down and climb in the rack too."

Satisfied, Loy swam down the access ladder to the mid-deck. Feeling overcome with exhaustion, she took off her socks and stowed them in a drawer, then peeled down to just a T-shirt. She set the alarm to sound in eleven hours. When the alarm went off, she and Reno would have to eat something light but fortifying, then spend another forty-five minutes sucking on an oxygen line, washing the remaining nitrogen from their biological systems, in order to be completely ready to don the suits. As she always did, Loy slipped her chronometer from her wrist and caught one of the strings that floated near her rack, tying the chronometer to it. She rigged the string so that the chronometer would be drifting close to her ear while she slept.

A rush of hot and cold went through Loy. Reluctantly, she acknowledged the sensation as a mix of mad excitement and sheer terror about the pending space walk. *One thing at a time*, she told herself.

Her sleep compartment was built into the mid-deck wall like a high shelf, with Reno's compartment the next shelf down. Loy hoisted her near weightless body and guided herself feetfirst into her rack. As she slipped in, she pulled a suspended sleeping bag over her feet, then up and over the rest of her body. Grasping the inside zipper, she tugged it along its track, enclosing herself in the bag. She heaved a sigh, closing her eyes.

*Mother's blood, I hate that spacesuit!*

Trying not to think about the immense void waiting for

her outside the ship, Loy tried to make herself go to sleep. After a while, her mind began lingering on Mika Reno, and she was soon lost in dreams.

Roughly thirteen hours later, Loy opened the outer hatch. She could hear her breathing speeding up, and she reprimanded herself. *Calm down. You can do this.*

She stepped from the confines of the depressurized external airlock and gave the switch by her right hand a slight tap. The manned maneuvering unit she wore like a self-contained backpack emitted a brief burst of nitrogen gas from the jet nozzles beneath it. The short emission propelled Loy off the hatch lip, out into the microgravity of the cargo bay. With the next controlled emission of gas, Loy began rotating, allowing her to check the safety line that ran from her EMU to the airlock door. Anxious, she wanted to be sure the line was playing out freely.

In the airlock behind her, she saw Reno's gleaming white, helmeted figure step to the lip of the hatch. Loy waited for her, idly examining the dazzling white structure of the cargo bay that surrounded her. Then, suddenly, an exuberant whoop of delight coming through the headset earphone startled Loy.

"This is so cool!" Reno enthused, using her own MMU to coast across the bay.

"Stay on task, Major," ground control cautioned, audible to both Loy and Reno on the multichannel communications carriers in their suits.

"Well, well," Loy couldn't resist remarking, "I never thought I'd hear anyone tell *you* to stay on ta —"

"Think you've got me all figured out?" Reno was steadily moving closer to Loy.

Laughing, Loy directed her MMU toward the knobby, metal shoulder portion of the robot arm. With a gloved hand, she grasped the wide metal pole as she passed. For the moment, in the shadowed shelter of the wall where the shoulder attached, Loy felt relatively safe.

"Can't quite figure myself out," Loy told Reno, watching the other suited figure drift closer. "Let alone *you*."

Reno landed beside her. Like Loy, the helmet visor she was wearing was a glare shield, protecting her eyes from the overly bright sunlight. The bronze-colored visor also prevented Loy from being able to see anything of Reno's face.

"And here I heard you were so smart," Reno replied.

Their ground control contact choked on a laugh, then relayed, "Crew, we are go for external RMS check."

Surprised, Loy noted Reno had no pale, thin cable traveling in her wake. "Wait a minute," Loy said. "Major, you didn't clip a tie line to the hatch."

"I've got the MMU," Reno answered, her voice slightly patronizing. "A tie line would just get in the way."

The underside of Reno's MMU puffed two small white clouds of nitrogen gas, and then Reno was traveling the length of the robot arm, heading for the elbow joint about nine meters distant. Concentrating on slowing her breathing, Loy maneuvered her own MMU and followed her.

Uneasy about Reno's free flight as they moved away from the ship, Loy persisted. "At least use a proper tie line out by the elbow. It would be foolhardy to do repair ops without a —"

"Without a safety line. I know. Okay. Sheesh!"

In a deviation from their discussed plan, Reno scooted around the pole, looping it in circles as she rose. "These things are great!" Reno crowed. "I can't believe I'm flying around out here, 400 kilometers above earth!"

Sounding like an indulgent parent, ground control spoke up. "The manned maneuvering unit is not a toy, Major Reno."

"Okay, okay," Reno responded, settling down into a straight, steady rise. "I'll try to behave."

As they moved silently closer to their goal, Loy gazed at the vibrant, blue-white ball above them. Unnerved by the vast panorama, it occurred to her that they were dreadfully exposed. Compounding her anxiety about bobbing through space on a tiny MMU was the fact that she was relying on the life-support functions of the EMU to keep her alive.

Swallowing hard, she felt the jittering edge of claustrophobia gnaw on her composure. She didn't like being enclosed in the space suit. She didn't like listening to her own breathing. And she hated having the damned helmet on her head.

Then, to her horror, she felt a familiar trembling. Aghast, she looked down at her left hand. On the armrest of her MMU, the bone-white glove shimmered in the harsh sunshine as her hand shook uncontrollably.

Reno dropped back from above her, moving into place on Loy's left side.

"C'mon, Chief," Reno called, her voice soft. "I need the Phillips."

It was a joke they had shared earlier. Just after they'd woken from their long, crisis-imposed nap, Reno had said, "Bet we can fix this whole mess with a Phillips screwdriver."

As Loy continued to stare at her glove, the tremor abruptly stopped.

"See? No problem," Reno said, even softer this time.

*She knows*, Loy thought.

"Everything okay up there?" ground control asked.

"Sure, sure," Reno answered. "Just admiring the view."

With deliberate care, Loy used both hands on the MMU controls, landing close to Reno on the elbow joint of the robot arm.

Loy reached into a pocket on her EMU, drawing out a second tie line. Unable to find a ring-shaped place to clip the line, Loy looped the line around the arm itself. Loy maneuvered the MMU and created the anchor for her work station. She clipped the line to her suit, on the opposite side of the original tie line she still had to the airlock hatch.

"Watch you don't get tangled up in all that," Reno commented.

Reno's helmet was turned toward her, and though Loy couldn't see her face, she could almost feel the concern radiating from her.

Automatically, Loy checked to see if Reno had created a tie line for herself. Her eyes traced the length of thin cable that snaked loosely from the waist of Reno's EMU to the television camera positioned a half-meter above the robot arm's elbow joint.

Turning to Reno, Loy proposed, "That camera mount isn't very sturdy. Let's retie you — secure you to the arm."

Reno didn't move or say anything in reply, although Loy was positive she heard a short, impatient sigh over her helmet radio.

Impulsively, Loy went by her. As she reached for Reno's tie line, she instructed, "Get a grip on the arm while I do this."

Obediently, Reno held on to the metal pole, watching as Loy unfastened the hook and looped the tether around the thicker structure of the arm.

"I almost forgot. I'm traveling with the overly cautious Ms. Chen."

Caught by the affection in that teasing remark, Loy looked over at her. *Mother's blood — I can't see a thing through that visor, and she knows it!*

Then, claustrophobia forgotten, Loy used the MMU to move back into place. "Ready for RMS repair," she told ground control.

As Loy examined one side of the elbow joint, Reno moved to the opposite side. From the tool pack she carried, Reno had selected a long metal bar with an adjustable socket wrench on one end and a flat edge on the other. Using the flat edge, Reno prodded the circumference of the circular joint.

Within a few minutes, Reno was moving along the underside of the joint, away from Loy. "Wow, look at all these pings and scratches," she breathed.

"What?" Loy asked, not liking the sound of that.

"There's some sort of dust here," Reno commented. Loy heard her puffing with effort. As Loy moved around the joint, toward her, she saw Reno working with the flat edge, using it like a crowbar. "I'm finding pieces of debris."

"Micrometeors," Loy guessed.

Reno wedged the long bar into the portion of the joint that controlled yaw on the RMS. As Reno pushed down, a fist-sized rock lodged in the joint sprang free.

Propelled by its sudden release from the squeezing pressure of the elbow joint, the rock shot out at Reno, passing within centimeters of her helmet. Then, instantly, the robot arm jerked back, directly into Reno, striking her. While the arm seized up, its sudden motion abruptly arrested, Reno went soaring away from the arm and out into space. The tie line Loy had secured just moments before reached its full extension in the space of a breath, and then snapped Reno to a dead stop.

The robot arm jerked again and swung toward the cargo bay and the satellites that lined the inside wall. As the arm traveled away from her, it left Loy adrift until her own tether yanked.

Seconds later, her right side slammed into something hard and unyielding. Stunned and nearly paralyzed by the fierce pain, Loy spun around and grabbed for whatever she had hit. Confused, it took her a minute to comprehend she was once more holding on to the robot arm, but this time farther down the length of it, closer to the shoulder joint in the cargo bay.

The long pole was now stationary, and in its fully retracted position. Before her, on the inside wall of the cargo bay, the six satellites sat in their deployment order, unharmed.

Ground control was insistently repeating, "What's going on? We just saw someone moving way too fast, then crashing into the arm! The elbow-joint camera feed went offline, but the cargo bay cameras have one of you on camera now. Chen, Reno — whoever is able — report! Over!"

"Mika!" Loy yelled, swinging around to look for her.

The fire along her right side made her double over, and she cried out. It took several minutes to explain to ground control what had happened. Then, as they grew insistently demanding about details, Loy finally told them they'd have to stand by.

"Find Mika," she whispered to herself.

Moving slowly against the sharp ache in her ribs, she looked for Reno. As she ran her gaze along the length of the robot arm, she saw the tie line near the elbow joint. Scarcely breathing, her eyes traced the tie line to its end. There, roughly twenty-five meters away from the robot arm, a gleaming white spacesuit drifted in a semicurled posture.

"Ground control, I have Reno in sight." Frightened, Loy added, "She's in neutral position." Loy knew ground would interpret that as meaning what Loy already suspected. Reno was unconscious, if not worse.

Gritting her teeth. Loy checked her tie lines and found they were corded over one another in a braided knot. She paused for a moment, knowing what she had to do yet terrified of the next step. She looked above her again. The yawning opening of the curved cargo-bay doors framed a scene that turned her blood to ice. Against the bright blue-and-white backdrop of a planet, Mika was an impossibly small, white figure at the end of a long, thin cable.

*You've got to do this*, she told herself. She reached for the clips that attached to each side of her EMU and released them.

The tie lines drifted free.

Holding her breath, Loy tested her MMU controls. When they worked without incident, the relief was so intense tears filled her eyes. Feeling like an idiot, she blinked hard, trying to clear her vision.

"I'm coming, Mika," Loy said aloud. She didn't know whether Reno could hear her or not, but the phrase reinforced her own resolution.

Concentrating on reaching Reno as quickly as possible,

Loy decided to forego the safer, more comforting approach of following the robot arm and then the tie line out to the place where Reno hung. Instead, she was manipulating the MMU, heading out of the cargo bay in a straight line, chancing a long, free fly across the distance separating her from her friend. As she passed the halfway point, it struck her how far away from the *Independence* she was. Determined to hold steady, Loy wouldn't let herself look back at the ship, wouldn't let herself look at the beautiful, blazing scenario all around her. Instead, she kept her eyes on Reno.

Ground control was speaking to her through the earphone, but she was having trouble concentrating on what they were saying. They wanted her to check the oxygen readouts on her EMU. Affirming their diagnostics, the microcomputer mounted on the chest of her suit emitted a series of warning beeps.

"You are losing oxygen," the impersonal female voice of the microcomputer announced. "No corrective action available. You have seventeen minutes to return to the ship."

Following the message, panic almost engulfed Loy. *Does that mean the suit's failing? Am I going to die out here?* She struggled to make sense of it, to get a grip on her emotions. *There's no point in freaking. I can't leave without Mika — so I'll just have to go and get her.*

Dimly, Loy heard some kind of away-from-the-microphone dispute going on at ground control. She realized the argument that had broken out concerned whether she should go after Reno or just go back to the ship. Rather than wait for the girls on the ground to come to a consensus, she decided to focus all her faculties on Reno.

She took one brief glance down at the elbow joint, noting that the line seemed sturdy enough near its anchor about the arm. Then she realized that the camera and its slender metal mount were gone; only a small stub remained where they had once been.

*Without the line, that swat from the arm would have batted*

179

*her miles away.* Loy tried to extinguish the next thought before it began, but it pushed through, anyway. *I would have never been able to find her!*

As Loy closed in on Reno, she reached out and grasped the tie line. Grunting involuntarily against the pain in her side, Loy hauled Reno's motionless, near-weightless form to within a few feet of her.

"Hey, buddy," Loy said, moving around Reno, doing a fast check of her EMU readouts. Finding them all functioning at normal levels, Loy asked, "Can you hear me?" Reno didn't reply and didn't move.

*Please, Mika, please be all right.*

Trying to sound decisive and reassuring, Loy stated, "I'm taking you back, now, Major Reno."

Keeping her breathing slow and even, Loy pulled a tie line from Reno's EMU pocket. Minutes later, she had rigged it to the length of two meters and had secured Reno to her own waist.

Ground control was snapping out orders in her earphone again, telling her to return to the ship.

"Roger that," Loy told them, and the incredulous laugh that escaped her made her wince. *Hey, geniuses — I want nothing more than to get back inside the* Independence!

She directed the MMU down, towing Reno behind her. She had traveled only a third of the way when the mild strain on her waist grew increasingly painful. A burning ache was spreading all along her right side. Trying to ignore it, Loy kept her focus on the ship that was growing steadily larger below her.

*Almost there,* Loy told herself. *Almost there.*

It became a chant as she went back, a mantra to keep her centered. Her vision seemed to be tunneling; on the periphery of her sight a blurring fog was encroaching. Loy sensed that pain or lack of oxygen was diminishing her faculties. She steadily advanced until the ship filled her view and she drifted down to the lip of the external airlock hatch. She felt as if she were outside of her body, watching two figures in white as one grappled with the hatch release, finally getting it open and clambering inside, and the other was pulled in behind her.

Ground control cajoled her along, gently coaching her what to do next. She surrendered to letting someone else think for her, and somehow, she got the hatch pressurization going. She focused her limited cognition on complying with directions. Her thought processes were severely impaired, and she knew it by the dependence she felt on that voice in her ear telling her to link a specific hose in the airlock to her suit. She did it, and then realized the hose was coming from a tank labeled OXYGEN. She spent what seemed like a long time hanging in the tight quarters of the airlock and simply breathing. She had no idea how long they'd been there. Ground control was telling her repeatedly that it was all right to open the internal airlock hatch and enter the ship. She raised her arms, took off her helmet, and set it aside. Then she disconnected the oxygen feed hooked up to her suit.

Though she tried to ignore it, pain came with each exertion. Getting the internal hatch open and maneuvering herself into the ship was a cumbersome process. She banged into the airlock walls, the internal hatch, the ship walls. Though she tried to take care with Reno's entry, it was nearly the same ordeal. She swung the hatch closed and secured it. She unfastened the manned maneuvering unit and slipped out of it. Then, biting her lip with worry, she reached for Reno and unclasped her helmet.

As Loy pulled the helmet off, red drops rolled out. Reno's eyes were closed, and a bloody gash extended across the plane of her forehead.

Cursing to herself, Loy took off Reno's Snoopy hat and examined the lump around the wound and ran through a basic vital-signs check. She retrieved the medical kit from the mid-deck and pulled out the bandages-and-medications pack. She cleaned and dressed the wound.

Loy managed to remove Reno's MMU, her portable

life-support system, and her gloves. Waves of agony from the injury to her side were washing through Loy, and she had to stop for a while to fight the nausea that came on the heels of it. When she was easing off the upper torso of Reno's EMU, she realized that Reno's eyes were open.

Reno stared at Loy with consternation. "Hey . . ."

"Mika," Loy gasped.

Reno squinted, then purposefully adopted a cavalier disregard for how wrong things had gone. "Are you getting fresh?" she wisecracked, "or am I getting lucky?"


Several hours later, Loy swam through the flight-deck hatch. She maneuvered her nearly weightless body into the commander's seat and used the seat belt to keep herself anchored.

The anti-inflammatory medication had taken the harsh edge off her rib injury. After palpating the area and reading the computer's diagnosis-assist, she was fairly sure she hadn't broken anything, but nothing was certain. Reno, meanwhile, had more than likely sustained a concussion — possibly a severe one. Reno was below, on the mid-deck now, a bag of synthetic ice taped lightly over the top of the bandage she wore. Forbidden sleep for the next few hours, Reno was dealing with her monstrous headache by plotting their next session of satellite seeding.

*She's nuts!* Loy thought, shaking her head as she brought the communications computer online. *Gaea knows, though, this next pass over the Northern Hemisphere is going to be key. We've got to get all six remaining satellites offloaded and into orbit. It will be an intense pace, but I think we can do it.*

She paused and pinched the bridge of her nose, thanking the Goddess that after their attentions during the EVA, the robot arm had proven to be operable once more.

Sighing, she leaned over the flight deck console and

accessed the afternoon e-mail, then had the computer decode the messages. She rerouted the requests from ground control for specific readings and calculations regarding the flight to the computer for processing and response. One message was a status update regarding the most recent fix Kali had written into Maat's Border program. Loy read it and stored it, reluctant to contemplate what might be underway in Freeland if she eventually got a message that said *Complete Border failure.*

In the back of her mind, Loy was aware that if the shuttle was traveling in a "zone of exclusion," out of range of any of the old NASA ground transmitters, the *Independence* would never receive such a message. Only persistent no-response feedback would alert Loy to the development she feared most — the final collapse of the satellite net.

One message had a privacy indicator on it. She finished the work-related mail, then, bemused, typed her password and opened the note Whit had sent.

*Thought you'd like to know: Per Captain Razia, Hypatia Rousseau has confessed to delivering chip copies of the cold-fusion fuel requirements to General Medusa in exchange for inducements of cash and advancement opportunities within the Vandenberg staff. You are ordered to apologize to Major Reno at once, in the manner you think best.*

Stunned, Loy stared at the screen, then reread the last sentence. "Whit," she whispered. "I'm over 400 kilometers away and I can still hear you laughing."

Loy dropped her head back, awash in a rising tide of relief, exhilaration, and then, as realization fully hit, guilt. *I was so sure it was Mika. Why?*

Confounded, she closed the e-mail application. As she relaxed, her body assumed the usual half-curled neutral position common in microgravity. Conscious only of the firm pressure of the seat belt straps against her waist and shoulders, Loy allowed herself time for self-examination. The truth did not take long to surface.

*I was ready to believe she'd betray me. After what happened with Arinna, I expected it. I thought that anyone who seemed interested in me was only trying to use me, to hurt me.* Raising one hand, Loy traced the scar on her jaw with her fingers. With difficulty, she swallowed. *I never even gave Mika Reno a chance.*

She gazed out through the front window, watching the brilliant blue-green, white-clouded planet that filled the top-right portion of the glass. *I'm willing to ride an experimentally fueled set of rockets and a century-old shuttle out into the stratosphere, but I'm not brave enough to take a chance on love.*

The insight made her involuntarily groan.

She remembered the fervent, hopeless, yet so-determined look in Reno's light-brown eyes when she stood before Loy on the airfield at Vandenberg, minutes before all hell broke loose. The words echoed in Loy's ears. "I know this is the last thing you want to hear, but I'm in love with you."

*Sweet Mother, the courage it took to tell me that, especially knowing full well that I thought her to be Medusa's puppet.*

Without allowing herself a moment to reconsider, Loy let emotion carry her. She detached the seat belt harness, pushed over to the hatch, and pulled herself along the ladder to the next deck down. Her hand on her ribs, she looked across the mid-deck to where Reno was hovering in space.

Reno glanced up at her, then back to her palm computer. "Any news from below?" she asked.

Loy watched Reno's index finger tapping busily over the palm. The synthetic ice bag was taped to the folded-down work station table beside Reno, as if discarded some time ago. Still, Reno's coloring was pale and her eyes looked red. Concerned, Loy wondered how Reno could run logistical coordinate calculations when she obviously felt bad.

"As a matter of fact, there was something," Loy offered.

Across the mid-deck, Reno's lifted her eyes in question.

Behind her, Reno's braid was drifting on the small jets of air that blew in the sleep compartments nearby. The air vents were designed to keep someone sleeping in a bunk from drowning in her own carbon dioxide. It struck Loy that she felt like she was drowning.

Her heart pounding in her ears, Loy touched the side of the galley, using it to move closer. Reno looked so sleepy, so young, so vulnerable. Loy felt overcome with a staggering tenderness. She found herself leaning closer, until her lips brushed over Reno's. In the contrary awkwardness of microgravity, their noses bumped, inadvertently sending Loy away from what she sought.

Loy slipped an arm around Reno, pulling her in against her. Their lips met. Slowly, deliciously, they kissed, as if savoring the reclamation of something precious. Then, after a moment, Loy's long-banked need rose, urging her on. In some distant awareness she felt her ribs aching with the press of their embrace, but all the same, the kiss became passionate.

Their breathing intensified, until the constant background hum and clicks of the spacecraft faded in comparison. One of Reno's hands moved through Loy's hair, while the hand holding the small, square shape of the forgotten palm computer swept along the back of Loy's white rugby shirt.

Suddenly, Reno ended the kiss, moving back to examine Loy's face. "Why?" Reno whispered. "What's happened? Has the Border —"

"No," Loy answered, smoothing a hand over the side of Reno's distressed face. "Just got a message from Whit about who gave Medusa the fuel documents." Sheepish, Loy mumbled, "Wasn't you."

Reno's eyes flickered with impatience, then she opened a pocket on her flight suit and tucked away the palm computer. "For someone who masterminded a shuttle launch, you are so dense, sometimes."

Loy managed a short, self-conscious laugh before Reno

demanded details. Loy relayed the message Whit had sent, including the order for Loy to apologize to Reno — in the manner Loy thought best.

Reno laughed softly. "I think I'll need more apologizing, then." She gave Loy a quick, conciliatory kiss on the nose. "Maybe when my head doesn't feel like it's had a big party and I wasn't there for it."

Feeling suddenly shy, still held close by Reno's hand in her hair, Loy whispered, "I can be a real hothead, you know. Quick to anger and slow to —"

"Like I don't know that." Reno proceeded to kiss Loy so completely that Loy lost track of everything — where she was, what she intended — everything. There was only Reno, only shuddering defenselessness when Reno kissed her.

When Reno released Loy again, Loy's body was on fire with sensations. Overwhelmed, she closed her eyes. After five days in the relative touch-deprivation of microgravity, she was starving for sensual attention, and Reno seemed to know it. Reno's arm wrapped snugly around Loy's waist, and Reno's silken lips tantalized Loy until she felt nothing but their passage and the savage ache between her legs.

At last Reno stilled, holding Loy in her arms. "I don't think we should allow this to go much further while we're still up here, do you?" Reno murmured.

Then, Reno's restless hands were moving over her, again, renewing the voluptuous onslaught. Loy had the distinct knowledge that Reno was reluctant to stop.

Loy opened her eyes and realized they were in a slow roll, gliding weightless through the cabin. Their arms and legs had managed their own instinctive grasp of the other's body, and they were pressed along the length of one another.

Struggling for a semblance of reason, Loy tried to order her priorities. "Um, yes, the mission is primary," she agreed. "We can't let anything take our focus off of that. We're here to do a job."

As they separated, their hands glided down one another's arms to grasp hands and then part.

Reno sighed. "At least that made my head feel a little better."

In answer, Loy placed a light kiss on the surface of the bandage. "Are you sure you're feeling up to running the RMS?"

Reno began moving toward the access ladder, ready to return to the aft crew station and their work there. "You didn't save my skilled ass for nothing, Chen."

*Here we go!* Loy thought, as she followed her in the swim up the ladder.


That same night, Kali came through the door of the Leader's office, and stopped. As she had guessed, Whit was still at her desk, her head resting on her crossed arms, sound asleep. Before Whit's inert body, a small computer slate glowed with a graphics map of the city-colony. Papers and chip boxes were scattered around her, and one hand still grasped a slate stylus.

Going to her lover, Kali leaned down, brushed back Whit's hair, and found an ear to nuzzle. "Come to bed, Tomyris."

With a muffled "What?" Whit lifted her head.

"It's past one o'clock in the morning," Kali said quietly.

Befuddled, Whit sat up straight, looking around her.

Kali ran her fingers lovingly through Whit's hair.

"Humph," Whit responded, then scrubbed both hands across her face. "I have to review the defense plans one more time."

Not even bothering to dignify that remark with a response, Kali reached over and thumbed the slate's Off button, shutting down the unit.

"Hey!" Whit protested angrily.

"Enough," Kali ordered. "You know the plans by heart. You're exhausted. These crazy hours you've been working have caught up with you." Giving a don't-argue-with-me look, she took Whit by the hand and gently tugged her out of the chair.

Looking contrary and ready to resist, Whit stumbled to her feet. Kali slipped under her arm, hugging Whit close to her side and supporting her.

"I'm too heavy for you," Whit grumbled. She regained her balance and cautioned, "The baby — you shouldn't."

"Okay, then, come on," Kali returned softly, continuing to lead Whit toward the door.

Whit stopped outside in the hallway, closing the door after them, then said good night to the two sentries posted there.

Satisfied to simply be this close to Whit, Kali walked along beside her, her arm loosely circling Whit's waist. She looked up to find Whit gazing down at her.

After what sounded like a distinctly guilty sigh, Whit said, "There's something I haven't told you."

"You're heading the Scramble Squadron," Kali returned mildly.

"I'm heading —" Whit huffed, "You know!"

"I guessed," Kali explained. "With this pregnancy, my telepathic skills are not as sharp as they once were. And you blocked me very well, love. But when you are so obviously blocking me, I know something's going on." She leaned into Whit, confessing, "There's a sudden shortage of pilots, and from what I hear, you were once considered an ace. Stands to reason you'd go where you're needed." Kali added wistfully, "As ever."

Whit stopped walking and pulled Kali into an embrace. "I didn't want to worry you."

"I know," Kali murmured, feeling a heady rush of desire for the strong, tall woman in her arms.

"If there's an air-raid alert, I've made arrangements with Captain Razia for you to be taken directly to the computer chamber below the Cedar House," Whit went on, her voice low and calm. "It's probably the safest, most impenetrable place in Isis."

"Whit, promise me you won't be reckless," Kali began, but Whit quickened their pace, pulling Kali toward the doorway to their private suite, saying, "I'm never reckless."

"Oh, what a fib."

Laughing, Whit nodded perfunctorily to the sentry posted by the suite door and touched the DNA plate. Once they were inside and the door closed, Kali's eyes brimmed with tears. She couldn't see much in the darkened room as Whit led her forward.

Gentle and sweet, Whit was undressing her, breathing endearments into Kali's shoulders and neck. Her large, graceful hands were sliding over her, making delicious promises. Then Whit was pulling back the bed covers and laying Kali down. Kali watched Whit strip and, moments later, Whit's splendid, warm, athletic body eased against her.

In the intoxicating hour that followed, Kali focused all her errant supernatural talent on weaving a spell. While she succumbed to Whit's kisses and melted beneath her, Kali kept one small, detached portion of her mind on the chant she was silently repeating. *Wherever she is, on earth, air, or sea, flesh and mind, bind her to me.* Whit steadily brought her closer and closer to orgasm, and Kali focused on harnessing the energy flaring through her, on using the transcendent maelstrom to fuse the enchantment. *Wherever she is, on earth, air, or sea, flesh and mind, bind her to me.*

She didn't realize she was saying the words in the incoherent ravings Whit caused, until Whit gathered her close against her, murmuring, "What's that you're yelling, wild girl?"

Sluggish and satiated, Kali only shook her head and luxuriated in Whit's embrace. Deep inside, she was certain the hex had gone true.


Whit sat bolt upright, so disoriented that for a full three seconds she merely stared around herself. *What the hell is that insufferable noise?*

In the predawn light streaming in from the windows, Whit saw the horror on Kali's face and realized what they both heard was the air-raid siren across the street blasting an alert.

Whit leapt out of bed, urging, "Get dressed, Kal," and grabbing the clothes she had shed only a few hours earlier.

Having pulled on the rumpled outfit, Whit turned to Kali.

In Kali's dark brown eyes was utter panic. She sat frozen, her hands gripping the sheet tightly against her chest.

"It's going to be all right," Whit soothed. "I have to go to the airfield. You have to go to the Cedar House." Her voice gentle, Whit coaxed, "Razia will be here for you any minute."

Kali's breath was coming fast. "This is how it started last time," she managed. "First the sirens, then the napalm." Kali shuddered. "Then the Regs — everywhere I turned — so many Regs —"

"Kal," Whit said firmly. "Look at me."

Eyes wide, Kali looked back at her.

"It won't be like that this time," Whit stated. "It's not a sneak attack. We're ready for them."

Some of the panic left Kali's face.

"Now, do your duty," Whit instructed. "Can you get our little daughter to safety?"

Kali gulped, then whispered, "Yes."

Whit turned to go, but Kali was off the bed and in her arms in a flash. They exchanged a deep, fevered kiss, then Kali released her and began yanking a shirt over her head. Whit took one last, longing look at her, then made for the door.

\* \* \* \* \*

Whit's motorcycle sliced across the airfield tarmac. *Perhaps the hours and hours of training have paid off.*

All nineteen Peregrines were ready, engines engaged, side by side in a long line, ready for action. Once a pilot climbed aboard and belted in, there would be only a quick acceleration down the runway before takeoff.

Whit had barely brought her cycle to a screeching halt before she was setting the kickstand and racing toward the Peregrine she had assigned herself. A mechanic met her with her insulated flight coveralls, boots, and helmet. Whit stripped and donned the outfit, aware of the transport from the barracks roaring up nearby. Other pilots were arriving, dashing before their Peregrines and changing into flight suits.

"What's the news, Corporal?" Whit yelled over the noise of the Peregrine. Even with the decibel-squelch devices in place, the jets were loud.

"A big section of the northern Border fell about three and a half hours ago. Like last time, the failure never showed on any of our monitors. Per Warrior Command, some Tubman scouts flying the perimeter sighted a wave of thirty bogeys." The corporal knelt to tie Whit's boots while Whit gathered her hair into a short, high ponytail and pulled on her helmet. "The scouts say all enemy aircraft are making straight for Isis."

"Just as we expected," Whit said to herself.

The young warrior glanced up at her, then rose and stepped back, saluting. "Mother's luck to you, Leader Whitaker."

"Thanks, Corporal," she responded, returning the gesture.

Whit peered down the line. Most of the other pilots were close to being fully dressed too. Anxious to get started, Whit hoisted herself up onto the wing of the Peregrine and climbed into the cockpit.

She settled in quickly, securing the seat harness, triggering the canopy retraction, and checking her gauges. Then she radioed the tower, asking for the latest weather report and the last known position of the bogeys.

The tower responded. "Weather all clear from the coast to the Rockies. Bogeys coming from the southwest, following the Sacajawea River. We expect them to turn toward Isis after they use the natural gateway of the river gorge to get beyond the Cascades."

"Whitaker and company, requesting permission to take off," she radioed.

"You are cleared for sortie."

Whit pushed the power lever slightly forward, and the Peregrine rolled out onto the tarmac. She swung wide, turning the point of the jet to face the long runway, then advanced the power lever. With a discernible roar, the Peregrine raced along, smooth and fast. It jounced a bit as Whit pushed the lever fully out, tugged back the joystick, and kicked the pedals that controlled the lifts on the wings. The jet leapt up, leaving the runway and streaking into the sky. As she climbed higher, gaining altitude, she banked the jet and saw the other Peregrines leaving the runway and climbing behind her in a well spaced and continuous single file.

"Form up for action," Whit radioed the squadron.

Moments later the jets were flying in three separate chevrons of five. Whit was at the point of the fourth chevron, which had only four jets. She looked through the Plexiglas at the Peregrine on her right, giving a thumbs-up sign to her young friend Danu Sullivan.

For a few seconds, she wished the radio-silence order could be retracted. She wanted to warn Danu, a known overachiever, to just do her best and not get tempted into making impulsive, self-sacrificing decisions.

*She's a trained warrior and pilot,* Whit reminded herself. *Trust her to do her job.*

The Peregrines were traveling so fast that the squadron was already passing the blasted-out crater of Mount Saint

Helen. Whit returned her attention to her radar. The graphics screen showed an array of Elysian aircraft moving out of the Sacajawea River Gorge and turning north.

Whit flipped the safety cover off the laser-gun trigger mounted on top of her joystick. *Gaea, help us stop them.*

# Chapter 9

On Whit's left, the first rays of sun broke over the jagged, snowcapped heights of the Cascades. Two large lakes reflected peach-colored light back up at her. Whit checked the coordinates on her NAVSTAR Global Positioning System.

*Thank the Goddess GPS is still up and running,* Whit thought, wondering just which satellite had to fail before they lost this most necessary of technological weapons. Glancing below, she squinted at the shine of water and calculated. *That's Guinevere and Hebe, the two lakes surrounded by miles and miles of the Skamania Forest.*

Whit checked the radar again, then stared through the Plexiglas canopy, straining for visual confirmation.

Seconds later, a host of dark shapes appeared in the sky.

In a deafening roar, the nineteen members of Whit's Scramble Squadron intercepted thirty Elysian jets. Most of the Elysian F-24s attempted to hold their course, but, instantly under attack, they were soon forced to abandon whatever mission they had. Thirty Elysian F-24s began to climb and weave, vainly trying to evade the predators that shadowed them like the brave peregrine falcons for which the Freelandian jets were named.

Peregrines were small aircraft, designed for the heightened speed and distances made possible by cold-fusion fuel. Constructed of composite plastics and layers of vinyl-steel, the jets sported a radarproof skin outside and state-of-the-art microcomputer support inside, making it a lethal piece of weaponry.

The F-24s were slower, larger, and clumsier in comparison. Whit knew, however, that eighty-five years ago, when the jets were brand-new, they had been formidable opponents. With their heat-seeking missiles and automatic-targeting machine guns, only skilled and constantly evasive pilots could avoid elimination. The F-24s Whit saw in the air around her, trying to gain the advantage of altitude in this unfolding dogfight, were ancient, endlessly repaired remnants of the last glory days of the United States of America. Since the end of the briefly fought Great Rift, the jets had seen little action. They had been warehoused and regularly maintained, cared for like deadly *objets d'art*.

Large sections of replacement parts, dents in the wing superstructure and fuselage, and areas discolored by rust or fire were visible. *Why?* Whit wondered. *Are these the same jets that attacked Tubman and Susan B. Anthony? Or is there an insurrection or something we don't know about going on in Elysium?*

The last information Freeland had from an undercover operative stationed in Elysian was two years old; Whit had smuggled out data on a bandit satellite transmission. There had been no mention of a rebellion in that massive download from the Reg's mainframe computer, only a seemingly odd lack of Reg presence in the land once called West Virginia.

As substandard as the Elysian jets looked, Whit couldn't be sure which of the two war birds in the air today — the Peregrine or the F-24 — would be the superior apparatus.

Within moments, Whit was operating on well-honed reflexes, relying on old skills acquired in flight school over a decade ago and polished in the Peregrine simulator all winter and spring. Whit was rolling, diving, banking, and climbing, blasting the laser weaponry at every F-24 that came into her sights. The sky was filled with swooping, soaring jets. Suddenly, she saw several explosions, and two Elysian F-24s fell from the sky in flames.

*Good thing it's been an unusually wet spring. Little chance of a forest fire spreading.*

Seeming to recover from their initial surprise at finding a hostile welcoming committee flying out to meet them, the Elysians retaliated by double-teaming the closest Peregrine. A few minutes later, Whit was dismayed to see billowing black smoke from a Peregrine wing.

"Head home, smokey," Whit ordered. "All others, make them come after you and use what Gaea gave us."

The Peregrines fanned out, taking up more space. When the F-24s pursued, the Peregrines dove, flying lower and still lower, cruising over the treetops, then banking toward the mountains. Almost immediately, an F-24 unused to skirting along a rim of towering granite made a fatal miscalculation. Trying to mimic a Peregrine's swift dodge, the F-24 got caught in an updraft. The less maneuverable Elysian jet tried to jerk free and instead went directly into a cliff face. The F-24 behind it fought off the same powerful current of air, then hit another F-24 while trying to correct its direction.

"One on your tail, ma'am," came Danu's voice through the radio in her helmet.

Whit glanced at the top right section of her helmet

viewscreen. The datalink code was orange — the F-24 chasing her had automatically targeted her Peregrine.

"Bank left," Danu instructed.

Whit dove and swerved, and a slim, heat-seeking missile streaked by her. The missile slammed into a steep, stony slope of mountainside. A huge eruption of dust and broken boulders blew out over the timbered landscape below the rocky heights. As Whit slid into a U-turn, she saw a fireball erupt in midair and knew Danu had taken out her antagonist.

"Good eye, little sister," Whit called.

In answer, Danu's forward laser guns discharged a series of short, bright bursts, which zipped close by Whit's right side, causing her to wince involuntarily. A shock wave from the rear buffeted Whit's Peregrine. Whit accelerated into another U-turn and saw an Elysian F-24 spiraling down into the forest.

"They're all over us," Danu radioed.

Whit recognized what sounded like first-action jitters in Danu's tone. She called back, "You're doing fine. Stay alert."

Toward the end, Whit was flying more by instinct than by technology. Soaring and swirling, sometimes evading machine-gun fire by less than a few feet, Whit tried to be unpredictable. The battle had no plan; it was all a blur of action and reaction. Whit listened to and relied upon Danu's occasional direction, trusting her, working as one with her. The two of them were steadily firing at and dropping F-24s one by one, until Whit had lost count of their kills.

Then, unexpectedly, two Peregrines suffered hits simultaneously. Relieved, Whit saw the pilots safely eject before the jets plummeted into the fir forest. She murmured a quick prayer to the Goddess, hoping the pilots wouldn't be injured as their parachutes dropped through the dense stand of trees.

Disturbed, Whit swung wide and made a fast tally. Sixteen Freelandian Peregrines were still in the sky, dogfighting nine Elysian F-24s.

"Two breaking away, ma'am," Danu reported.

Whit peered through the canopy and saw the two F-24s Danu meant, rolling free of the seven F-24s that were still engaging the Peregrines. Flying south, as if retracing their route, the two were either deserting in the face of action or planning something more sinister.

"Scramble Squadron, proceed with sortie," Whit ordered. "Take them down! Danu and I are on a pair of running dogs."

Whit turned south, with Danu flying high and tight just to her right. They soared toward the Sacajawea, the mighty river that divided Old Washington territory from Old Oregon. All the way, the two dark shapes flew before them. Ahead, a wide ribbon of water shimmered blue and metal wings glinted as the F-24s banked east into the morning sunlight.

"I'm reading friendlies," Danu warned.

Whit glanced down at her GPS sensor scan and saw what Danu meant. Ten recognizable signatures were sending positions and trajectories on her amplified graphics screen. This was the only craft Whit knew that was invisible to radar, so friendly jets sent encoded GPS data to receptive computer chips in like craft in order to forewarn that an encounter was about to occur.

*Peregrines*, Whit surmised.

A new, crisp voice came through Whit's helmet. "Captain Griffin, here. You're in Boudica airspace, now, ladies." There was a laugh, then, "Let us get those two chickens."

Whit countered tensely, "No — they're mine. I have a feeling about them —" She didn't add, *And from living with a mage I've learned to trust my instincts.* "I think one of those guys is carrying a nuke — that they came all this way to do to Isis what they did to Lang."

"We'll help you get 'em," Captain Griffin immediately offered.

"Problem is," Whit argued, "if we take them out here, we'll fry ourselves, and radioactive fallout will be unleashed over Freeland. I'd rather ride herd on them, chase them and any nasty junk they've got onboard back to Elysium."

"Roger," Captain Griffin agreed.

Thankful that she could leave the dogfight behind her with an easier mind, Whit requested, "Still a bit of a fracas over the Skamania Forest if you really want to get in on the action."

"We're there!" Griffin answered.

The ten Peregrines streaked by Whit and Danu, the lead jet dipping its wings slightly as it passed. "We've been watching the engagement on combined readouts — both extended radar and GPS monitoring," the Boudican pilot called. "They'll be using it as a textbook lesson in air tactics for years. Damn fine show, Whitaker."

"Thanks, Captain Griffin," Whit called back. "How'd you know it was me, anyway?"

"That whiskey voice of yours!" the pilot laughed. "Go get 'em, Leader."

Whit grinned, and headed east. Soon she was readjusting her radar tracking and concentrating solely on the two F-24s heading away from her and Danu.

"She just blew your anonymity," Danu asserted quietly.

Whit realized it was true. Trying to downplay the incident, Whit said, "I hardly think it matters, as long as we can chase these guys back across the Border and into Elysium."

Her voice resolute, Danu responded, "Let's do it, then."

For the next two hours, at supersonic speeds, Danu and Whit pursued the Elysian F-24s, which had left low-level altitude as they flew over what had once been the boundary between Washington state and Idaho. The F-24s climbed miles above the ground to gain more speed, and Whit and Danu followed them. Whatever plan the Regs might have had for backtracking and approaching Isis from another direction seemed to have been abandoned.

During the long flight, lulled by the continual dull roar of the decibel-squelched jet engines, Whit found her mind wandering. She thought of Kali, and fervently hoped the Boudican pilot, Griffin, would pass on Whit's decision to "ride herd" on the fleeing Elysians so that one of the Scramble Squadron members could in turn relay the information to Kali. She was sure Kali would understand her compulsion to personally escort the two breakaway craft back to Elysium.

Despite the relative ease of the long chase, Whit felt a niggling fear between her shoulder blades and up her neck. She was certain that at least one of the F-24s racing before her carried a small thermonuclear bomb, similar to the one that the Elysians had dropped over Lang. She suspected that the Regs on board, having been prevented from delivering the weapon as originally intended and then relentlessly stalked when the backup plan was attempted, had reached the end of available options.

Despite the lack of actual military intelligence on the matter, Whit was certain she was right. The chain of command in Regulator hierarchy was rigid and distinct; in the face of adversity, pilots were simply not allowed to develop creative strategic solutions. Among Elysians, only tribunes and procurators made strategy decisions; pilots followed orders.

*Mother's blood, I hate that place*, Whit thought vehemently.

Restless, she shifted her torso, trying to move her legs and arms in the tight cockpit and get a little blood flowing. It wasn't just the long flight; the mere thought of again getting this close to Elysium was making her nervous. She knew they were entering the edge of Old Nebraska territory, a mere twenty minutes or less from the Border.

Ugly and irrepressible memories of her undercover work in Elysium drifted through her mind. Roughly two years ago, Whit had spent a two-year hitch there that seemed interminable. Top brass had since closed the undercover postings, and subsequently, no one else had gone into Elysium. The information Whit brought out with her had been the last spy data gleaned.

Frowning with distaste, Whit remembered the filthy, poverty-stricken cities ruled by feudal law, where plague bearers were hunted with a merciless religious zeal. After all, everyone "knew" AGH was God's punishment. Anyone showing signs of AIDS/genital herpes was arrested and shipped off to an AGH farm or a labor camp, doomed to live out their days in the backbreaking labor of serfdom. In comparison to the citizens of Freeland, even Elysium's average citizens were starved and destitute. Meanwhile, the wealthy and politically powerful minority — the reverends, the procurators, and the tribunes — lived above the horror and terror in the lush comfort and safety of high-walled estates.

For Whit, however, beyond the harshness of daily life in Elysium, what she could never get over was the meanspiritedness of its people. In the founding days of Elysium, their ancestors had driven plague bearers, people of color, and non-Christians out of their country. Later, those same Elysians had murdered thousands of AGH victims in cold blood.

More recent generations of Elysians appeared to be just as self-centered and grasping and cruel. Neighbors informed on neighbors, selling the Reg authorities anything from idle gossip to complete fabrication, all for a few potatoes or sticks of firewood. No one shared food or medicine, or even the refreshing gift of good humor or song. No one went out of their way to help another, unless it was a thinly disguised attempt to curry favor with the Regs.

It had taken all Whit's will to keep silent in the face of the routine misogyny, to turn away from the many spousal beatings she'd witnessed, to just play the role of a nerdy, unkempt computer tech. She had spent two years trying to look as unattractive as possible, trying to repel male attention; two irretrievable years of brutes and idiots and madmen bossing her around. Though she had eventually succeeded in breaking into Elysium's central core computer and using a NASA satellite to download all its highly secret material to a computer in Freeland, Whit had never fully recovered from the experience of life in Elysium.

*By now, most of that stolen data has to be out of date.*

When she thought about what the Regs had done to Kali and to Isis, her hatred for all things Elysian nearly consumed her. It was only her conviction that hatred was a dangerous, self-destructive indulgence that kept her from dwelling on thoughts of vengeance against Elysium and its people.

Danu's alarmed voice broke into her reverie, "Enemy craft breaking formation, ma'am!"

Startled, Whit focused on the radar readout of the craft ahead of them and realized Danu was right. One of the F-24s was circling wide, heading back toward them.

Taking a few quick breaths, she evaluated the situation. *One flees while his wing man runs interference. The one on the run must be the one carrying a nuke.* Whit took a moment, trying to decide what to do. *Gaea knows when or even if the new satellite network will kick in, or what will happen to the Border! I have no choice. This guy is just going to land, refuel, and then try another sneak attack later. I'm not going to risk Kali or our baby or anyone else in Isis. If the Elysians are so fond of this bomb from hell, then let them deal with a return delivery — right over Andrews Air Force Base, if necessary! At least it will be one bomb that never leaves Elysium again!*

"Danu, you take the bird circling back," Whit ordered. "I'm on the other one."

"Roger," Danu replied, her voice calm and even.

Danu's Peregrine shot away, heading for the Elysian jet. Though Whit could still see Danu's craft on the GPS gauge, she wondered if she would ever see Danu herself again.

All at once, there was a slight haze ahead of Whit's Peregrine. Whit blinked, trying to clear her vision. The strange haze seemed to curve near the top, like a roof. Straight ahead, a puzzle piece was missing in the blanket of haze; a vast section of sky was decidedly brownish-yellow. The two Elysian jets raced into the yellow, and Whit roared along right behind them. As thick, amber clouds surrounded Whit, she knew she had just flown through a hole in the Border.

Wide awake, she was encountering her worst nightmare.

She was back in Elysium.


Loy popped another salt pill, then reached for the drink bag floating nearby. She swallowed more water, then tightened the safety straps on the pilot's chair.

On the other side of the flight deck, Reno was already strapped into the flight commander's seat. Like Loy, she was dressed in a launch/entry suit. She took a sip through her drink bag straw, and grimaced.

"If I drink any more of this I'm going to barf," Reno muttered.

Loy grinned in response.

For the past few hours they had been readying their cardiovascular systems for the return to Earth's gravity. After they had they left Earth, their blood volume had steadily decreased to adapt to the microgravity of the shuttle flight. In order to avoid lightheadedness or sudden thirst when they landed, they were both working to increase their blood volume before deorbit.

Loy glanced at the clock on the instrument panel. "Two minutes to retro fire," she announced. She gulped down more water, then let the drink bag go. As it drifted away from her, Loy reached for her helmet.

Securing her own headgear, Reno commented, "Who would have thought water weight gain could be a good thing."

Loy reacted with a delighted laugh, then stopped abruptly at the flash of pain along her right side. She opened her eyes to find Reno watching her.

"I'm okay," Loy told her, but it took another few moments before she was able to get her helmet on properly.

She wondered if the giddiness she felt was the result of sheer exhaustion or utter relief at their success. All twenty satellites had been released and were now proceeding in their predetermined orbits. She knew that down below, in Freeland, the satellite team was reconfiguring the Border software, eliminating the changes made to Maat's original program, and getting the new satellites online. Meanwhile, on the *Independence*, the cargo-bay doors were already closed and they were flying backward, tailfirst, prepared for deorbit burn.

Ground control came through the radio in Loy's helmet. "Chief Chen." Loy knew the voice well enough to hear the anxiety beneath it. "Reentry G forces are going to play hell with your ribs."

Through the open helmet visor, Loy looked over at Mika. "I'm willing to bet Major Reno's head ends up hurting her more," she said with a grin.

Ground control stated, "Just so you're both aware."

Reno rolled her eyes. "I take it you're daring me to something."

"Of course," Loy said. "Whoever yells first buys the other dinner at her restaurant of choice."

"H'm," Reno returned, meeting her eyes. "You're on."

They both felt the shimmer in the cabin as the orbital maneuvering system engines fired for the next two minutes, slowing their speed by 320 kilometers per hour. When the OMS engines stopped, Loy used the instruments before her to turn the shuttle around so that it was traveling nosefirst again. She raised the nose to a 28- to 38-degree angle, holding the shuttle steady as it began to fall.

"Control," Loy radioed, "We are in entry attitude."

Smoothly, Loy prepared the next step of the descent, which was to pump overboard the cold-fusion propellant left on the ship by unloading it through the forward reaction control system. This would shift the orbiter's balance for point for reentry. Loy and Reno silently watched the globules of water-based fuel stream from the RCS thrusters on the nose of the ship.

"Control, this is *Independence*," Loy said. "RCS dump complete. Over."

"Roger, out."

With a plop, Loy's drink bag ceased floating beside her and dropped to the flight-deck floor. She knew they were only at about two-tenths of what was considered normal Earth's gravity, but her body was already feeling heavier.

She was so busy with the reentry checklist and her pilot's instruments that the next half-hour passed quickly.

"Altitude 122,000 meters," Reno announced. "Entry interface about to commence."

Ground control remarked, "We'll pick you up on the other side, *Independence*."

"Roger that, ground," Loy acknowledged. *We're on our own, now.*

She knew that as the orbiter dropped, atmospheric drag was going to generate tremendous heat around the *Independence*. The heat was going to strip electrons from the air around the shuttle, surrounding it in a sheath of ionized air that was going to block all communication with the ground. The blackout would last approximately twelve minutes.

Ground control signed off, saying, "Good luck, *Independence*. Out."

Reno turned to Loy and said, "Oh, and about my dinner?"

Chuckling, Loy looked over at her.

"I'll be wanting a candlelit supper in your cabin. In your bed, to be precise." She fixed Loy with a gaze full of meaning. "So you just go ahead and yell whenever you feel like it."

Desire shot through Loy. She answered Reno with a stunned nod, before turning back to the control panel.

The full force of reentry hit as the *Independence* encountered earth's atmosphere. It was not the 3-G force of liftoff, when they were going up in a straight line. This time, because they were coming in at an angle as the shuttle glided lower, they were meeting a 2-G force. The strain on Loy's body as it was forced into the flight chair was shocking. Loy knew their bodies had weighed next to nothing for the past five days, and as a result the G forces felt stronger now. Gasping, she placed a hand against her ribs, clenching her teeth against the pain. She felt the entire shuttle shaking around her, vibrating as the friction of the earth's atmosphere slowed them from an orbiting speed of twenty-five times the speed of sound to two times the speed of sound.

The burning pain along Loy's right side began to spread, and despite her best effort, a whimper escaped her.

Above the roar of noise, Reno urged, "Let me win this bet, okay?"

Loy was helpless against the agony, and a cry tore from her throat.

Suddenly the G forces diminished. Loy felt the tug on her safety harness, which meant the orbiter had dramatically lost speed. Gasping uncontrollably, she leaned back in her chair, valiantly scanning the instruments. The reaction-control system was beginning to shut down, and the aero-control surfaces were starting to take effect. The pain in her side was rapidly abating. She lay there, taking quick, shallow breaths, trying to focus her attention on the tasks required of her. Shakily, she began manipulating switches, causing the *Independence* to execute a series of S-turns. The S-turn maneuvers used the air to slow the shuttle the way a skier uses snow to slow the downhill run.

"Great," Reno told her. "You're doing great."

Loy looked over at her. "How's your head feel?"

"Like it doesn't want to go through reentry again anytime soon," Reno joked, "but otherwise, okay."

Nodding, Loy turned back to business. "Control," Loy called, "This is *Independence*. Do you copy? Over."

Ground control rejoined them. "We've got you on GPS, *Independence*. You look good." The unmistakable sound of women cheering came through in the background of that transmission. "Ready for TACAN?"

Tactical air navigation — the radio-electronic system that gives both range and bearing measurements. Ground control would be sharing computer control of the approach landing with Loy, but only Loy would be making adjustments. Once the shuttle was down to 5,500 meters, the microwave landing system would kick in and Loy would be out of it completely.

"Roger, control," Loy acknowledged, then changed the body FLP switch to auto.

"TAEM go," control responded. "Computers have you committed to touch down at Cochran Space Center in twelve minutes."

Loy responded with an affirmative, but she was already worriedly watching the computer display screens, checking the descent trajectory. TAEM — terminal area energy management — was in effect. Guidance, navigation, and flight-control software transmitted from ground ops were now running the shuttle. Enough altitude and speed for the final approach was essential to reach the final touchdown point.

The *Independence* had no power of its own. They couldn't go around for a second attempt at Cochran's runway if the TAEM phase went wrong. The shuttle had to glide to the ground in a single attempt, or the mission was going to end in a spectacular crash.

Reading the gauges before her, Loy realized their descent was too fast. "Applying speed brakes," Loy announced, asserting her capacity to make changes to the computer programs.

Reno leaned toward her, watching the altitude/vertical velocity indicator. "Good call."

Loy cut another S-turn.

Somewhere below them, a pair of huge metal cylinders sat side by side, about eleven kilometers from the runway. These heading alignment cylinders were going to guide them home. *All the software has to do,* Loy thought, *is line up the shuttle with one of the cylinders, follow the curve, and the* Independence *will be on mark with the runway entry point.*

The safety harness tugged Loy against the seat, displaying again how much speed they were losing. The orbiter began shaking, as if encountering turbulence.

"Cochran," Loy radioed, her eyes on the alpha-mach meter, "we have buffeting."

Beside Loy, Reno murmured, "Just over the speed of sound. That means about two minutes to landing, doesn't it?"

Loy nodded, then said, "Almost there."

Control called, "We've just heard two sonic booms, and we have you on visual. We're ready to bring her in."

Loy peered through the pilot windows, searching the fir forest below her for the heading alignment cylinders. Finally, she spotted the two round, gleaming objects sitting in a valley, surrounded by a dark-green forest of Douglas firs. The cylinders shone in the bright June sunlight like welcoming beacons. A strange mix of elation and melancholy moved through Loy.

She knew the autoland phase was about to begin. Ground control personnel were going to do the landing sequence once *Independence* cleared heading alignment cylinder Way Point One. In a few moments, Loy would be just a passenger on an amusement park ride.

Automatically, the *Independence* swooped around the curve of one cylinder, then followed the line that ran between the two of them.

"*Independence,*" control called. "Have you acquired autoland? Over?"

Glancing at the indicator, Loy replied, "Roger. Autoland captured. Out."

Gazing out at the runway approaching them, Loy was amazed to realize that this was the end.

"Yeehaw!" Reno yelled, raising her fists in the air.

The last steps of the flight unfolded. Preflare was initiated, and the landing gear was lowered and locked in position. Then the shuttle nose rose up, and all Loy and Reno could see was blue sky.

Traveling at 346 kilometers per hour, the back wheels of the *Independence* touched down lightly. With a soft bump, the nose came down, and the shuttle was rolling fast down the long length of tarmac. Loy and Reno both watched the gauges while ground control kept the speed brake at full forward.

Gradually the orbiter slowed and finally coasted to a stop.

"Mission accomplished," Reno breathed. She half turned in her chair and, hand over heart, gave a salute. "Damn, Loy. I'll fly with you any time."

Loy returned the salute. "Feeling's mutual, Mika."

They grinned at each other. On the radio, they could hear control ordering the special transport van out onto the tarmac for egress. It was going to be at least another hour before they completed the long orbiter shutdown checklist and got their "earth legs" back well enough to move around in their forty-one kilogram launch/entry suits.

Yet they were home and were safe. And they had at last acknowledged aloud that they were in love with one another. For Loy, that was more than enough.

Desperately, Whit did a barrel roll, then abruptly steered her craft lower, escaping the trail of fiery-red tracers from the F-24 on her tail. No matter what she did, she couldn't seem to escape the Elysian.

She had chased the F-24 all the way to northeastern

Virginia, and then unexpectedly the Elysian jet had turned on her. Now she was in full retreat, unable to target him. Instead, she was trying frantically to stay out of his missile lock.

*This is just like the program in the Peregrine simulator,* Whit thought. *The program I was engaging the day Kali came to tell me she was pregnant.* She swallowed hard against the near panic she felt, trying to control her breathing. *I was shot down that day!*

That day, she had abruptly dropped speed, let the F-24 on her tail fly by her, and then she'd climbed above the Elysian to eliminate it. However, the computer-generated F-24 had followed more closely in back of her. This real-life Elysian pilot was giving himself enough room to react to a trick like that.

*What can I do?*

Suddenly, she wasn't sure where the Elysian was any more.

Intuition took over. *Don't think. Move, move, move!* Her brain shrieked at her.

She initiated a series of sharp zigzags, then yanked the stick back, sending the Peregrine into a sharp climb. *I'm going to get above this jackass if it kills me!*

A line of tracers zipped by her left wing. She heard a soft *bip, bip, bip.* She was hit. And then Whit was soaring over the F-24.

From her position above the Elysian jet, Whit unleashed a punishing volley of machine-gun fire. Black smoke billowed from the rear of F-24. Immediately afterward, the jet broke off the engagement, curling away from Whit in a smooth arc. As Whit swooped around to follow, the F-24 flew low and fast, due east.

Unexpectedly, the radio earpiece in Whit's helmet crackled to life. "Mayday, Mayday, Mayday!" Danu's voice called.

Whit checked on the Elysian F-24 and realized he was fleeing, a thin, dark smudge spewing in his wake.

Instinctively, Whit swung her Peregrine into an about-face maneuver. "Where are you," she radioed Danu.

"GPS 12.3 on my gauge," Danu said.

Whit manipulated her radio controls, trying to boost the fading reception.

"Objective completed," Danu went on, informing Whit that she had taken out her F-24. "Sustained no damage, but am losing altitude. Can't figure out why." Danu's voice was terse. "I'm going down."

"Bail out!" Whit ordered, locking her auto pilot on the GPS location Danu had relayed. "I'm coming for you."

"But —"

"Follow orders!" Whit yelled. "Bail out!"

"Yes, ma'am," came the faint message.

Whit glanced toward her left wing and saw the steady stream of cold-fusion fuel slipping out, emptying in a straight line behind her.

Her crippled Peregrine was dropping lower, only several hundred feet above the mountain treetops when Whit roared into Old West Virginia territory.


Kali sat at Whit's desk, gripping the arms of the plush desk chair, her eyes on the wallscreen. Breaking news reports were streaming by in a ribbon of print along the bottom of the screen, while a newswoman was interviewing Scramble Squadron pilots on the tarmac of the Isis Airfield.

Seventeen women had returned from the mission. Even the two flyers shot down over the Skamania Forest had been recovered, though one had a broken leg and the other a shrapnel wound to the back. Meanwhile, twenty-eight Elysian jets and the Regs who'd flown them were only so much debris on the forest floor.

The comline reporter questioned jubilant pilots about their exploits, while the camera trained on one triumphant face after another. In the quiet office, alone, Kali focused on the stream of printed news at the bottom of the screen. A painful lump lodged in her throat, and her eyes burned with unshed tears. Vigilant, as she had been for three hours now, she watched the moving strip of words, searching for Whit's name and news on what had happened after Whit had followed the two escaping Elysian jets.

The office door slid open. Lilith and Styx came in, followed by Captain Razia and Tor Yakami. Kali's eyes went anxiously to Lilith, then closed, recognizing the restrained despair she saw on her face.

Lilith leaned over, embracing her. "Captain Razia just received an encoded message from Tubman." With a small catch in her breath, Lilith pressed on. "A Tubman patrol picked up Elysian aircraft on their extended radar. The patrol flew north to investigate, to the area where the Border had disintegrated. By the time they got there, the aircraft had flown through an enormous hole, into Elysium."

Stirring impatiently, Kali demanded, "Is this about Whit?"

Lilith stood up then, her hand stroking Kali's hair. "The Tubman surveillance group reports that they continued to track the F-24s on extended radar. Much to their surprise, they also started receiving encoded GPS bursts, with signatures that informed them they were receiving positional coordinates on Whit's and Danu's Peregrines."

Confused, Kali asked, "Danu and Whit flew into Elysium?"

"Yes," Tor whispered.

It was the first time Tor had spoken, and at last, Kali really looked at her. Her face was a frozen mask, her eyes dark and dazed.

Kali was suddenly sure she did not want to hear what Lilith was here to tell her. "No . . ." Her voice was hollow.

Raising a hand to her mouth, Lilith stopped, battling tears. After a moment, she said, "Danu got the F-24 she was chasing. She must have taken a hit before she got him, because the Tubman data states she seemed to have trouble controlling the Peregrine at the very end. Her GPS feed became sporadic before it faded and went silent."

Tor swayed, and Styx slipped a supporting arm around her waist.

"Whit?" Kali whispered.

Lilith took a deep breath. "Whit apparently went deep into Elysium. It seems the F-24 turned on her . . ." Covering her eyes for a moment, Lilith paused, then dropped her hand and plunged on. "She went through a series of evasive maneuvers, retreating from northeastern Virginia to the Shenandoah Mountains. From there, it all gets . . ."

As if trying to conclude the tale, Lilith spoke faster. "The Tubman patrol says her GPS feed to them ended suddenly. All we know is that the F-24 chasing Whit's Peregrine broke off the engagement and flew eastward again. Whit's Peregrine effectively disappeared. Meanwhile, the F-24 steadily lost altitude and speed and finally fell out of the sky just north of Andrews Air Force Base. A thermonuclear device must have been on board. The explosion took out everything in a thirty -mile radius."

Lilith's voice broke. She stopped, gathering herself, then finished.

"The Tubman patrol lingered in the area of the hole in the Border for over half an hour. They sent GPS signatures and even radio broadcasts, trying to raise Whit or Danu. As of a few minutes ago, the Border was fully restored. The hole is closed." Her voice very soft, Lilith ended, "Whit and Danu have been reported missing in action."

A strangled sound escaped Kali, but she clenched her fists and fought her agony into submission. *If I start crying, I'll*

*never stop. Think! Think! If Whit were dead, wouldn't I
already know? Wouldn't I have felt it like a knife in my heart?*

By her side, Lilith turned into Styx's comforting arms,
sobbing. Tor stared at nothing, obviously in shock. Beside Tor,
Captain Razia's usual ramrod posture was gone. She stood,
slumped, looking lost, her eyes filled with anguish.

From the wallscreen, another comline newswoman, this
one posted at Jackie Cochran Space Center, was intoning a
late-breaking news update.

"And the story here, Freeland, is that the Border is up —
restored to perfect working order! Maat Tyler's Border
program is now sending successfully to the twenty new
satellites placed in orbit during the past four days by Pilot Loy
Yin Chen and Flight Commander Mika Reno of the FS
*Independence*."

In the background, the camera focused on a group of
mission control team members. The raucous group was raising
their fists in victory and shouting. Distractedly, Kali noticed
the querulous astrophysicist, Hel Campanelli, looking uncharacteristically ebullient. The reporter's sensitive
microphone picked up Hel shouting, "We knew Loy would do
it!"

Through the desolation of the ghastly news Lilith had just
brought her, Kali felt a surreal inclination to laugh hysteri-
cally at Hel. *Sure . . . Now you're behind her.*

Over the film footage of the shuttle landing, the newswoman reported, "Ten minutes ago, the *Independence* safely
returned to Cochran Space Center. We hope to interview Chief
Chen and Major Reno within the next two hours."

Smoothly, the comline newscast shifted to other stories in
other cities, where wild revelry and solemn commemoration
ceremonies were under way. Cameras panned huge crowds of
cheering people gathering before the Leader Houses in the
seven remaining Freelandian city-colonies. The shot of Isis

showed Cammermeyer Street filled with a dancing, exuberant multitude.

Turning her head toward the wall of windows, Kali realized she could hear the voices of hundreds of women in the garden below the balcony, all of them yelling for Whit. Their emotion seemed to pierce Kali, elevating and enriching her spirit with some nameless force.

A surge of mage power, a low, rumbling wave of it, flared through Kali like distant thunder in a summer sky. "She's alive," Kali stated.

Lilith and Styx separated and looked at her.

"Whit's *alive*! I know it!" Kali declared.

Lilith glanced helplessly at Styx.

Eyes alight with hope, Tor crossed the room to Kali and laid a hand on her arm in silent supplication.

Kali closed her eyes and reached with all her psychic might, searching for the other end of the faint vibration she felt from Tor. "Danu too," she pronounced. "They're in trouble . . . I sense fear and danger . . . but they're alive."

Then, like a quick, unpredictable summer storm, Kali's power was blown out, and she leaned back in the desk chair, exhausted.

Nodding acceptance of Kali's words, Styx said, "We're going to have to go and get them."

Recovering from her surprise, Lilith pulled a palm computer from her pocket. "We'll need to get organized." She tapped quickly on the palm. "A search-and-rescue party will need supplies . . ."

Styx looked Tor over, then remarked, "You look healthy enough to me, but you'd better see a sympathetic healer and secure a medical clearance if you want to be on board."

Tor gaped at Styx, then raced from the office.

With effort, Razia mastered the expression of sheer joy that had overtaken her. She turned toward Lilith and snapped to attention. "I'll requisition your deployment aircraft, ma'am." A crisp salute followed, and then she, too, was headed for the door.

From her seat at the desk, Kali leaned forward and rested her head in her hands. Eyes closed, she whispered, "We're coming Whit. Hang on."

# Characters and Places

**Arinna** (Ah-RIN-ah).   Hittite name for the Great Goddess, Mother of the Sun. Worshiped by the Amazons that resided around the Black Sea until the fifth century. ( It was once called the Amazon Sea).

*Arinna Sojourner* was a Think Tank innovation, created at the same time as Kali, by Kali's mother, Maat. Arinna came to Isis during its refounding, as a systems director. Later, as a means of creating a power base, she tried to take control of both Isis and Kali. Arinna shocked everyone with a display of mage power never before witnessed. The mage power was a by-product of Maat's recombinant DNA engineering. It is generally thought that Whit destroyed Arinna by deflecting back onto Arinna a burst of electricity Arinna unleashed against Whit.

**Danu** (Dah-NEW).   Celtic name for the Great Mother Goddess, often associated with rivers (the Danube in Germany, the Don in both Russia and Ireland) as the Goddess of Waters of Life. Also, the leader of the Irish trinity of Fates (the other two called Bobd and Macha, collectively called the Morrighan).

*Danu Sullivan* is a Think Tank innovation created approximately nine years after Arinna and Kali were, in the final weeks of the program. Her enhancements are in mathematics and architectural design. She possesses a photographic memory. She first came to Isis as architectural director when she was seventeen, after submitting her designs on the comline to the Seven Leaders Council. After assisting in the building of Isis, she tracked Arinna Sojourner to her hiding place in the North Cascades and went there to seek vengeance for the death of a friend. Instead, she was captured and tortured. Tor rescued Danu, while Kali fought Arinna in a duel of mage power.

**Elysium** (Ill-LIZ-ee-em).   Greek name for the plain of the departed, the dwelling place for virtuous people after death. Also known as *paradise*, it was thought to be located in the underworld, or in the far west. A place of ideal bliss or perfect happiness.

*Elysium* is what the procurators and reverends of the New Order decided to call the nation they carved from the eastern United States during the Great Rift (civil war of 2013). Elysium is a fascist dictatorship ruled by the procurators and reverends, and holds to the beliefs of the Aryan nation and the fundamentalist Christian church.

**Freeland** (FREE-land).   The name of a town on Whidbey Island, in Washington state. Settled by former slaves and wandering idealists who were looking for peace and brotherhood following the War Between the States (1861–1864). The town still exists in Washington today.

*Freeland* is the name the Mothers decided to call the western half of the former United States. (The Mothers is what herstory calls the matriarchs who ended up leading small bands of villages after most of the men died in the AGH plague). Freeland consists of eight city-colonies and is a democracy. Multicultural by necessity of survival, diversity is cherished and encouraged.

**Gaea** (GAY-ah).   The primeval prophetess, our most ancient Earth. She came before everything else and brought the world into being. Fires were lit to her on mountaintops. Believers went into oracular caverns deep in the ground to hear what she would reveal of the future. She created heaven (Uranus) and she created the sea (Pontus) and took both as lovers. The Greek name for *Mother Earth*. Also known as Gaia, the Great Earth Mother, one of the earliest of humanity's deities.

**Hypatia** (Hi-PAY-shia).   Egyptian mathematician and philosopher who was the first notable woman in mathematics, (c. 370–415). In Alexandria, she fell victim to the fifth-century Christian persecution of intellectual women. While driving her chariot to an academy where she taught, she was assaulted by monks, who took her to a church, stripped her, and scraped the living flesh from her with oyster shells. After burning her remains, judicious bribes kept her murder from being investigated by officials.
*Hypatia Rousseau* is first assistant to Chief of Staff Loy Yin Chen. She is responsible for all second-in-command duties having to do with the shuttle project.

**Isis** (EYE-sis).   Egyptian goddess of fertility, generally thought to be the oldest of the old goddesses. Her name means "throne." Cleopatra wore her crescent mantel as warrior queen. She was a creating and destroying goddess. She was worshiped throughout the ancient world, including Rome, where many aspects of the Isis cult were absorbed into legends of Mary, the Madonna, the Mother of Christ.

**Kali** (KAH-lee).   Hindu goddess, born fully armed from the brow of her mother, the goddess in one of her earliest aspects, before fathers were recognized. She is also known as Dark Mother, a triple goddess of creation, preservation, and destruction. Kali the Destroyer is the reality that as death cannot exist without life, so life cannot exist without death. She is Virgin, Mother, and Crone. She is a blood-smeared face with a lolling tongue, the devourer of all existence. She is the ocean of blood at the beginning and end of the world. She is terrifying to Western man.
*Kali Tyler* is Maat Tyler's daughter, a Think Tank innovation

engineered with abilities in mathematics and science. She possesses a photographic memory. She was fourteen when Isis was attacked and burned to the ground by invading Elysians. Her mother was burned at the stake before her eyes, and Kali was taken into Elysium as a prize of war. She killed the tribune who had ordered her mother's death, and escaped. Following an emotional breakdown and a complete loss of memory, she spent the next ten years in Elysium masquerading as an AGH serf. She met Whit when Whit was evading Regulators, on her way out of Elysium following two years of undercover activity as a spy. After being wounded while helping Whit escape, she was takenout of Elysium and back to Whit's home colony of Artemis. Kali and Whit fell in love, became partners, and returned to refound Isis. Later, Kali ended up fighting Arinna Sojourner when Arinna decided to use Isis as a power base and Kali as an acolyte. In resisting Arinna, Kali discovered she had many of the same mage powers Arinna had developed: bursts of electric energy that can be directed in pinpoint blasts, psychic awareness of where others are and what they are doing, the ability to mind-read, to mind-bond, and a tenuous ability at foresight. Kali still bears the effects of her captivity in Elysium: she is deathly afraid of the Regs, and she has difficulty being in a closed room.

**Lilith** (LIL-lith).   Sumero-Babylonian goddess "Belili." Early Jewish rabbis tried to assimilate the strong and independent agricultural goddess by incorporating her into Jewish mythology as Adam's first wife, Lilith. As such, she was created at the same time and in the same way as Adam — from the dust of the earth. Lilith was Adam's equal. She would not be subservient to Adam. She would not lie beneath Adam in the "missionary position," instead preferring being on top and participating in a marriage based on mutual respect. When Adam tried to force her to his way, she damned him and left him, going to make her home by the Red Sea. The Hebrew God then created Eve as a more compliant mate for Adam. The story of Lilith was later removed from the canonical Bible.

*Lilith* is Kali's biological mother, having donated an ovum to her partner, Maat Tyler, which Maat joined with an ovum of her own, and then used in a recombinant DNA engineering experiment. Kali was incubated and born from a Delphi Unit in Artemis. Lilith was part of a happy family with Kali and Maat for twelve years, until Maat separated from Lilith and took Kali with her to participate in the founding of Isis. Lilith, a grain trader, was elected as Leader of Artemis (rather like a city mayor, except for additional senatorlike representation on the Seven Leaders Council). She served in Artemis, reelected as Leader for three consecutive five-year terms. She retired from the post to settle down with her new partner, Styx, then ended up being asked to take on the position of deputy leader in Isis when the elected deputy leader, Kali, had to step out of that role. Lilith is also Whit's adopted mother, having taken in the grief-stricken, nineteen-year-old Whit, when Whit's family were all killed in the fall of Isis.

**Loy Yin** (Loy Yin). Loy Yi Lung is one of two girls (the other being Gum Lin) in an ancient Chinese tale. Gum Lin, a poor starving peasant, comes to Wild Swan Lake to sing to the dragon's daughter, Loy Yi Lung. In singing of the plight of her fellow villagers, and the need for the dragon to release water to grow their rice fields, Gum Lin enlists the aid of Loy Yi Lung. Loy Yi Lung sings with Gum Lin, and the dragon comes to the lakeshore to hear his daughter. Gum Lin sneaks, unnoticed, past the dragon to his cavern. Though jewels, gold, and many riches there tempt her, she does not take anything. Instead, she faithfully searches for and finally finds the golden key to open the stone gate. Taking only the key, she opens the gate and allows the lake waters to flow through the countryside and down to her village. The dragon's daughter finds a new home near Gum Lin's village, and they often sing together by Ye Tiyoh (Wild Swan River), at the foot of Tai Ma Shan (Great Horse Mountain). In the light of the waning twenty-one-day-old moon, on the third month of the year, Chinese women go there to sing of Loy Yi Lung and Gum Lin.

**Yin Wang Chun** is a sixteenth-century Shaolin nun (also known as Yim Ving Tsun) who studied temple boxing under Ng Miu, another nun. She developed many kung fu training aides and a new style of fighting called Wing Chun Pia. This is a popular style even now. Bruce Lee was a follower of her technique, upon which he patterned his own.
*Loy Yin Chen* has a checkered past. She was Whit's first lover,

having met her while both were sixteen-year-olds at the Artemis Flight School. Loy was all flash and dare, and relied upon cheating on tests and charming instructors to make the grade. Following a tumultuous love affair, Loy and Whit became fierce rivals and finally enemies. Later, Loy left the warriors to serve as deputy leader in Boudica. She came to Isis as finance director, to participate in the refounding. Her actual goal was to get herself elected as Leader of Isis. She subtly but continually challenged Whit's authority while Whit served as the appointed city-colony military governor. She worked in league with Arinna Sojourner to undermine Whit, hoping to get her out of the way during the Leader election. When this effort failed, unknown to Loy, Arinna tried to kill Whit in what would appear to be an accident. Kali intervened and saved Whit. Unable to overcome Kali's resistance to her mage power, Arinna instead took Loy with her as a captive. Held against her will in a secret, heavily fortified SAC installation in the bedrock of the North Cascades, Loy was tortured by Arinna. When Kali came to battle Arinna in an exchange of mage power, Loy leveled the playing field by destroying Arinna's robotically-controlled defense system. Kali was able to face Arinna one-on-one. As punishment, Arinna viciously mutilated Loy's face and opened a vein in Loy's left wrist. Loy nearly bled to death before Tor found her while Tor was looking for Danu. Tor carried Loy out of the SAC installation. Loy returned to Isis. While Whit, Danu, Tor, Kali, Lilith, and Styx know the value of Loy's sacrifice, most other Freelanders can't get past her earlier alliance with and misdeeds for Arinna Sojourner. However, in confronting Arinna, Loy found her own self-worth. She finally knows who she is and what is important to her. She is still scarred physically and psychologically from her experience as Arinna's captive.

**Maat** (MAH-aht or Maht).    "Mother." A very early Egyptian goddess, the personification of Truth or Justice. She was the lion-headed goddess of both law and revenge. She was the original Eye of Heaven (before Hathor). She was also associated with the heart, as that is the place where judgments are made. She was the lawgiver in archaic Egypt, giving rules of behavior. She was the All-Mother. She is depicted as a woman, with an ostrich feather upon her head, a scepter in one hand, the life symbol of the ankh in the other. The same feathers of truth are worn by other aspects of the Goddess, such as Isis, who was the same sort of law-giving Mother. All other gods were required to "live by Maat." She was the manifestation of truth, justice, moral law and cosmic balance.

*Maat Tyler* was Kali Tyler's mother. Maat used an ovum donated by Lilith to fertilize her own egg in a parthenogenic procedure, then employed recombinant DNA engineering to enhance Kali's intellect. After Kali was born from a Delphi Unit, Maat, Lilith, and Kali formed a happy family unit in Artemis for twelve years. Earlier, as a very young woman, Maat developed the computerized manufacturing program that mass-produced the AGH vaccine she and other medical scientists had discovered. The vaccine eradicated AGH in Freeland and allowed them to survive. Later, Maat created the Border software, which reprogrammed the electromagnetic shield the Elysians had put in place in 2013. In doing this, Maat allowed Freeland to gain control of the Border and use it to keep contained the violent, medieval culture Elysium had become. Courted by dynamic younger women, Maat grew restless in her settled family life with Lilith. She ended their partnership and struck out for new experiences. Maat led the initial founding of Isis, and was elected the city-colony's first Leader. She was burned at the stake there, as a witch, during an Elysian invasion. Her ghost has since been seen in various parts of the city-colony.

**Mika** (MEE-kah).   Native American name: wise little raccoon.
*Major Mika Reno* is a naturally brilliant warrior pilot and astrophysicist. She comes to Isis as General Medusa's selected shuttle pilot.

**Medusa** (Med-DOO-sah).   She birthed the winged horse Pegasus (a horse is an Amazon link), but is most widely known as one of the three snake-haired Gorgons. To look upon Medusa was to be turned to stone. She was also the serpent goddess to the Libyan Amazons, a goddess of wisdom. She wore a veil because she was the Future and the future is always veiled.

**Candace Amanirenas** (CAN-duh-see Ah-mah-nir-AY-nahs). Queen of Ethiopia, who in 30 B.C. fought the campaigns of Patronius, governor of Egypt. Patronius wanted to extend Roman rule into Ethiopia and so brought his army there. She took the Egyptian city of Cyrene and sent Patronius and his legions on the run. While she lived, the Romans were never again in full control of southern Egypt.

**General Candace Amanirenas Medusa** is a three-star Freeland general. She has had a long career and is skilled both in the strategy of war and politics. She comes to Isis to wrest control of the shuttle project from the civilian task force running it thus far and make it into a military operation.

**Regulators** (REG-u-lay-tors).   A group in charge of regulations.
**Elysian Regulators** are the storm troopers of the New Order. They wear green uniform jackets, small caps, dark pants, and knee-high boots. They are allowed little initiative and follow orders to the smallest detail. They are known for enjoying the violence and terror they are enlisted to inflict.

**Styx** (Sticks).   Name for the mythological Roman river that led into the underworld.
**Styx** is city-colony herstorian, first for Artemis, and then later for Isis. Her overwhelming mission is to save as many printed paper books and other artifacts from Old America as possible. She studied Wicca with Baubo as a young woman, and has mastered some minor psychic skills. She was an early product of Think Tank experimentation, when a cystic fibrosis gene was engineered out of her DNA chain during mitosis. She was also given minor psychic gifts during that same genetic work. She is Lilith's partner.

**Tamatori** (Tama-TOR-ee).   A Japanese legend, Tamatori was an ama (nun). Under the sea, she battled a giant octopus and the dragon lord, while trying to recover a sacred jewel. When she realized she would be unable to make it back to the surface of the sea, she ripped her stomach open with her sword, and pushed the jewel deep within herself. Her corpse washed ashore and the sacred jewel was recovered.
**Tor Yakami** came to Isis as a lieutenant to assist Kali in readying to battle Arinna Sojourner. An expert martial arts champion, Tor was also gifted in channeling ki and the intricacies of Zen. While sharing quarters in the warriors' barracks with Danu, she fell in

love and the two are now deeply involved. Tor went into Arinna's mountain bastion with Kali. She rescued Danu and Loy, but was slain by a death spell Arinna had set before the doorway that had to be passed through in order to escape. Kali sought Tor's spirit in the netherworld and brought her back. Her body has never fully recovered from the trauma, and she is on extended medical leave from the warriors.

**Tomyris** (Toe-MY-ris).   Queen of the Massagetae (Celtish origins) in Central Asia (now part of Iran) in the sixth century. She was a brilliant military tactician and founded the city of Tomis. When her nation was invaded by Cyrus the Great and his huge Persian army, she promised him, "enough blood to sate your gluttony." In a savage battle, she and her warriors slaughtered 200,000 Persians; not even a messenger escaped to take news of the defeat back to Persia. Tomyris personally decapitated the captured Cyrus, and tossed his head in a skin filled like a bucket with human blood, saying, "I have fulfilled my promise. You have your fill of blood."

*Tomyris Whitaker*, nicknamed Whit by her friends, has spent most of her life as a Freeland warrior. Following the loss of her friends and family in the fall of Isis, Tomyris was formally adopted by Lilith, the Leader of Artemis. Lilith has acted as a mentor and mother figure as Whit has made her way through the ranks. While a major, after a frustrating involvement with the healer Cimbri Braun, Whit went into Elysium and spent two years there on an undercover spying mission. She worked as a computer technician, enduring the open misogyny and casual brutality of that primitive culture, and developed a hatred of all things Elysian, especially men. Eventually, while making a repair to the procurator's computer, she accessed the Regulators' mainframe, and downloaded every file stored there into a satellite transmission to Freeland. On the run from Regulators, Whit's stolen Elysian jet malfunctioned and she had to ditch in Kali's potato field, near the northern Bordergate. In a fight with two pursuing Regs, Kali saved Whit's life and was badly wounded. Unable to leave her, Whit broke a Freeland law that prohibited bringing Elysians through the Border, and brought Kali into Freeland. Together, they crossed the Wilderness, the huge abandoned section of the West, until a search party found them. Whit and Kali were taken to Artemis. Gradually, they had been falling in love with each other. Kali eventually recovered her memory of the fall of Isis, and with it, she remembered enough to incriminate the unsuspected person responsible for the disaster. In a fight to the death, Whit saved Kali from the traitor. Declaring themselves partners, Kali and Whit went into the ruins of Isis and began building a country home on Whit's family land. Other women from all over Freeland followed their example, and Isis was once again opened as a city-colony. Whit was made military governor, overseeing three directors (Loy, Arinna, and Danu). Kali worked on a construction team and took school courses on the comline in an effort to catch up on ten years of missed education. When accidents around the half-built colony escalated into catastrophe, no one knew what to think. Meanwhile, Kali was dealing with a discomfiting ability to read minds and influence others to do her will. Styx, Lilith's partner, informed Kali that her psychic gifts might be a by-product of her Think Tank origins. Eventually, the accidents and deaths that had occurred in Isis were explained when it was revealed that Arinna Sojourner had been operating on an agenda all her own. When her plans to take control of Isis and Kali were thwarted, Arinna fled Isis, taking an unwilling Loy Yin Chen with her. Isis was saved, but everyone knew it was only a temporary reprieve. Whit was elected Leader of Isis, and Kali was elected Deputy Leader. Kali resigned as deputy leader in order to prepare for her planned confrontation with Arinna. Asked first to fill the post as a temporary replacement, Lilith was subsequently elected as deputy leader in her own right. While aircraft and satellite searches were unable to find Arinna's hiding place, Kali trained to battle Arinna both physically and psychically. Thinking Kali was not Arinna's equal, Whit was opposed to Kali's decision to seek out and battle the Sorceress. The two partners had a bitter, and increasingly contentious disagreement over Kali's course of action. Lieutenant Tamatori (Tor) Yakami came to Isis to train Kali in martial arts, channeling ki, and using Zen to bring her psychic gifts to full development. Styx and Tor worked with Kali, with Danu Sullivan acting as a sparring partner. Seeing that Tor was interested in quiet, reserved Danu, Whit assigned Tor as Danu's roommate in the warriors' barracks. Despite their efforts to resist each other, Tor and Danu fell in love. Danu eventually discovered Arinna's bastion in a SAC installation high in the North Cascades. Instead of telling the others, Danu struck out alone, intent on vengeance for the death of a friend. Arinna captured Danu. When the others were able to piece together what Danu had found, Kali led Tor and a small party in a military strike against the installation. Unexpectedly, Loy disabled Arinna's robotic defense system, and Kali was freed to battle Arinna one-on-one. Tor found Danu, and led her back to the surface of the mountain while carrying the unconscious Loy over her shoulder. Tor purposefully stepped into one of Arinna's death-spell traps in order to allow Danu and Loy to go safely through after her and escape the fortress. Tor, Loy, and Danu all nearly died while still on the mountain. Whit arrived with backup, then went deep into the mountainside to confront Arinna with a specially devised weapon, just as Arinna was about to conquer Kali. Whit took everyone back to Isis, realizing that beneath her genteel civility and newly-crafted Leader persona, she was still a warrior. Whit and Kali were handfasted (married) in the sight of all the women of Isis, and a wild celebration followed.

# Glossary

**AGH**  AIDS/genital herpes. Ignored in its formative years, the plague spread silently through the American populace in the early twenty-first century. By 2013 mass death and a civil war had erupted. Most lethal to men, the plague killed two thirds of the people driven out of Elysium (eastern U.S.). Freeland (western U.S.) found a vaccine, and the plague no longer exists there. In Elysium, a milder version of the plague still kills two out of ten persons.

**APU**  Auxiliary power unit.

**cold fusion**  An environmentally safe, inexpensive means of producing energy by causing small atomic nuclei to join together (fuse) at room temperature into larger atomic nuclei.

**comline**  Freeland's satellite-based communications system. The melding of telephone, computer, and television functions into one system with many diverse uses. Wrist chronometers (wristcoms), desk top computers, computer slates, and palm computers are all linked on the comline.

**blackout**  Approximate twelve-minute period when a shuttle is reentering Earth's atmosphere. Shuttle and ground control are unable to communicate. When the orbiter descends, atmospheric drag dissipates its tremendous energy, which generates extreme heat. This heat removes electrons from the air around the shuttle, enclosing the shuttle in an pocket of ionized air that blocks all communication from the ground.

**Delphi Clinic**  Medical facility where parthenogenic procedures are done and a Delphi Unit is housed.

**Delphi Unit**  Supportive, artificial womb where a newly created being is able to grow from mitosis through embryo to fetus stages. The units were created to free women to continue vital community work during the initial depopulation crisis that followed the AGH plague.

**EMU**  Extravehicular mobility unit; spacesuit with self-contained life-support system.

**EVA**  Extravehicular activity; commonly known as a space walk.

**external tank**  Half a football field long, the tank contains 697,500 kg or 1,550,000 pounds of fuel. It is the large, fat tank located under the shuttle's belly.

**handover/ingress team**  The group of technicians who spend several hours in the shuttle crew compartment prior to launch, making sure everything is prepared. Once the crew arrives, they assist the crew members to crawl to their seats and get strapped in. They take care of any final readiness tasks.

**GPS**  NAVSTAR Global Positioning System. Navigational satellites read a signal sent from a transmitter on earth and place the object in relation to its geographical surroundings, which the satellite reads from space.

**mage**  A magician, wizard. A person talented with occult powers.

**MMU**  Manned maneuvering unit. A self-contained backpack that latches on to the spacesuit. It is propelled by nitrogen gas released in specific spurts from twenty-four nozzles placed around its exterior. It transports crew members on space walks.

**orbiter**  Another name for the space shuttle.

**PAM**  Payload assist module. The metal cradle that fits around a satellite while it is stowed in the shuttle's cargo bay. The PAM spins the satellite, which protects it from the heat of direct sunlight. The PAM also has small rocket boosters built into it, which, upon release, lift the satellite to a preset orbit.

**parthenogenesis**  Process by which a woman's ovum or egg shell is sliced open by a microlaser. Using an electron microscope, chromosomes from a donor's egg are removed and placed in the ovum of the mother to be. The fertilized egg is placed in a test tube and allowed to become mitotic.

**PSI**  Pounds per square inch.

**RMS**  Remote manipulator system. The RMS coordinates the shuttle's robot arm. It is operated from the aft crew station, which is located just behind the pilot's and flight commander's seats. The RMS is used to place satellites in space.

**SRBs**  Solid rocket boosters. Two reusable rockets used to launch the shuttle. On liftoff, they flank the external tank. They are the largest solid motors ever to fly. After they are emptied of fuel, they separate from the shuttle, deploy parachutes, and fall into the ocean. Two oceangoing tugs locate the SRBs by the tracking and sonar beacons they carry. Air in the casings keeps the SRBs floating upright. The open end of the SRB is sealed and the water pumped out of it, then it is towed back to port.

**TACAN**  Tactical air navigation. A series of ground stations send transmissions at specific frequencies, which are detected by the orbiter. After blackout, during the descent and landing of the shuttle, this radio-electronic landing system measures bearing of the craft and distance from the landing runway. This gives the angle of the shuttle's course and the desired path of trajectory.

**TAEM**  Terminal area energy management. Process of conserving energy during landing sequence. Begins directly after blackout.

**Think Tank**  Nickname given to a Freeland program in genetic engineering. Recombinant DNA technology used specialized enzymes to snip a gene from one organism and splice it to another. Developed by Maat Tyler in an effort to improve Freeland's chances of surviving the severe depopulation effects of AGH, Think Tank creations are enhanced intellects. They also meet fierce prejudice and suspicion because they are different.

**VAB**  Vehicle assembly building, where the external tank and solid rocket boosters are joined to the shuttle.

Jean Stewart was born and raised in the suburbs of Philadelphia, Pennsylvania. She was the neighborhood bad girl. After a wild childhood (lots of gallivanting around and brawling with bullies), at age twelve she stumbled upon *Jane Eyre*, and the earth moved. Soon, she had a voracious habit (five library books a week), was keeping a journal, and began what became a lifelong habit — writing scenes in her head whenever bored.

She later managed to earn Bachelor of Science and Master of Education degrees at West Chester University. For eleven years, she taught school and coached a variety of women's sports, then left teaching in order to concentrate on writing. Jean and her true love, Susie, have been together thirteen years and live very happily in the suburbs of Seattle with their three dogs and one cat.

Two of her earlier books, *Return to Isis*, and *Warriors of Isis*, have been nominated for Lambda Literary Awards. Jean is currently writing the sequel to *Winged Isis*, and plotting a sequel to *Emerald City Blues*.

Publications from
# BELLA BOOKS, INC.
*The best in contemporary lesbian fiction*

P.O. Box 201007    Ferndale, MI 48220
Phone: 800-729-4992
www.bellabooks.com

FOREVER AND THE NIGHT by Laura DeHart Young. 224 pp. Desire and passion ignite the frozen Arctic in this exciting sequel to the classic romantic adventure   *Love on the Line.*
ISBN 0-931513-00-7    $11.95

WINGED ISIS by Jean Stewart. 240 pp. The long-awaited sequel to *Warriors of Isis* and the fourth in the exciting Isis series.
ISBN 1-931513-01-5    $11.95

ROOM FOR LOVE by Frankie J. Jones. 192 pp. Jo and Beth must overcome the past in order to  have a future together.
ISBN 0-9677753-9-6    $11.95

THE QUESTION OF SABOTAGE by Bonnie J. Morris. 144 pp. A charming, sexy tale of romance, intrigue, and coming of age.
ISBN 0-9677753-8-8    $11.95

SLEIGHT OF HAND by Karin Kallmaker writing as Laura Adams. 256 pp. A journey of passion, heartbreak and triumph that reunites two women for a final chance at their destiny.  ISBN 0-9677753-7-X    $11.95

MOVING TARGETS: A Helen Black Mystery by Pat Welch. 240 pp. Helen must decide if getting to the bottom of a mystery is worth hitting bottom.                ISBN 0-9677753-6-1    $11.95

CALM BEFORE THE STORM by Peggy J. Herring. 208 pp. Colonel Robicheaux retires from the military and comes out of the closet.
ISBN 0-9677753-1-0    $11.95

OFF SEASON by Jackie Calhoun. 208 pp. Pam threatens Jenny and Rita's fledgling relationship.        ISBN 0-9677753-0-2    $11.95

WHEN EVIL CHANGES FACE: A Motor City Thriller by Therese Szymanski. 240 pp. Brett Higgins is back in another heart-pounding thriller.                       ISBN 0-9677753-3-7    $11.95

BOLD COAST LOVE by Diana Tremain Braund. 208 pp. Jackie Claymont fights for her reputation and the right to love the woman she chooses.                   ISBN 0-9677753-2-9    $11.95